From Cradle

Titles by Rhys Bowen

From Cradle
to Grave

RHYS BOWEN

BERKLEY PRIME CRIME
New York

BERKLEY PRIME CRIME
Published by Berkley
An imprint of Penguin Random House LLC
1745 Broadway, New York, NY 10019
penguinrandomhouse.com

Library of Congress Cataloging-in-Publication Data

Names: Bowen, Rhys author
Title: From cradle to grave / Rhys Bowen.
Description: New York: Berkley Prime Crime, 2025. | Series: Royal spyness mysteries
Identifiers: LCCN 2025027099 (print) | LCCN 2025027100 (ebook) |
ISBN 9780593641392 hardcover | ISBN 9780593641415 ebook
Subjects: LCGFT: Detective and mystery fiction | Novels | Fiction
Classification: LCC PR6052.O848 F76 2025 (print) |
LCC PR6052.O848 (ebook) | DDC 823/.914—dc23/eng/20250626
LC record available at https://lccn.loc.gov/2025027099
LC ebook record available at https://lccn.loc.gov/2025027100

Printed in the United States of America
1st Printing

The authorized representative in the EU for product safety and compliance is
Penguin Random House Ireland, Morrison Chambers, 32 Nassau Street,
Dublin D02 YH68, Ireland, https://eu-contact.penguin.ie.

From Cradle to Grave

Chapter 1

Dear Diary: It's been a strange start to this year, watching my cousin David, the former king, sneak away from England to join Mrs. Simpson in France, having renounced his throne for her. I do hope he realizes what he's given up. I really hope he is happy. I don't think she will be. This isn't what she wanted at all. She had set her sights on being queen. How silly. Anyway we have a new king and queen on the throne and I think they'll do jolly well. They are a really decent couple, and their daughters are dear little girls. I'm really fond of them.

I've been lax with keeping up with this diary this year as not too much has happened in my life that is worth writing about. I've been at home taking care of my baby son, watching him

grow and enjoying his every new move. Darcy has been
going up to London to work or seeing to the running of the
farm. Sir Hubert is away again. Granddad is back in Essex.
All is quiet and peaceful.

10:30 a.m. I should never have written this!

This story began when I looked out of the blue bedroom window
at the front of the house on a brisk morning to see an ancient
taxicab coming up the driveway. As I watched, it disgorged a
tall elderly woman. She looked around with an expression so
haughty and disapproving that I concluded she had to be at least
a Russian grand duchess, maybe sent to us by my friend Zou
Zou, who was more formally known as the Princess Zamanska.
I hastily patted my hair into place and smoothed down my skirt,
and hurried down the stairs to greet her myself.

I opened the front door just as she was about to knock.

"Hello," I said.

The expression became even more disapproving. "Are all the
servants in this house allowed to be so familiar with arriving
guests and to be dressed in such an inappropriate manner?" she
asked in a voice that could cut glass. "I wish to speak to Lady
Georgiana. Please go and inform her that I have arrived."

I noticed that she was wearing a gray cape over a gray skirt
with a gray pillbox hat on her head, matching her gray hair and
gray face. Only the eyes were a darker shade of steel. Golly, I
thought. Was I supposed to know she was coming? Had Darcy
or one of the servants forgotten to pass along a message that a

person of considerable importance was about to land on my doorstep?

"I am Lady Georgiana," I said. "Please do come in."

At this she raised an eyebrow. "Your sister-in-law, her grace, the duchess, told me that this was a lax household, but I had no idea that the lady of the house had to open her own front door."

"I just happened to see the cab draw up from the upstairs window, so I came down to greet you," I said. "So you know Fig, do you?"

"Her grace, Hilda, Duchess of Rannoch? Yes. I am familiar with her. A wonderful woman. Salt of the earth."

Anyone who could describe Fig as a wonderful woman was immediately suspect in my view. "And may one know your name?"

The eyebrow arched again. "You mean you were not expecting me? Your sister-in-law, her grace, the duchess, told me she was going to write to you announcing my arrival. Clearly the post office is not what it was, or maybe storms in Scotland have stranded the postal van again. I am your new nanny. Nanny Hardbottle."

I think my jaw dropped open and somehow I was unable to close it.

She was frowning at me now.

"But there must be some mistake. I didn't request, I mean, I had not hired . . ."

"Precisely," she said. "Her grace told me that you had been without a proper nanny since the birth of the child and it was about time you had one. So she took it upon herself to save you the trouble, and as luck would have it, she learned that the last of the Aubrey-Fulton sons has just gone off to a military academy and that I would now be free."

I still couldn't make my mouth work to say anything.

"I had considered retiring," she continued, "and growing begonias in a cottage in the Lake District, but given your obvious need and the way her grace, the duchess, almost got down on her knees to beg me, how could I refuse? The young master is going to be raised to be a leader of the empire, after all." She paused, examining me with utter disdain. "Now, if you would be good enough to have a member of your staff show me to my quarters? I presume that there is a suitable room for me in the nursery suite, next to the young master?"

The young master was, at this moment, not in the nursery at all. He was in his cot in my bedroom, since I had been nursing him myself and wasn't about to go walking around the corridors and up the stairs in the middle of the night. Also I wanted to be close to him if he woke up and cried. I knew, in theory, that I needed a proper nanny. James was being raised, as she said, to be a future leader of the empire, and families like mine were expected to employ nannies. But I had put it off, enjoying the closeness and the ability to watch every new achievement, every smile and gurgle. Until now my personal maid, Maisie, had helped me take care of him, doing the less pleasant tasks like his laundry, changing nappies and watching him when I was out. My mind was racing, trying to think of a way to tell this woman that she was the last person on God's earth that I'd want taking care of my child, but my brain refused to work.

I opened my mouth to tell her to go away and never come

back, but instead I heard myself saying, "If you will come into the morning room, I will summon my housekeeper. She will know about nursery arrangements."

I led her into the morning room, bade her sit and rang the bell. Our footman, Phipps, appeared instantly. "You rang, my lady?"

"Yes, Phipps. Please tell Mrs. Holbrook I would like to speak to her."

I was conscious of Nanny Hardbottle's steely gaze sweeping the room. Since it was the nicest room in the house, its wallpaper a soft blue-and-yellow pattern, its furnishings in pale blue silk and its tall windows looking out over the grounds, she could find no fault with it.

"This is your husband's family home, is it?" she asked. "It has a very pleasing aspect." (I half expected her to say "a pleasant little wilderness." The resemblance to Lady Catherine de Bourgh was striking.)

"No, the house belongs to Sir Hubert Anstruther, the famous mountaineer and explorer. He has invited us to live here. I am his heir."

"Really? He does not have a royal connection, does he? I know that you do. Her grace made it quite clear to me that you are a great-grandchild of Queen Victoria. So you inherit through your mother's family, I presume?"

I tried to keep a straight face. I was dying to tell her that my mother came from a humble two-up two-down house in the East End of London and that her father was a former policeman. Perhaps if I told her that, she'd be so horrified that she'd leave. But I also didn't want to make her despise my mother and grandfather. So I replied, "Sir Hubert is my godfather. He was once married to my mother."

"Oh yes. The actress." So she had heard about her, probably in lurid detail from Fig. "How very fortunate to be heir to such a fine property. The young master must be raised to appreciate that such privilege comes with responsibilities."

I wished Mrs. Holbrook would hurry up. I decided this might be the time to play the submissive female. "We will, of course, need my husband's approval before we take you on," I said. "He is currently up in London."

"At his club, no doubt."

"No, he works for the government," I said. "He had some kind of conference this weekend."

"He works?" She could not have sounded more disapproving if I'd said that he sold cockles and winkles from a barrow on the docks. Now she sounded like Lady Bracknell delivering her famous line: "A handbag?"

"Mr. O'Mara is not the type of man to be idle," I said. "He has done great service for his country."

This did not remove the critical stare. "Mr. O'Mara? Do I understand that your husband is a commoner?"

"Not at all. I should have said the Honorable Darcy O'Mara, heir to Lord Kilhenny of Ireland."

"Oh. An Irish peer. I see."

For a second I almost wished that I had done what my family wanted and married Prince Siegfried of Romania, aka Fishface. Even she couldn't look down her nose at second in line to a throne, albeit a foreign one! I decided I might have had enough.

"If you suspect that this household is not right for you,

Nanny, then please feel free to go to the Lake District and rear your begonias," I said.

I seemed to have scored a point. For a second she looked a bit put out. But then she recovered, saying, "We shall have to see, shall we not? At least give the situation a chance, until the duchess arrives."

"The duchess?" I think my voice came out as a squeak this time. "My sister-in-law is coming?"

I think she looked a little smug at this. "She assured me that she would take the trouble to come down to England herself to make sure I had settled into my new position, just in case you needed some guidance on the role of a nanny in a household of your caliber. She gave me to understand she would be writing all this to you in a letter, which mysteriously has not yet arrived."

The way she looked at me seemed to suggest that she suspected me of having burned it. I gave a sigh of relief as Mrs. Holbrook came in.

"You wished to see me, my lady?" she said, then froze. "Oh. We have a visitor. I'm sorry. I wasn't informed. I did not hear the front doorbell."

"Don't worry, Mrs. Holbrook. I answered the door as I happened to be passing. This is Nanny Hardbottle. She has been sent from my sister-in-law to take care of James."

Mrs. Holbrook shot me a swift querying glance. "Very good, your ladyship."

"So she will need to be shown to her quarters."

"Her quarters, your ladyship?"

"In the nursery suite. There is a suitable bedroom and sitting room for a nanny, I take it?"

"Yes, there would be. But as you know, it's not currently in use." Mrs. Holbrook was looking worried.

"Not in use?" Nanny Hardbottle said. "Do you not have a nursemaid of sorts? Where does she sleep? Who attends to the young master should he awaken at night?"

This was getting more awkward by the minute.

"Actually I have had James's cot in my own bedroom at night," I said. "I have been breastfeeding him myself and it seemed most convenient."

If her eyebrow had arched any higher it would have disappeared under that steel-gray hair. "Well, I never," she said. "One hears that such practice is the modern thing to do. How old is the young master?"

"Almost seven months," I replied.

"And not started on a solid diet yet?"

"He has started on solid foods. I am in the process of weaning him, but he does find nursing so comforting. And so do I." I did not want to admit to her that James was showing less interest in nursing and the fact that he had developed teeth had made it less appealing for me too.

"Well, I suppose arrangements can be made for him to be brought down to you at the appropriate hour, should you wish to continue this strange practice," Nanny Hardbottle said. "And has potty training begun, may one ask?"

"Not yet." I felt as if this was turning into the Spanish Inquisition.

"All the babies in my households have been quite trained by the time they are eight months old," she said. "It's only a matter of routine and making sure the child knows what is expected of it. Every child should know the rules by the time they are a year old at the latest."

"If you will excuse me, my lady," Mrs. Holbrook said, "I will find Maisie and we will get the nurse's quarters up and running if it's your wish."

"Thank you, Mrs. Holbrook," I said. "We will give Nanny time to see if this position is right for her. And in the meantime perhaps you could have some tea sent up?"

"Of course." Mrs. Holbrook gave a grave bow and retreated.

"You seem to have well-trained staff," Nanny Hardbottle commented. "I presume they came with the house and belong to Sir Hubert?"

She really was quite insufferable. Why couldn't I find the courage to tell her to head straight back where she came from and to tell my sister-in-law what she could do with her nanny? Instead we sat in uneasy silence until the rattle of teacups was heard outside the door.

"Oh good. Tea," I said.

The door burst open and in, bearing a tray, came Queenie.

"Whatcher missus," she said.

Chapter 2

SATURDAY, FEBRUARY 20

EYNSLEIGH

Oh golly. What am I going to do? I can't very well get rid of her
    before Fig comes, can I? And I can't think of any way to stop
    Fig from coming. Help!

My former maid, now our assistant cook, entered the room giving her usual impression of a runaway cart horse. The cups rattled alarmingly as she skidded to a halt, staring at the visitor
open-mouthed. "Oh blimey," she said. "I didn't realize you'd got
someone from outside 'ere. I'd have put a slice of my lardy cake
with the tea things." Her cap was askew and one of the front
buttons of her dress uniform had come undone or had split
open, revealing a hint of a rather gray and unappealing under-
garment.

"That's quite all right, Queenie," I said. "This is Nanny Hardbottle. She has come to take care of Master James."

"But I thought you said you didn't want no nanny," Queenie went on in her usual tactless way. "You said no dried-up old prune was going to raise your child. I heard you myself."

"That will be all, Queenie," I said. "Please put the tray down carefully on the little table."

"I can be mother, if you like," she said.

"No. I can manage, thank you." My gaze told her that the sooner she left, the better. Queenie was never quick on social cues. "I don't mind at all," she said. "I ain't got nothing more to do since I already peeled tonight's spuds and Chef is making one of them Frenchie puddings. He called it a po de crème." She giggled at the mention of the word "po." Cockneys seemed to find the mention of anything to do with lavatories or bodily functions highly amusing.

"You may go, Queenie," I said.

"Bob's yer uncle, then." She gave Nanny Hardbottle a big grin. "Nice to meet you, I'm sure."

There was a silence as I poured two cups of tea.

"What an extraordinary woman," Nanny Hardbottle said. "Who on earth is she? Surely not one of your maids?"

"My assistant cook," I replied. "I'm afraid she's a little unorthodox. But she does bake rather well. Usually we keep her safely in the kitchen, but I expect the other servants were occupied elsewhere, or, knowing Queenie, she took it upon herself to bring up the tea."

"Extraordinary," Nanny Hardbottle repeated. "Your housekeeper seems a competent woman. Can she not teach this person the rudiments of polite behavior?"

I had to smile. "She has tried, I'm sure. We have all tried. Either nothing sinks in or Queenie deliberately doesn't want to learn."

"Then why not give her the sack?"

"Because she was once my maid and she was awfully brave. She saved my life in Romania. I feel responsible for her. And as I said, she does make rather good cakes and biscuits."

Nanny Hardbottle said nothing this time, merely shaking her head. I handed her a cup of tea. She sipped suspiciously, as if Queenie might have done something unmentionable to it. I drank my own. When we had finished, Nanny Hardbottle put down her cup decisively. "I suggest you might introduce me to the young master. James, you said his name was?"

"That's right. James Albert Darcy."

She nodded at this. "After the old king, your great-grandfather. Very suitable."

"Actually after my own grandfather, and my husband," I said. "And James after my uncle who was killed in the Great War. I never knew him."

"So many young men lost in the Great War," she said, sounding almost human for once.

I stood up. "I'm sure Maisie has bathed him and taken him up to the nursery by now, if you'd care to follow me."

I led her up the grand staircase, along the hall and up a second, less grand one. "There is a servants' stair at the other end of the hall," I said, pointing in that direction. "It leads straight down to the kitchen and servants' hall."

She turned back to stare at me. Clearly she objected to the suggestion that she might be classed as a servant or expected to use a back staircase.

"I shall expect my meals, and those for the young master, to be brought up to me on a tray," she said. "And I expect my food to be piping hot, so no dillydallying, and please, do not have that person bring me my food."

"She wouldn't make it up three flights of stairs," I said, chuckling.

I could hear voices coming from the nursery end of the corridor. Maisie's soft high tones and Mrs. Holbrook's cultured lower ones.

"So what's she like?" Maisie was asking. "Am I supposed to be working alongside her? Jamie won't like it if someone else takes care of him. He's used to me."

"I'm sure Nanny will be most grateful to have you working with her," Mrs. Holbrook said tactfully.

"I'm bringing Nanny up to meet James," I called, warning them not to say anything we'd all regret later. "He's awake, isn't he?"

Maisie popped out of the nursery bedroom. "Oh yes, my lady. He's had his bath and he's playing with his toys. Such a good little chap. Entertaining himself."

We went into the nursery. A fire was burning in the hearth and the room was pleasantly warm. The big rocking horse I had ridden as a child still stood in the window. James was sitting on the braided rug in the middle of the room, busy with blocks of various shapes and sizes. He turned over when he saw me and started to crawl toward me.

"Ma ma ma," he said, holding out his arms to be picked up. He was just learning to say some words, having mastered "Dada" and "ball." He was now trying "Mama" occasionally.

"Hello, darling," I said, "I've brought a lady to meet you. This is Nanny. She's going to help look after you."

James stared at her warily, looked back at me, and for the first time in his life he said a new word. "No no no!"

"I can see Master James has a mind of his own," Nanny said. "No. Do not pick him up, your ladyship. A child must not get used to having his own way. Now, if I might suggest that you go downstairs and let me get better acquainted with your son." And she almost physically shoved me out of the room. I stood in the corridor feeling angry and helpless, ashamed of myself for letting her boss me around.

"Now, young man," I heard her voice coming from the room, "I can see the sooner you have settled into a proper routine, the better."

I went downstairs. Part of me whispered that she was right. James was going to inherit a peerage one day. He needed the same upbringing as the rest of our class. And Maisie was there to give James the necessary love and hugs. I went back to the morning room and tried to settle to reading the morning papers, when Phipps came in with the midday post on a salver.

"A letter for you, my lady."

I took it and recognized the crest immediately, also the bold, spiky handwriting of my sister-in-law. With trepidation I opened it.

My dear Georgiana,

I hope this missive finds you in good health and good spirits. All is well here in Scotland although we've had some particu-

larly fierce gales recently which have blown down some trees on the estate. Binky has had a nasty cold, but luckily has not passed it on to the children. Podge is making good progress with his studies and we hope he will be ready to start school at Lynwood House near you in September. Addy seems to enjoy taking part in his lessons so I suppose we'll have to think about a governess for her in the future. All costing money we don't have, of course.

The reason I am writing, my dear Georgiana, is that I have finally managed to find a suitable nanny for you. I was most disturbed when I last visited to find that you had no qualified nanny for James and that he was in danger of becoming hopelessly spoiled. I therefore made it my quest to search out a nanny for you, and have finally succeeded. She comes with the highest credentials, having been engaged by the Aubrey-Fulton family for their six sons and before that for the sons of the Duke of Huntington. All these young men have entered Sandhurst or Dartmouth successfully to start their careers in either the army or navy.

Nanny Hardbottle will be arriving a few days after you receive this and I hope that you will welcome her, handing over the running of the nursery to her immediately. I have decided, even though it is a great sacrifice, that I will pay her wages for the first six months, to give her time to settle into her new position. I have also decided, however inconvenient at this time, to come down to Sussex myself next week, just to make sure that Nanny is being given the appropriate help and support from your staff and that I shall be able to give you pointers on leaving the upbringing of your son in her very capable hands. Make the most of her, Georgiana. You are getting a treasure.

Your loving sister-in-law,
Hilda, Duchess of Rannoch

PS: Binky sends his love. He would come too but is occupied with the Highland cattle.

I put down the letter. "Oh crikey," I said. The thought of not only a terrifying nanny but also Fig in the house at the same time was daunting to say the least. If only Darcy would come home. If only Granddad were in the house. I needed an ally. Actually I could hear my grandfather's calm Cockney voice. "It's your house, my love. You tell her to take a long walk off a short pier if you don't want her." That's what he'd say. But it would have to be Darcy's decision as well as mine. Perhaps he wanted his son to be raised to be a leader of the empire.

I ate luncheon alone, then went up to give James his two-o'clock feed. I was met at the door by Nanny, who held up a finger to tell me to be quiet.

"Master James has just been put down for his afternoon nap," she said. "We wouldn't want to disturb him, would we?"

"But I usually nurse him at this time," I protested.

She shook her head and calmly ushered me into her sitting room. A fire had been lit in there and the room felt cozy and pleasant. I had seen the room before, without taking too much notice of it, but I remembered it as quite nondescript. It was as if she had waved a magic wand over it in the first two seconds, making it her own. She offered me a chintz-covered armchair and I sat.

"I came up to nurse him," I said. "He usually has a two-o'clock feed."

"Master James has had pureed carrots and a little semolina," she said. "He seemed to take to both quite quickly. I'd say he has been ready to move on to more grown-up food for some time. I suggest we make the most of his newfound interest and give up this notion of breastfeeding being good for him."

"But I can't just stop," I said. "I feel uncomfortable at this moment."

"I quite understand that," she said. "It must be a gradual process. I shall bring him to you at six in the morning for his first feed of the day, and at six at night before bath and bed. I shall also offer him warm milk in a bottle until we can progress to a cup. As soon as this transition is complete, say, within the month, then he will be brought down to you at teatime, at four o'clock sharp, for his hour of socializing with his parents. I hope this meets with your approval?"

"You want me to see my son for just an hour a day?" I demanded.

"I'm sure you're aware that this is normal procedure for a noble household? Were you not subject to such a schedule yourself?"

"I hardly even knew my parents," I said. "My father was mostly on the Riviera and my mother took off when I was quite young. I was lucky enough to have a kind and caring nanny so I didn't feel that I lacked anything. I want James also to be raised with love and warmth."

"He is a boy, my lady," she said. "He must learn strength and courage from the start. I'm sure your husband will agree with me. I presume he was sent off to school at a young age?"

"He was sent to boarding school," I said. "But also I gather his mother was a warm and gentle woman who was involved in the raising of her children. Unfortunately she died young."

"An Irish family, you said." The voice was icy. "I'm sure they are a little more lax over there. Now, if you will excuse me . . ." She stood up. "I shall bring the child down to your bedroom for you to feed him."

Then she went, not waiting to be dismissed.

THE AFTERNOON DRAGGED on. I kept one ear tuned to hear if James was crying, but heard nothing. I kept glancing at the clock, praying that Darcy would be home soon. Tea was served but I didn't feel hungry and was not tempted by Queenie's shorty whirl biscuits. Then, just before six, I went up to my bedroom. There was the brisk tap of feet along the hall, a tap on my door, and in came Nanny with James in her arms. He saw me, let out a huge wail and clung to me like a limpet.

"It's all right, my sweetheart. Mummy's here," I said, stroking back his dark curls.

"Now, Master James, remember what I told you," Nanny said. "You're a big boy now. And big boys don't cry or make a fuss." She gave me a warning look. "I shall return for him in half an hour."

I was left alone with my son. I don't know if it was because he had been upset by the change in routine, but he fussed and wouldn't nurse properly. I wondered if that woman had fed him a large meal right before he came to me. I wouldn't put it past her. In the end I gave in and rocked him on my shoulder, singing softly to him. His soft cheek against mine felt so perfect. When I heard feet approaching, I braced myself for the entrance of Nanny. Instead Darcy came in. He paused in the doorway, a smile spreading across his face. "Well, that's a sight for sore eyes," he said. "My two favorite people." He came over and kissed both of us. "How was your day?"

Then he stopped, staring at me. "What's wrong?" he said.

"Everything," I replied, fighting back tears. "Fig sent us a nanny. She's taken over the nursery and is trying to stop me from nursing James or seeing him too much."

Darcy perched on the bed beside me. "Fig sent her?"

I nodded. "She said she had been looking for the right nanny ever since she saw I didn't have one."

"I suppose I could say 'damned cheek,' but it is true. We have put off finding a proper nanny. I presume this one comes with good references?"

"This one has trained generations of boys for military service," I said. "She's terrifying, Darcy. She wants James on a routine and only brought down to us at teatime."

Darcy stroked my shoulder. "I suppose it had to happen, old thing," he said. "It is the done thing for our kind of people."

"I don't want to do the done thing," I exploded, making James stir and whimper on my shoulder. "I want my child with me. I want to enjoy his every moment."

Darcy slid an arm around my shoulders. "I do understand," he said, "but there should be a happy medium. James will eventually go away to school. We don't want him to be too clingy or dependent, do we? And what about you? You need the freedom to leave him at times, to travel with me, perhaps?"

"The last time I traveled with you, I nearly ended up being shoved down a lift shaft," I reminded him.

"Well, travels on your own, then," he said, laughing. "Trips up to London to see Zou Zou or your grandfather and not have to worry about getting back in time to take care of James."

"All right," I conceded, "I agree that we do need a nanny, but not a hard and horrible person like this one. A nanny more like mine, who would put me on her knee and sing to me."

"Then you have to make an effort to find such a person," Darcy said.

I glanced up at him, frowning. "I thought you'd be on my side," I said.

"I'm always on your side," he replied, stroking my cheek. "I'm just trying to be reasonable. We both agree we need a nanny. I have a job in London and the running of the home farm. The house and the servants are your responsibility. So if you want another nanny, you have to find one."

I was still frowning. A small voice whispered that he was right. I had put off the nanny problem, the way I put off anything I was going to find unpleasant. "I don't even know where to start. . . ." I began.

"Go and see Zou Zou," Darcy suggested. "She knows everybody. She'll probably wave her magic wand and a nanny will appear from a cupboard."

Now I had to laugh. "She probably would," I said. "That's exactly what I'll do, except . . . I can't go running off because Fig is due any day now."

"Fig is coming here?" A look of utter horror crossed his face.

I nodded. "She sent me a letter to announce the arrival of Nanny Hardbottle—don't laugh, Darcy, that's her name and it suits her—and added that she was coming down from Scotland herself to show me the ropes of dealing with a nanny."

"Bloody cheek," Darcy muttered, then corrected himself. "Sorry for the swearing. Show you the ropes indeed. So I think you should get to work on finding a replacement nanny right away. Then when she comes you can say thank you very much for your efforts; however, you had your own person in mind and she can take her candidate back to Scotland with her."

I nuzzled my face against Darcy's cheek. "Oh yes. That's exactly what I'll do," I said. "I'll go up to London on Monday and let Zou Zou work her magic."

Chapter 3

EYNSLEIGH

Feeling a little more hopeful this morning as I head up to
London. Zou Zou really is a miracle worker and she knows
everybody. She'll find me the world's most lovely nanny and
everything will be all right.

Accordingly on Monday morning I took the train with Darcy
from Haywards Heath up to London. It felt sort of forbidden
and exciting to be running away from home with my husband,
and I had to admit that it would be nice to do this kind of thing
occasionally. Zou Zou would give me a lovely lunch. She might
even take me shopping and allow me that glimpse into her own
glamorous world. (For those of you who haven't met Zou Zou,

she is a Polish princess who fled from her native land when her husband, the Prince Zamanska, was hacked to pieces by peasants, luckily not before he had transferred his fortune to Switzerland. So Zou Zou has been living a life of fun, adventure and extravagance in London, when not zooming around the continent on the little plane she pilots herself.)

I left Darcy heading from Victoria Station to Whitehall, where he now had an office. I stopped off at a Lyons to have a cup of tea and a bun since I was pretty sure Zou Zou would not be up and ready to receive visitors at nine thirty. Then I set off for Zou Zou's house on Eaton Square. It was only a short walk and I relished every moment. It was a lovely, crisp and breezy day. The sycamore trees that lined the streets were already showing the first hint of green buds. In the gardens of Eaton Square, daffodils were blooming and the birds were singing with gay abandon. It felt good to be alive. If I had a twinge of guilt about leaving James, I told myself that at least he'd be safe and cared for. No harm could come to him.

I glanced at my watch before I ascended the steps to Zou Zou's house. It was very like my family's own London residence, a tall white building with a pillared portico in the middle of Belgravia—the poshest part of London. Quarter past ten. Zou Zou should be up and around by now. I took a deep breath and pressed the doorbell. I heard the distant jangle, then the front door opened to reveal Clotilde, Zou Zou's maid.

"Lady Georgiana," she said, a fleeting look of surprise crossing her face. "How very nice to see you," she added in her strong French accent.

"Bonjour, Clotilde. Is Princess Zamanska at home?"

"She is, my lady," she replied. "You have just caught her in time. She is getting ready to depart on a journey."

"She's going on a trip?" I asked. "She didn't mention this last time I saw her." This was not too surprising. Zou Zou was a creature of impulse. One day she'd be having a fitting for a new gown and then suddenly decide to fly her little plane to Monte Carlo. Or pop to Ireland to see her racehorses (and Darcy's father, although that romance did not seem to be moving along as it should).

"Would you please tell her I'm here?" I said. "I won't take up too much of her time."

"But of course. Please come in." Clotilde stepped aside for me to enter. She took my hat and gloves before ushering me into the well-appointed sitting room at the front of the house. Warmth came from radiators around the walls. There were Persian rugs on the floor and a Monet over the fireplace. The whole room shouted money and taste. I went over and sat on a chair by the window, looking out at the tempting blue sky and picturing Zou Zou's plane soaring up and over the Channel. I was quite surprised when I heard the tap of high heels and Zou Zou entered dressed in a smart black Chanel suit and small black hat with a veil. Her dark hair with no hint of gray was swept back into a neat chignon and she was wearing only the minimum of rouge and lipstick.

"Georgie, my darling girl." She held out her hands to me. I stood to be kissed on both cheeks before she pulled me down to sit on the sofa beside her. "How well you look! Positively blooming. Motherhood agrees with you. And married life, of course. Who wouldn't be happy married to the delightful Darcy."

I rather suspected she'd had a little fling with my husband herself several years ago, so she was giving an informed opinion.

"I'm sorry to have arrived on your doorstep without warning," I said.

"In other circumstances you know I'd always be delighted to see you." She was still clasping my hands and smiling at me. "But unfortunately I'm rushing off. I have to catch the eleven thirty train north."

"Are you going anywhere exciting?" I asked. "You look frightfully smart."

"Nowhere exciting." The smile faded. "Positively depressing, in fact. I'm going to a funeral. In Derbyshire of all places. It will be cold and dreary at this time of year. Probably snow on the ground." She gave a dramatic sigh. "Usually I don't mind funerals at all. Quite like them, in fact. Although Zigmund's was a little over the top with all those bishops and people sobbing. It's a chance to get together with old pals one rarely sees and there is usually a good old booze-up afterward." She gave her trademark naughty grin. "But this one will be very sad. Quite tragic actually. It's for the son of an old friend. She was one of the first people I met when I came to London after Zigmund's death and she was so kind to me. Her son, Sebastian, was a horrid little boy at the time—you know, the type with a runny nose who kicks things—but he was sent off to school and turned out quite well. Went to Cambridge and then had been doing adventurous things around the world, rather like your adorable godfather. I sent him a present for his twenty-first but haven't seen him since."

She paused for breath, staring out past me now at the lovely flower arrangement on the low glass-topped table. "We sort of lost touch after she moved away. Her husband inherited a rather splendid estate in Derbyshire and they moved up to run it. We've exchanged Christmas cards but not much more until I received this funeral notice. Of course I have to go. Poor Tilly will be devastated. Her only son, you know."

"So he was still a young man?"

She nodded. "Couldn't have been more than thirty. Not married, as far as I've heard."

"How did he die?" I asked cautiously because I could see the pain on her face.

"Tragic accident. That's all it said." She stood up. "Look. I must dash. Have Clotilde make you anything you want to eat and drink and let's get together when I return. I don't suppose I'll stay more than one night. Not in Derbyshire."

As she talked she walked around the room, picking up her handbag, straightening her hat in the mirror. "Did you want to see me about something special or was this just a friendly visit because you happened to be in town?" she asked.

"I had a favor to ask," I said. "I wanted to pick your brains. But it can wait."

"Ask away now while I wait for the cab," she said, "then I can be thinking about it on the train."

I followed her toward the front door. Clotilde stood there, holding out her dark mink coat. She slipped it on and nodded to herself in the mirror with satisfaction. "At least I don't intend to freeze. My overnight bag, Clotilde?"

"I bring it to the voiture for you," Clotilde said. "I send a boy to find a taxi."

"Brilliant," Zou Zou said. "You're a treasure, Clotilde."

Clotilde blushed. "Thank you, madame."

"Now. What was your problem?" Zou Zou asked as she stood on the steps.

"I wanted your help in finding a nanny for James."

Zou Zou laughed. "I should have thought I'd be one of the last people who knew about nannies, having had no children of my own and actually trying to avoid them whenever possible. There must be agencies, surely."

I felt a bit crestfallen. "I just thought that you always knew people who knew people."

"I'll mull it over," she said. "Tilly's son, Sebastian, had a nanny, I remember. Perhaps she can remember where she found her. Oh, here's the cab now. Must fly, darling. I'll telephone when I return and we'll have lunch somewhere." She pecked a quick kiss on my cheek and dived into the cab, waving as it sped away.

I stood on the pavement in the empty square feeling let down and alone. Then I gave myself a pep talk. I didn't often have the chance to come up to London, I told myself. So I should make the most of a whole free day. There were things I must need at Harrods or Selfridges. Whether I could afford them was another matter, but there was no harm in looking. So I set off in the direction of Knightsbridge and Harrods. On the way I realized I was passing the mews where my best friend, Belinda, lived when she was in London. I stared down the narrow cobbled lane with a sense of longing. I missed her. She was quite different from me—daring, sexy, bubbly, sophisticated, the naughty girl at school who had climbed out the dorm window to meet ski instructors and who had taught me to smoke. For the past year or so she had been living in Paris, honing her designing skills with none other than Chanel. I hadn't heard from her recently— Belinda wasn't the best of letter writers—but I presumed she was still in Paris, up to her eyes as they prepared for the spring collections.

I don't know what made me walk down the mews and tap on her front door. It wasn't until I had done this that I realized Belinda might have let the place to strangers. Feeling foolish, I was about to turn away when the door opened.

"Georgie!" a delighted voice said, and Belinda stood there dressed in a lovely purple silk dressing gown trimmed with ostrich feathers. Her usually sleek cap of black hair stood up in all directions and she blinked at me, her eyes reacting to the bright sunlight.

"Belinda, you're back!" I exclaimed. "How wonderful!" Then I checked myself. "Sorry," I said. "I didn't mean to wake you. I just stopped by on the off chance that you might have come home, and here you are."

"That's right. Here I am," she repeated. "You absolutely must be psychic. I only came home yesterday and I was going to telephone you today, when I'd had the telephone reconnected. Come on in. The place is a frightful mess with boxes and trunks everywhere, but I expect I can find you somewhere to sit while I get dressed."

She led me into a tiny sitting room that was indeed piled with luggage, but she threw a hatbox off the sofa. "Sit there. Don't move. I'll get dressed and be down," she said. "I want to hear about everything."

Then I heard her feet going up the stairs and the sound of

water running as she presumably took a bath or shower. I waited patiently. The room was rather cold, since no fire had been lit and any central heating there might have been had not been turned on. Eventually Belinda returned, now wearing a cashmere jumper and well-cut woolen slacks. It was a simple outfit, but it screamed Paris and her mentor, Chanel. It only needed a string of pearls to complete it. She removed another item of luggage and sank into an armchair.

"Are you home on a visit?" I asked. "You seem to have brought an awful lot of luggage with you."

"Not a visit, darling. I'm home for good. I'd decided I'd had enough of Paris. I think I've learned all I can from Chanel. Besides, she's got a new beau and is spending a lot of time on his yacht in the Med. I certainly didn't want to find myself in the role of unpaid lackey while she's away. And I have grown weary of Frenchmen."

"Really?" I tried not to look amused. Belinda and her men were a constant source of interest to me, having led a terribly sheltered life myself.

"And Italian men. And Continental men in general," she added. "All the Frenchmen I meet tell me they adore me, write me long, passionate letters, then want to set me up as their mistress while they marry a pure and virginal Catholic girl of good family. Or they live with their mothers. I have a great yearning for a plain and simple British bloke who drinks beer at the pub, plays rugby and calls a spade a spade."

"You had one," I pointed out. "You let him go." (Belinda had met a nice Cornishman and they seemed perfect for each other, but the difference in class got in the way.)

She wrinkled her nose. "I know. Silly of me. I expect he's found someone else by now."

"You could go down to Cornwall and see. . . ."

"I'll think about it." She toyed with the fringe on a cushion.

"So what do you plan to do now you're back?" I asked. "Set up a salon in London?"

"I don't know about that either," she said. "Frankly. I'm tired of dealing with rich spoiled women. They want everything about the dress altered to their taste, then they try to walk away without paying. You know, I might go down to Cornwall and get to work on my grandmother's old house. But first I'm going to enjoy London for a while. And seeing my old friends. I have to come and see your little son. He must be a few months old by now and I haven't even seen him. Terrible of me."

"Yes. Please do. I'd love it. You'll keep me sane."

"Don't tell me Darcy is driving you round the bend?" she asked.

"Not Darcy. He's still wonderful. No. I've acquired a frightful new nanny and my sister-in-law, Fig, is coming to stay. I have to endure both until I can find a nanny to replace her."

"Gosh. How grim. Why did you select a frightful nanny in the first place, darling?"

"I didn't. That's the point." I heard my voice rising. "Fig chose her and sent her to me, and has paid her wages for six months. What's more she's coming down any day now to make sure Nanny is settled in and I learn to behave properly."

"Bloody cheek," Belinda said, echoing Darcy. "Is the nanny really grim?"

"The grimmest," I said. "A face that would curdle milk.

Plans to put James on a strict routine and only let me see him at teatime. I hate that, Belinda. I want to be part of the upbringing of my son."

"Don't put up with it, darling. You're letting yourself be bullied by that frightful sister-in-law. Tell her you thank her for her kind thoughts but now she can go and take the dreadful nanny with her."

I chewed on my bottom lip, something I did when stressed. "I don't want to cause a huge family rift," I said. "But I don't want her nanny either. Darcy suggested I find a nanny I like and then tell this one we've made other plans. That's why I'm up in town. I was hoping Zou Zou might know the right sort of place to find a good nanny, but she's off to a funeral in the north."

Belinda had been nodding sympathetically. "I tell you what," she said, her face brightening up. "I've got to find a new maid. I've had enough of looking after myself. Let's go to some agencies together this morning."

"Oh yes, let's," I said. "Have you used a good one before?"

"When I hired my last maid," she said. "But that was years ago. We can try them and if they don't specialize in nannies we can ask for a recommendation. Are you free all day?"

"As a bird, as it happens. I'm meeting Darcy to catch the train home at five."

"Then let's do servant shopping, then go out to lunch. I've been dying for good old English food—fish and chips. Shepherd's pie . . ."

"If you come to us, then Queenie can cook all those things for you."

She shot me an alarmed glance. "Queenie? She is still with you?"

"As assistant cook. I have Pierre, the chef we met in Paris, who cooks divinely."

"Oh yes. Of course. And Queenie hasn't poisoned anyone yet?"

"She has not, although Pierre was suspected of poisoning guests at a dinner party. He didn't, of course. And Queenie is not a bad cook, as it happens. Come down and I can guarantee a jam roly-poly or a steak and kidney pud."

"How divine." Belinda reached across and grabbed my hand. "I have missed you, old thing."

"You could have come to stay at any time," I pointed out.

"I know, but I was so busy in Paris, and frankly I thought of you with your happy family and I felt somehow superfluous."

"Don't be silly. I've really missed you too."

She jumped up, pulling me to my feet. "Come on. Let's go nanny hunting then have lunch somewhere posh. The Dorchester? Ritz?"

I laughed, nervously. "Belinda, do I need to remind you that I am a housewife whose money goes on bibs and nappies?"

"But darling, I am rolling in the stuff," she said. "And I actually sold several of my creations in Paris, so it's my treat. We might even do a little shopping on Bond Street."

She grabbed a smart but mannish tweed jacket that obviously also came from Chanel, then almost dragged me out of the house. We set out for Hyde Park Corner, then crossed into Mayfair, walking up Park Lane. The agency was on Mount Street, next to an expensive-looking hat shop and a solicitor's. I glanced at Belinda as we approached.

"I'm terrified in these places," I said. "They are always run by women who are so frightfully snooty that I feel I have to curtsy to them."

"Just remember that you are the employer and you are doing them a favor by keeping them in business," Belinda said. "And you are related to the king, for heaven's sake. Make sure they know that. Nobody can be snooty to a royal. If you like, I'll do most of the talking."

With that she strode up to the agency door, flung it open and stepped inside.

Chapter 4

It's so wonderful to know that Belinda is back in England. I've missed her.

A bell jangled. We found ourselves in a foyer that was spare and efficient in appearance. The floor was parquet. On the wall was a tasteful print of the Scottish Highlands. Facing us was a big mahogany desk and behind it sat the sort of woman I always dreaded meeting. Her graying curls were perfectly in place. She wore a burgundy silk blouse with an opal pin at her throat and a little too much makeup. Her little dark eyes darted around, ready to strike.

"May I help you ladies?" she asked in an accent that would make the queen sound as if she came from the East End.

"Good morning." Belinda stepped forward. "I am Belinda Warburton-Stoke and I am here with Lady Georgiana Rannoch, the king's cousin. We are both in need of household help."

The woman's eyes lit up. "Of course. Of course. Miss Warburton-Stoke. I remember now. We supplied you with a personal maid a few years ago. I hope she proved to be satisfactory. We do like satisfied return clients. So happy to oblige. You've come to the right place. Please do take a seat."

With that she ran out of breath. We sat on the two upholstered chairs facing the desk.

"Now." The dragon fixed us with her steely gaze. "What manner of staff should you be requiring?" I heard now, under the cut-glass accent, hints of humble beginnings. The accent had been carefully practiced, as had my mother's.

"I am just returned from Paris and in need of a maid," Belinda said.

"Of course. Of course. That would be a lady's maid?"

"Actually I'd like more than that. I only have a small mews flat, so I'd like someone to take care of my clothes, but also keep the place clean and cook for me. . . ."

"Cook for you as well?" The woman gave Belinda a severe frown. "My dear Miss Warburton-Stoke, I am not a miracle worker. If you are in need of a skivvy, I can assure you that you'd find plenty of willing applicants in Whitechapel or Shoreditch. We only handle domestic help of the highest quality."

"When I say cook," Belinda said hastily, "I mean make me tea and coffee, the occasional egg for breakfast. I shall not be eating at home much. And I intend to travel a lot."

"I really don't know how I can help you, but let me see what I have on the books right now." She opened an impressive ledger, running a finger down the page and making tut-tutting noises as she went. "These women would not take kindly to being asked to cook and clean," she said. "They are ladies' maids of the highest caliber." Then she paused. "Wait a minute. Would it matter if the girl was foreign? As it happens I have an Austrian young lady, newly arrived in England and anxious to find work. Her English needs improving but she has been in service in her own country."

"I don't mind her nationality," Belinda said.

"She did stress that she was Austrian," the dragon said. "So many people are not willing to take on a German servant at the moment, given the frightful situation over there." Then she paused. "I must apologize, Lady Georgiana, since your royal family connections obviously have German roots."

"Not for a long time," I said. "My great-grandmother Queen Victoria was born in England after all."

"Quite. Quite." She looked pleased. "And what manner of domestic employee are you looking for yourself?"

"A nanny," I said. "I have a young baby and the current nanny is not proving to be suitable."

"Oh dear. I'm afraid this is something I cannot help you with. You need a specialized agency for that. I can refer you to an agency that supplies nannies to all the best families. So you have recently had a child. An heir, I hope?"

"Yes, it's a boy."

"Your husband must be pleased. As will the family."

"My husband is pleased," I replied, slightly annoyed that

everyone welcomes a boy more than a girl. "So am I, actually. He's an adorable little chap."

"When was he born?"

"Last August."

The expression changed. "And you are now looking for a new nanny?" The look seemed to say that I must be the one responsible for the relationship not working out.

I nodded. "I have a nursery maid, but I wanted to be involved with the care of my son in his early days."

The woman shook her head in pitying fashion. "Such a modern attitude. I gather that even the king and queen liked to be present at the princesses' bath time. You know them, I presume . . . the little princesses?"

"Oh yes," I said. "I saw them at Sandringham last Christmas."

"They seem such delightful children."

"They are. Very sweet, both of them."

The woman sighed. "How I envy you, being on intimate terms with our new king and queen. I think they'll do a good job, don't you? Of course we regret losing dear King Edward, but that woman would never have done as his consort, would she?"

I didn't like discussing my family with a complete stranger, so I merely nodded. "The name of the agency, if you please?"

"Of course." She wrote down the name and address. Not far away, on Curzon Street. "And Miss Warburton-Stoke, would you like me to send the young Austrian girl to you on a trial basis, to see if she might prove suitable?"

"Yes. You can do that. You have my address in your files, I think."

"I'm sure we do. I bid you both good day, ladies."

༄

"WELL, THAT WAS simple enough," Belinda said as we came out into a brisk breeze. "A hefty *Fräulein* straight from the mountains might be a good idea."

"As long as she's not too hefty and doesn't clomp about in the early mornings while yodeling."

Belinda chuckled. "You do have a point there."

"And she doesn't ruin your good clothes, after being used to washing things in mountain streams. You wouldn't want another Queenie."

"True enough. As long as she's willing to learn, and not speaking English might be an advantage because she can't let on about anyone I might bring home."

"I thought you'd given up men."

"Foreign men, I said. I'm still on the hunt for a decent English bloke. There must be one around who hasn't been snapped up. Come on. Let's find you a nanny on Curzon Street."

The second agency was even more intimidating than the first. The woman took down all my details, then looked up. "What exactly do you require in a nanny?"

"Someone kind and gentle," I said. "Someone who will love my child as I do. None of this old-fashioned starch and routine and discipline."

She looked shocked. "I think you will find that most nannies are trained in routine and discipline. It prepares the young for a future at boarding school and then in the army or colonial service." She flicked through her books. "Nanny Peacock? No, perhaps not. She is known for her rigid rules. I do have Nanny

Ramsbottom at the moment. Just back from taking care of a family in Switzerland. A first-class woman. Of course she comes at a price." And she named one that would have bought me a new Bentley. I thanked her politely and left feeling dispirited.

"How am I going to find the right person?" I asked Belinda. "I just want a nice, simple woman who will make my child happy. I'm not raising James to go into the army."

Belinda took my arm. "Let's leave it for today. She has your telephone number. A suitable candidate might turn up." She paused as an idea came to her. "Obvious! Why didn't we think of this before? We'll put advertisements in *The Lady*. You can say you're looking for a special nanny who is warm and caring and I can say I want a maid who is versatile enough to take care of my every need."

"I wouldn't say that," I said. "It sounds rather suggestive."

Belinda laughed. "I suppose it does. I'll work on the phrasing. But it's brilliant, isn't it? We spell out exactly what we want and we'll get it."

"I think you should give Brunhilde a chance first," I said. "She might be quite good and bake you strudels."

I broke off as Big Ben tolled twelve, resounding through the air.

Belinda looked up. "Come on. Let's go have lunch at the Dorchester, or how about the Ritz? Or Fortnum's?" She listed these as if lunching at any of them was a usual occurrence.

This was all rather heady for me. "I don't mind. They all sound marvelous. You choose."

"All right. Then let's do Claridge's. That's close by." Belinda set off through Mayfair until we came to the hotel on the corner of Brook Street. The large, square redbrick building had never struck me as elegant, but I had to admit it was imposing. I felt horribly provincial and underdressed as we entered the dining room, but Belinda strode out as if she ate at places like this every day. "Not quite as grand as the Ritz in Paris," she said, looking around, "but I suppose it will do."

The maître d' took in the Chanel jacket and ushered us to a table. Belinda insisted on ordering a bottle of bubbly—"to celebrate your return, darling"—and oysters.

"May I recommend the duck, madame?" the waiter said.

"Oh God no," Belinda replied. "I've just come back from Paris. I've had enough duck to last a lifetime. You don't have a good steak pie, do you?"

He looked mildly surprised. "If you require something English, then I can recommend the roast beef with Yorkshire pudding."

"That sounds perfect," Belinda said. I agreed.

The champagne had been opened with a satisfying pop and we had just started on the oysters when two men came to sit at the next table, involved in animated conversation.

"When was this?" one asked.

"Only last week."

"Well, that's a rum do," one was saying. "Poor fellow. I can't say I remember him, but I've read about his exploits recently."

"Yes, he was making a name for himself, wasn't he? Who'd have thought it? His pater is devastated. Would be, of course. He was an only son. Now the title will go to a cousin."

I thought the voice sounded familiar. I glanced across at the same time as the fellow looked up. Our eyes met. I saw recognition in his. "Good God. It's Georgie. It's been ages. How are you, old bean?"

Augustus Gormsley had been a chubby youth and had turned into a portly man with a round red face and a self-satisfied sort of expression. We had moved in the same circles during my post-deb period. I had had several encounters with him, not all pleasant, but I smiled politely.

"Very well, thank you, Gussie," I said. "And you?"

"Fair to middling, I suppose. I've been away in Australia. Trying my luck, you know. Mining. Sheep farming. Actually got sent there by the pater when I ran up some rather uncomfortable debts. But now all is forgiven and I'm back home and ready to settle down. How about you?"

"Already settled down, thank you," I said. "I'm married with a baby."

"Well done. Did they force you to marry foreign royalty? I know they were trying to once. Wasn't his name Prince Siegfried?"

"No. They did not. I married a chap of my own choice and we're very happy. Darcy O'Mara. I expect you know him."

"Good God. You managed to tie down old Darcy? I saw him as the perennial man-about-town." He looked across at his seatmate. "You know Georgie Rannoch, don't you? Binky's sister? Well, she's married Darcy O'Mara."

"Oh. Right." The other man looked at me with interest. "No. I don't think we've met, although I knew your brother at Eton. I'm Rowdy. Rowdy Ruffles." We nodded politely to each other. "And you're married to old Darcy? I never thought any girl would get him to settle down. Not old Darcy. He must have finally been worn out with all that . . ." A warning glance from Gussie made him not finish the sentence.

"This is my friend Belinda Warburton-Stoke," I said. "Belinda—Rowdy Ruffles and Augustus Gormsley."

"Oh, Gussie and I go back a long way," Belinda said.

Gussie's eyes lit up as he recognized her. "I say, Belinda, you're looking absolutely spiffing," Gussie said. "Don't tell me you're also hitched with hundreds of children."

"Free as air, actually," Belinda said. "I just returned from living in Paris."

"One can see that," Rowdy said, "from the clothes."

They were both now ogling Belinda, I, the married woman, having been forgotten. But that was how it always had been with Belinda. Beside her I was invisible. Not that I minded anymore. . . .

"I say, Belinda," Gussie said, "if you're in London and free as air, so am I. Do you fancy going to a nightclub? The Astor was quite good, I remember. Or the Café de Paris? Or we could see if any new ones have opened."

"Why not?" Belinda said. "I haven't had my toes trodden on by a true-blue English gentleman for quite a while."

"Oh, come on, old bean. That's not fair. I am told I trip the light fantastic rather well. And it's not the only thing I do rather well, as it happens." He gave her a knowing look. Having managed to escape once from Gussie's clutches, I thought I'd better warn her.

Conversation waned as their cocktails were brought along with a plate of pâté and a bowl of soup. We finished our oysters and sipped our champagne.

"So have they held the funeral yet?" Rowdy asked.

"They just did. Up in Windermere, where he was racing that damned boat. I attended and just got back last night. I didn't know him that well but I thought one should do the right thing and support an old Trinity College classmate."

"Quite right," Rowdy said. "He wasn't at school with us, was he?"

"No. Winchester, I gather. Rather a brainy chap I remember from college days. A little too intense for me. Actually studied and passed his exams."

"I suppose it was an accident waiting to happen," Rowdy said. "Pushing speed records like that. Boats weren't meant to go that fast. Punts on the Isis were more my style."

"Sorry for interrupting," Belinda said. "But are you talking about the chap who was trying to break the water speed record? His boat crashed on Lake Windermere?"

"That's right," Gussie said. "Algie Beauchamps." He pronounced it *Beecham*, of course. One does. "I just attended the funeral. I must say it's sobering when it's one of our age who has popped off. Still, he did like living dangerously. I suppose I took a few risks myself in Australia. Met a shark once when I was surfing. Nearly fell down a mine shaft. Maybe it's about time I lived a sober and godly life."

Rowdy laughed at this. "You'd die of boredom."

Gussie grinned too. "You're right. I would." He went back to tucking into a large helping of pheasant.

We turned our attention to a plate piled high with thin slices of pink roast beef, a round puffy Yorkshire pudding, crispy roast potatoes and brussels sprouts. For a while there was silence apart from a sigh of content, then Belinda looked up suddenly. "I meant to tell you. You'll never guess who I met in Paris." She paused, a wicked smile on her face. "The one and only Mrs. Simpson, soon to be Mrs. Former King."

"Oh golly. Did you?"

Belinda nodded. "She came into Chanel to see the spring collection. Items for her trousseau, I gather. Although the things she picked were not quite as grand as they would have been for Queen Wallis." She took a sip of her wine. "Are you invited to the wedding? She was very fond of you, you know."

"I don't think Wallis Simpson is fond of anyone but herself," I corrected. "We have not received an invitation, and if we did I think we'd have to turn it down. Darcy says that the king and queen want no members of the royal family to attend. It will be in France, I presume."

"Probably. They are staying in a château near Paris at the moment. I wonder where they will choose to live after their marriage."

"I wonder what they will do with themselves. She won't like not being the center of attention any longer. And between you and me, Belinda, I heard that she was having second thoughts about marrying him. It was only the idea of queen that appealed to her. Once they are stuck in exile together I think she might regret it."

"How sad," Belinda said. "So he really gave up the throne for nothing. Do you think Bertie will make a better king? He is so shy and has that awful stutter."

"But he has Elizabeth beside him. She's strong and determined. I think they'll do very well."

"I hope so," Belinda said. "I think the world is in for tough times ahead. I met so many people in Paris who had decided to leave Germany. It's getting worse there by the minute. If you say anything about Hitler you are taken away in the middle of the night. Neighbors are turning in their neighbors. It's frightful, Georgie, and your mother is there."

"I know. I've tried talking to her, but you know Mummy. She loves being adored and the center of attention. Max adores her. All the Nazi hierarchy adore her. She'll just turn a blind eye to anything she doesn't like. There's nothing I can do."

"I hope she won't leave it too late," Belinda said.

Chapter 5

After an absolutely decadent luncheon we came out of Claridge's feeling replete and a bit squiffy from the champagne. At least I felt squiffy—not used to drinking at lunchtime. Also my body was reminding me that I had not given my son his two-o'clock feed. I hoped I wasn't leaking.

"You made quite a hit with Gussie Gormsley," I said.

"I'm not sure I want to be a hit with someone like him," Belinda answered. "I remember him from years ago. Wandering hands. A little too eager for the old rumpy-pumpy, as he put it."

I laughed. "I had to fight him off once. But you did say you wanted a good old British bloke. He's as British as they come."

"I think I can do a trifle better than that, but I don't mind being taken to a nightclub to get me back in the swing of things."

"He'll probably want you to pay," I commented.

We headed toward Bond Street. The day had clouded over, the way they always do, and dark clouds were building to the west.

"It's strange that I was just reading about that speedboat accident on the train coming over from Paris," Belinda said. "I wonder why people want to set records all the time. Or climb unclimbable mountains like your godfather."

"Don't ask me," I said. "I'm all for a quiet life with my husband and baby. Golly, I hope James is all right with that awful nanny. The agency didn't sound too promising, did it? If only Zou Zou . . ." I broke off. "That's a coincidence, isn't it? She was off to a funeral today. I wonder if it was the same chap." I corrected myself. "No, it can't have been, because Gussie just came back from Algie whatsit's funeral."

"Another young man?" Belinda asked.

"Yes. Another tragic accident too. I suppose young men like to live dangerously so it's not too surprising."

"I've always found that things like that come in threes," Belinda said. And we moved on to other subjects. Belinda insisted on shopping in Bond Street, while I looked on with just a slight twinge of envy.

"One wants to look British again," she said. "A good old pleated skirt and a jumper."

I laughed. "When have you ever worn a pleated skirt and jumper?"

She laughed too. "Well, maybe not that British. But something suitable for country weekends. A jersey dress. A hacking jacket. Good old-fashioned brogue shoes, you know."

We shopped without too much success while she declared

British clothes to be deadly dull and that she'd just have to design and run up a few things herself. Then we parted ways, me heading for the tube to Victoria Station and she back to her flat. I met Darcy at the station.

"Had a good day?" he asked.

"Lovely. I saw Zou Zou briefly, and you'll never guess! I met Belinda. She's back in London."

"That's good news," he said. "Back in London for good or on a visit?"

"For good. I've invited her to come down to Eynsleigh."

"Good idea."

We couldn't talk during the train ride home as the compartment was packed with businessmen in bowler hats returning home from the city. Darcy drove me home from the station. We came into the front hall to be greeted, as usual, by the puppies, Holly and Jolly, making a fuss of us as if we'd been away for years. Mrs. Holbrook appeared immediately. "Oh, I'm so sorry, sir, my lady. I don't know who let them out. They really are a bit of a handful."

"I know they are," Darcy said. "I think I'll have to take a stern hand to them. Although in my experience Labs are usually untrainable and wild until they are two, then instantly become calm and adorable. So be patient." He stroked Jolly's head as he spoke. Jolly looked up at him adoringly. Holly, the jealous one, tried to nudge her brother out of the way. I bent to pat her.

"I'm glad you've come home, my lady," she said. "That new nanny was in a fair tizzy when she brought young James down for his feed at six o'clock and you weren't home."

"Goodness," I said. "It's only just gone six, isn't it?"

Darcy consulted his watch. "Six oh seven," he said. "You'd better fly straight up or it will be no supper for you." He chuckled.

As I made for the stairs, Mrs. Holbrook put out a hand to restrain me. "Don't go yet, my lady. I should warn you that you have a visitor."

"A visitor?" What now?

"Her grace, the duchess, is in the sitting room. She arrived at midday."

"Oh golly." I gave Darcy an exasperated glance. "Not Fig. Not yet. There is a limit to my endurance."

"Which of them do you want to face first?" Darcy asked, still looking a little amused, which made me want to slap him.

"I'd better nurse James. He won't be happy, poor little chap. You go and entertain Fig."

With that I ran up the stairs to my bedroom, taking off my jacket as I went. I could hear James's protests as I hurried along the hall. I came in to find Nanny Hardbottle sitting in the chair at my dressing table holding in her arms a squirming and red-faced baby.

"You are late," Nanny Hardbottle said, glaring at me. "Your son is quite distressed. This is why you should wean him as quickly as possible now. I will always make sure his meals are on time." She stood up and handed him to me. "I will return to collect him in half an hour."

James put out his arms to me and gave a big sob as I took him. "It's all right, darling. Mummy's here," I whispered. We settled down on the bed and he started nursing greedily, although I think it was the comfort he wanted more than the nutrition. I smoothed back his curls and gazed down at him, tears springing into my own eyes at the thought of him unhappy. "I love you so much," I whispered. "I don't want someone else to take care of you."

I toyed with the whole concept of a nanny. Maisie was good with him, wasn't she? She bathed him and sang to him. What more did I want? I thought about my own nanny. She had been kind but also firm. She made quite clear what was expected of me, the rules of polite behavior. A lady never does this. A lady always does that. Silly little things like "Got, hot and lot are words a lady never uses." One is never hot. It's a trifle humid in here. It's never I've got a lot of things. I have plenty of things. Nanny had all sorts of sayings that stuck. Wills and won'ts and shalls and shan'ts are naughty words for boys and gals. I smiled now. So she did instill good behavior and etiquette into me. Would Maisie be able to do that for James? I could do so myself, but would I want to spend all my days in the nursery? And Maisie was a simple country girl. I'm afraid her vocabulary and accent were not suitable for James to imitate as he learned to speak.

James had just fallen asleep in my arms when Nanny returned on the dot of six thirty.

"There we are. Quite content. A lot of fuss over nothing," she said as she took him. "I'm afraid he's been rather too indulged and spoiled, your ladyship. Rather too used to getting his own way. Well, that will soon change, you'll see." Then she stalked out of the room before I could say anything.

"Number one task for tomorrow morning," I muttered to myself. Buy a copy of *The Lady* and place an advertisement for a nanny. I brushed my hair, powdered my nose and made myself presentable before I went down to face Fig. She and Darcy were sitting beside the fire, Fig holding a glass of sherry and with a plate of cheese straws beside her. They both looked up as I came in.

"Ah, there you are, Georgiana," she said. "I was surprised to find that your staff were not expecting me and my room was not ready. I thought I gave you ample warning of my arrival."

"There must have been a holdup with the post," I said. "Your letter arrived after your nanny did. It was an awful shock, I can tell you, both for James and me."

"Ridiculous postal service," she snapped. "Just because we live in a slightly remote area is no excuse for not collecting the letters daily. I know there was a bit of a snowstorm, but really. If a postman can't walk through a foot of snow, what good is he?" She took a gulp of sherry. "Anyway, all is now well. I see that Nanny Hardbottle has worked her magic on her nursery quarters, just as I had expected. You have acquired a treasure, Georgiana. I hope she is with you for many years to mold and direct all your future children. The Aubery-Fultons could not say enough about her. They were told by the military academy that no child has ever come as prepared as their youngest, Peregrin. A proper little soldier with a fine sense of duty, they said."

I shuddered and tried not to look at Darcy.

"Actually it's up to Georgie how comfortable she feels with the nanny," Darcy said.

"Comfortable? She's not supposed to feel comfortable. All she needs to know is that the nanny is competent and will raise the children as befits your station. You are not bringing up James to be a middle-class bank clerk. He is destined to be a future leader of the empire."

"Podge is also destined to be a duke," I pointed out, "and yet your nanny seems nice enough."

"A little too nice at times," Fig said. "She allows Podge to have feelings. Says he is a sensitive child. Utter rubbish."

"He is a sensitive child, Fig," I said. "So was Binky."

"That's just the point, Georgiana. I certainly don't want him to grow up like his father. Binky is far too softhearted. Do you know he actually cried when one of his favorite calves died, and he refused to let me take the meat for veal cutlets? I think he cares about those cows more than he does about me."

That would not be hard, I thought but did not say.

"Anyway, Fig, we'll give Nanny a fair trial," Darcy said. "It's up to her to fit in with our ways, not the other way around."

"But that's just the point," Fig said. "You have no ways. That child has been without a proper schedule. You've been bringing him down to the sitting room whenever you feel like it, letting him be held and passed around, and still being nursed when he's close to a year old. It won't do, Georgiana." She leaned toward me. "Now, I know you are young and inexperienced. You need guidance, and that is why I am here. Nanny and I only want to make your life run smoothly and simply. I have told Binky he must do without me. I am prepared to stay on as long as you need me."

And to my horror she reached across and patted my knee.

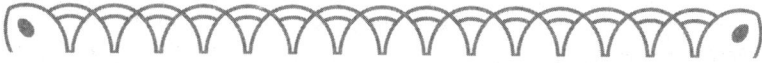

Chapter 6

How am I going to handle this situation? Fig and Nanny at the
same time! Although I do realize now that she is right about
one thing. James should be weaned. Those little teeth are
horribly sharp and he likes to practice biting.

The rap on my door at six o'clock in the morning was a rude
awakening. I sat up in bed, adjusting my nightgown as Nanny
came in carrying a bleary-eyed James.

"Time for the early morning feed, my lady," Nanny said. She
looked wide-awake and efficient with a starched white pinny
over her gray uniform. Darcy turned over and grunted. I nudged
him before he said or did something inappropriate.

"Nanny has brought James for his morning feed," I said.

"Good show," he muttered and went back to sleep.

James seemed distracted and not that interested. I suspected he wasn't quite awake yet. I realized with a jolt that Nanny might be right in this instance. In addition to his sharp little teeth, he might be losing interest now that he was being introduced to other food. Maybe I was at fault, not wanting him to move on because I enjoyed the closeness. He nursed for a few minutes, then squirmed and wanted to be active. I handed him back and went over to my writing desk while I awaited my morning tea.

First I composed the advertisement to *The Lady*. "Wanted for noble household: an experienced nanny. Must have good credentials but also be kind, loving and adaptable." Yes, that should do it. Salary? What did one pay a good nanny? I had no idea, also no idea how much we could spend. I knew the home farm was now producing income and Darcy was being paid regularly. Sir Hubert left money in the bank for the running of the house, but I didn't like to take his money for a nanny. So I'd leave the mention of a salary out.

I then took a sheet of writing paper.

Dear Belinda,

Fig has arrived. Please come as soon as you can and let me know when you have a telephone installed. Nanny and Fig in my house at the same time! I need support!

I addressed the envelope, put a stamp on it, then tied my dressing gown, tiptoed downstairs and left it on the hall table for when the postman delivered the early post. With any luck, Belinda would get it by the end of the day. I hoped she'd take pity on me and come flying to my aid. The day passed, then the next while I entertained—no, make that endured—Fig as she tried to lecture me on the proper treatment of servants.

"You are far too kind, Georgiana," she said. "Servants take kindness for weakness. They should tremble every time you summon them."

"You've just told me that Nanny should be in complete control of the nursery and I should consider myself a guest there," I pointed out. "I don't notice Nanny trembling when I look at her."

"Well, Nanny is different. The nursery is her own little kingdom," Fig said. "The same as the chef. The kitchen is his domain. They should both be treated with respect and caution."

"But it's my son she's looking after," I said. "And my meals that the chef is preparing with my money."

She patted my hand, something I found horribly annoying. "Georgiana, you have to learn. You are still so young and inexperienced, and of course you grew up with no guidance. You had no parents to show you how to run a great house. My mother, on the other hand, was a superb example of a mistress."

I had an overwhelming desire to giggle. Fig's mother, Lady Wormwood, would never have been a candidate for anyone's mistress. She resembled a stick insect with a toad's face with the most supercilious expression on it.

"My servants all seem quite content, Fig," I said.

"Content? They are not supposed to be content."

I said no more and wondered when I could politely tell her to go home. I waited anxiously for Belinda to telephone me. No call came. On the second day I received a letter.

Dear Georgie,

I'm so sorry to be leaving you in the lurch with the two witches, but I'm stuck here at the moment. When I inquired about having a telephone reconnected I was told that it wouldn't be before the end of the month. The man said that there was a big demand for telephones at the moment. Ordinary people now wanted them for their houses. I ask you, Georgie, why would ordinary people want telephones? If the woman from the bakery wanted to talk to her cousin Mabel she could see her in the baker's shop or just walk down the street. I seriously think this is giving people ideas above their station. I'm sorry if I sound like a snob, but I am a snob. I was brought up to be one.

In other news, Brunhilde has arrived. Her name is actually Trudi and I think she might possibly do. She's clearly from peasant stock, very humble and shy. She curtsies every time she speaks to me, calling me "Gnädige Frau." Her English is practically nonexistent, but when she understands she nods with enthusiasm and says, "Ja, ja. Gut!" But she has been in service to a count in Austria and seems to know about taking care of clothes, which is the main thing. Of course she hadn't a clue about making English tea. I had to show her, step by step, but a passable cup did appear at my bedside this morning, so there is hope.

I went to a nightclub with Gussie yesterday. Contrary to his belief that he's a good dancer I came home with bruised toes. He was amusing enough and we met people we both know, but he escorted me home and expected to be asked in. I told him I had just arrived home and none of my bags had yet been unpacked so he left, disappointed. Frankly, darling, I just did not fancy him. I mean who would? I've become more choosy in my old age.

So chin up, darling, and be bold. Don't let the witches get you down. I'll come down as soon as I can. In the meantime hold the fort and give little James a kiss from me.

Yours,

Belinda

I scowled at the paper in frustration. I needed that ally. Belinda wouldn't be intimidated by Fig or a nanny. Darcy was also being annoying. He announced at breakfast that he had to go away for a few days.

"You can't leave me with Fig," I said. "That just isn't fair."

He stifled a grin. "Sorry, old thing, but I do have a job. Maybe you should pretend to appreciate Nanny and all that Fig has told you so she can go home."

"I was never good at telling lies," I retorted.

"Then telephone Binky and ask him to summon her home."

I had to laugh at this. "As if Binky has ever summoned anyone in his life. And he's also too guileless to lie and say that he needs her or wants her back."

"Then go up to visit Belinda if she won't come to you."

I considered this. "I hardly like to when she's just settling in."

"Then go and see your grandfather."

"Oh yes. I could do that." This made me perk up. "I haven't seen him in a month or more. Good excuse to be out all day. I'd bring him back here with me, but I know he runs a mile when Fig is in sight."

"Who wouldn't?" Darcy said. He looked around. "I must say I miss having James around. I haven't seen him properly for a couple of days."

"You weren't here at teatime when he was brought down," I said. "Poor little chap. He's been very fretful and clingy every time he sees me. This can't go on, Darcy. I do hope we get some good replies from *The Lady* soon."

"Give it another week, until I get back from . . . wherever I'm going . . . and then tell them both it's not what you want. I'll be back to give you reinforcements."

"Where are you going?" I asked.

"I can't tell you, I'm afraid."

"It's Germany again, isn't it?"

He gave me the look that meant he wasn't going to tell. I hated it when he was going to Germany. It seemed rather dangerous these days. And who knew what he was doing there? Helping to smuggle out another important Jewish scientist? I kissed him good-bye the next morning, then told Fig I had to go and check on my grandfather and I hoped she didn't mind being on her own for a day.

"Not at all," she said. "I actually quite enjoy being down here. The rooms are warm, the food is good and there is no Binky around to annoy me. Frankly, the conversation is sadly lacking. He comes in, looking like a scarecrow, to tell me the latest exploits of his Highland cattle. Facts that I absolutely do not need to know."

"I'm glad he's become so involved with them," I said. "They are an ancient breed and need to be preserved."

"As long as they make good joints of beef, that's all I care about," she replied. "Which reminds me. Those piglets of yours now seem to be big and fat enough to make into bacon."

No, I wanted to yell. I knew, realistically, that the piglets were being reared to become pork one day, but I had grown fond of them. I think my farmworkers felt the same. I couldn't see any of them willing to butcher the piglets. Being a farmer is hard.

I dressed and headed up to London, then changed to the District Line out on the eastern side of the city to Essex, where my grandfather lived. I got out at Upminster Bridge and walked up the hill, battling a fierce wind that promised rain at any moment. I was halfway up the hill when the rain came. I had brought an umbrella with me, but the wind would have turned it inside out in seconds. I arrived at Glanville Drive looking like a drowned rat. My grandfather opened the door and gaped in surprise.

"Blimey, ducks. You look as if you've been dragged through a hedge. Come in, quick. Don't let the heat out." He dragged me inside and helped me out of my raincoat. "Why didn't you tell me you were coming? I'd have got something nice in for you to eat."

"It was a spur-of-the-moment thing," I said. "I realized I missed you and wanted to see how you were."

"Not too bad, all things considered," he said. "The old chest ain't playing up too much and I started planting out some veg during last week's mild spell."

"Granddad, we have plenty of veg for you at Eynsleigh if only you'd come back."

He shook his head. "I never feel right there, ducks. When you have your posh relatives and guests I feel like an intruder. Especially that sister-in-law of yours. The way she looks down her nose at me . . ."

"She is pretty frightful, I agree," I said. "She's staying right now, as a matter of fact. She's found me a dreadful nanny and she's lecturing me on how to raise my child."

He had walked ahead of me into the kitchen and put the kettle on the stove, ready to make a cup of tea. "She's found you a nanny? Did you ask her to?"

I perched on a stool at the kitchen table. "Of course not. And the nanny is awful. She's cold and stern and full of rules and regulations. Not at all what I want for my son."

"Why haven't you told her to bugger off, then?"

"Fig is paying her salary for six months, so that I have time to get used to her. So it's rather awkward." I chewed on my lip.

"It seems to me those ruddy relatives of yours interfere a darned sight too much. They planted themselves on you before Christmas and found a school for their son near you so you can entertain him for half terms, and now that Fig woman has given you a nanny you don't want and didn't ask for." He paused as the kettle shrieked, sending out steam. "Tell me, were you looking for a nanny? Do you actually want one?"

I watched him heaping tea leaves into the brown ceramic

pot, then pouring on the boiling water. "In theory I have to have one eventually. I'm supposed to do more than play with my baby all day, even though I enjoy it. And I have to confess I am glad that Maisie does the less pleasant tasks like changing nappies and bedding."

"So what's wrong with keeping Maisie on like she is right now?"

Again I hesitated. "The only thing is that she's a village girl. She's not very educated. A good nanny brings up the child to know how to behave in polite society. It's how it's done. But I'd like her to be my ally, not my enemy. This one makes me feel I'm doing everything wrong with James and I'm an intruder who is not welcome in the nursery."

He poured a cup for me, put in the milk and handed it to me. "Then you tell her either she fits in with what you want or she goes. It is your house and your son, after all. You call the shots."

"You're right," I said. "It's just having to deal with a Fig who is not getting her own way is so awful."

"Then send her home too." He put a hand on my shoulder. "Come on, ducks. It's not like you to be cowed by someone else. Look how brave you've been all your life. You grew up with no parents around. You went on your own to school in Switzerland. You learned to make your own way in London. I'd say you'd always shown spunk. Show it now."

I nodded. "I was hoping Belinda would come down to Eynsleigh and back me up," I said. "Darcy is off again somewhere abroad. He won't say but I bet it's Germany."

"Don't talk to me about that place," Granddad said. "I don't like what I'm seeing. That Hitler bloke is going to cause trouble. You mark my words. And your mum is still there, I take it."

"Yes, she is. She won't be reasoned with."

"Let's hope she don't come a cropper, and find she can't get out," he said. "You wouldn't catch me staying there, the way they are behaving. She better not leave it too late."

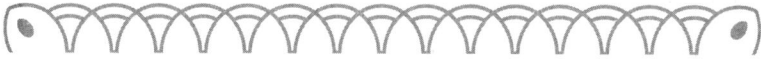

Chapter 7

Golly, I seem to be rushing around after months of non-activity.

We had a lovely visit all morning. Granddad made me toasted cheese as a midmorning snack and his little kitchen felt warm and safe. It was with reluctance that I walked back to the station. Luckily the rain had abated for the moment. He had promised to come down to Eynsleigh for Easter, which cheered me up. By then Darcy would be back, the nanny situation would be sorted out and Fig would be gone. As I came to Victoria Station, the temptation to see Belinda and get a peek at her new maid was too strong. I strode out to Knightsbridge, propelled by the strong breeze off the Thames, and rapped on the door. It was opened by a person who was not at all what I had expected. I had pictured a large red-faced blond girl with plaits around her head, wearing a dirndl. Instead she was small and slender with mousy brown hair held back in a severe bun and sharp features.

"Hello," I said. "You must be Trudi. Is Miss Belinda at home?"

The girl shook her head. "She gone," she said. "Not here."

"Oh, do you know where she's gone and when she'll be back?"

Trudi shrugged. "She go *vater*."

It took me a moment to work this out. "Oh. To her father? Is something wrong? Is her father sick?"

I saw her process this. "*Nicht gut*," she said and accompanied this by shaking her head.

"Oh no. Poor Belinda. You don't have a telephone yet, do you?"

When she looked confused I mimed picking up a telephone receiver. "No telephone?"

She shook her head. "*Nein*."

"Then, when you see her, please tell her that I called," I said. This was met with a blank stare. "Lady Georgiana. Me." I fished in my handbag and produced a calling card. "My card. You give her when she comes back. Okay?"

She nodded then. "I tell."

I left, fighting back worry and frustration. Belinda was not close to her father, since he'd remarried a woman she didn't like, but it must be serious to make her go running off to him. I realized I didn't know the family's address or how to contact him. Besides, Belinda might want to be left alone at a time like this. So it seemed I should head back home to face the twin horrors, unless . . . I paused. Unless Zou Zou was back. I looked for a public telephone box, went in and miraculously found her number in my little address book. I dropped in the three pennies and the phone was answered by Zou Zou herself.

"Georgie, sweet girl. How lovely to hear your voice. Where are you?"

"I'm in London. A few streets from you. I wondered if you'd returned home and if you were busy."

"No. I'm not busy. I'm recuperating after a tiring journey north."

"Do you want to be left to recuperate or could I pop in for a visit?"

"Of course. Come over immediately. Have you had lunch?"

"Sort of." If a slice of toasted cheese at eleven counted. "A midmorning snack."

"Then I'll have some sandwiches and things whipped up. Hurry over, darling. I need cheering up."

I needed no more urging. Seeing Zou Zou was always a tonic. It had started to rain again by the time I reached Eaton Square, and Clotilde skillfully divested me of my wet things before ushering me through to the drawing room. Zou Zou was lounging on the sofa, looking languid in a quilted velvet jacket over purple pajamas. She held out a hand to me.

"You're soaked, poor child. Come and sit by the fire. Clotilde, tell Robert to make a hot toddy when he brings up the sandwiches. Plenty of rum in it."

I held up a hand to protest that I shouldn't be drinking plenty of rum in the middle of the day, but Zou Zou ignored me. "Come. Sit."

I sat on the chair close to the fire.

"You're looking worried," she said. "What's the matter, darling?"

I told her about Fig and the nanny. She shook her head. "How absolutely frightful. Your sister-in-law alone is anyone's nightmare, but two of them . . . We must do something. Would you like me to come down to Eynsleigh and get rid of these women instantly?"

I had to smile at this. "Much as I would love it, I don't want to cause a big fight. You know Fig. She'd hold the grudge forever. It would be much smoother if I find a nanny I like; then I can tell this one that her services are no longer needed."

"So how do you propose to find this paragon? Aren't all nannies bossy and territorial?"

"I suppose so. Actually I just want someone to help me take care of James, not to take over my child completely."

"Of course you do. I'll put my ear to the ground, although at my age my friends' children are beyond the nannying stage."

"Which reminds me," I said. "How was the funeral?"

"Ghastly, darling. Poor Tilly sobbed the whole time. Half the congregation was dabbing at eyes with handkerchiefs or blowing their noses. An only child, you know. Only son, who was going to inherit the title and a rather nice property."

"You said it was an accident?"

"Quite tragic. His motorcar went off the road at a sharp bend and into a ravine."

"Was the road wet or icy?"

"I think roads are always wet in the Peak District. It seems to rain when I'm there anyway. But the point is that he was an expert driver. He prided himself on his driving skills, in fact he had actually done some motor racing. He came third at Brooklands once. Not bad. And he'd taken that corner so many times. So what went wrong that particular time nobody can tell."

"Might his brakes have failed?"

She sighed. "We'll never know. The car fell onto the rocks at the bottom of the ravine and caught fire. His body was retrieved, quite charred." She broke off and looked up as Clotilde came in, bearing a tray on which were all sorts of delectables: finger sandwiches, slices of quiche and terrine, a small plate of olives, an assortment of cheeses, grapes, jars of pickles and beside them a steaming mug of hot toddy. "That will warm you up," she said as Clotilde put the tray down on the low table beside me.

Zou Zou waited until her maid had left, then leaned toward me. "What nobody mentioned was whether it was intentional or not."

I looked up sharply from my hot toddy. "Murder, you mean?"

She stared at me, horrified. "Oh no. Not that. What I meant was whether he took his own life. I'd say he was always a little highly strung. Had something been bothering him that he never confided to his parents? I know nothing about his love life. Had he been jilted by a girl?" She leaned forward to take an olive, popping it into her mouth. "As far as one could tell, he had everything—a bright future, enough money, a lovely property to inherit one day. But one can never know what is going on inside a person's head, can one?"

I took one of the sandwiches. It was anchovy and shrimp. Quite scrumptious. I ate in silence, then helped myself to some quiche.

"I have invited Tilly to come and stay down here. She'll need something to distract her, poor woman. I don't know how one recovers from the loss of an only child. I managed to get over Zigmund's death quite well, but then I'd only ever been mildly fond of him at the best of times. And we never managed to have children."

As she was speaking I pictured losing James. The emotion that surged through me after this thought was so strong that I had to resist the urge to run out and catch the next train home. Instead I sipped my hot toddy and listened to Zou Zou's plans. "My little plane is pining for me, and I have a great yearning for the South of France after that sad business, but the Grand National is coming up and we have a promising horse running, so I'll have to go to my stables in Ireland and see how it's shaping up."

"That's exciting," I said. "Will you go up to Aintree to watch the race?"

"Oh absolutely, rather," she said. "Wouldn't miss it for the world. But I should pop over to Ireland first, just to check on my horse, don't you think?"

From the little questioning smile, I got the feeling that she might want to check on Darcy's father, who ran her racing stable. We had thought those two were a match made in heaven, but his stupid pride had hindered him from going any further, since she was rolling in money and he wasn't.

"I think you should definitely go to Ireland," I said.

"Yes." She nodded agreement. She paused, then added, "So I gather that darling Hubert has gone off again?"

Like my mother, she hedged her bets. Unlike my mother, she could exist perfectly well without a man in attendance, adoring her.

"He's giving a lecture tour in Australia and New Zealand. 'My Life as a Mountaineer.'"

I saw her considering this. "Perhaps I could fly out and surprise him. Wouldn't that be a hoot!"

"To Australia? Zou Zou!"

"Remember I did attempt to fly my little plane to Australia once. I didn't make it, unfortunately. Came down in the desert and they took three days to find me. Not very pleasant. I thought I might have to drink my own pee. So perhaps it's not such a good idea. Ireland it will be, then."

Chapter 8

THURSDAY, FEBRUARY 25

EYNSLEIGH

I'm going to try and be assertive and let Nanny know who is in charge. At least I hope so. . . .

I left Zou Zou's house feeling warm and well-fed as I hurried to make the five-o'clock train. Seeing both Granddad and Zou Zou had bucked me up a lot. I made a vow I was not going to be cowed by either Fig or Nanny. I had to remember that I came from a family of warriors. Robert Bruce Rannoch didn't hesitate when he faced the English army even though he was out-numbered and eventually hacked to pieces. I reached Eynsleigh just in time to take off my coat and meet James in my bedroom. He was clearly pleased to see me but again less interested in nursing. I was going to have to accept that my baby was ready to move on to the next stage of life. I noticed that Nanny looked smug when she came for him.

"He really seemed to enjoy his cereal this afternoon," she said. "And mashed banana. He's developing quite an appetite."

Of course he is, you horrible woman, I thought. You're deliberately feeding him before he nurses so that he's no longer interested. Then I made a decision. This stops right now.

I slept fitfully with Darcy away, but the next morning I awoke with resolve. When I had finished nursing James, I did not wait for Nanny but carried him back up to the nursery myself.

"I have made some decisions, Nanny," I said. "I wish to be more involved in my son's life. I don't like the thought of him shut away all day. I shall be coming up to visit James during the day when I feel like it. I shall sometimes want to feed him his meals, give him his bath. I may even want to bring him down to be with me when I have time to spare. This should give you some free moments during the day to take a walk around the grounds. Get some fresh air."

I watched her face as I said it. It was most gratifying. Finally she said, "I don't think you realize that young children thrive on a routine. If you upset this routine they feel insecure. If they find they are taken down to play with Mummy they will soon learn to have tantrums if this doesn't happen."

"I don't wish to do anything to upset his routine," I said. "I agree that meals, sleep, bath, should all be at a regular time, but while he is awake and having to amuse himself, he would benefit from having a playmate from time to time." I stared at her. "Tell me, Nanny. Do you actually play with him? Peekaboo?

Building blocks and knocking them down? Pretending you are the big, bad wolf?" I tried not to grin as I said this.

"Play with him?" She stared back. "My job is not to play with him, Lady Georgiana. My job is to keep him safe, fed and educated. One hopes that he will soon have siblings to join him in the nursery; then he will have playmates."

"Until that happens his mother will be delighted to play with him. So I shall be dropping in from time to time. Thank you, Nanny. That's all." I handed her James and made a grand exit. It felt wonderful.

Later that morning I took James out in his pram. We went down to the farm and he looked at the chickens and pigs. The dogs came with us. We all enjoyed every moment. I wondered why I had been so hesitant until now. When I returned James to the nursery I said, "He really enjoyed feeding the chickens, Nanny. Perhaps you can take him down to the farm yourself every day when the weather is fine and I am not available. Fresh air will do you both good."

"The chickens, my lady?" she asked, the disapproval showing in her voice. "The farm?"

"Yes, the home farm. It's a nice long walk down the track. You can just see the farmhouse chimney from here."

"I hope it was a wise decision to take him out in a cold wind today," Nanny said. "He is teething at the moment and therefore quite vulnerable to colds and ear infections." She took him from me. "Look at you, Master James. Drooling down your chin in that cold wind has already produced a nasty chapped face. Oh, and I can see that a nappy needs to be changed. Did Mummy take you out with a dirty nappy on?"

She was clearly settling down for a good fight, but I wasn't going to be cowed.

"When you have changed him, I think I'll bring him down to the morning room for some play on the rug."

"And what about his morning nap? Babies can get very cranky if their nap time is disturbed," she said. "He needs the right amount of sleep if he is to grow and thrive, my lady."

I hesitated. Obviously I didn't want to disturb James's nap or make him cranky.

"You're quite right, Nanny. Let's put it off until this afternoon, then. He usually is brought down around four. Let's bring him down early today. Shall we say three thirty?"

I felt as if I had scored a small point. Now all I had to do was handle Fig. What could I give her to do that was so repugnant that she'd want to go home? I knew what she thought about bringing James into the morning room and playing with him on the rug, but I was determined to do it anyway.

Fig did look quite surprised when she came into the sitting room to see me sitting on the floor with James and the dogs.

"Gracious," she said. "Is it teatime already? I must have dozed off."

"No, not teatime yet. I just felt like playing with James today. It's not good for him to be shut away with Nanny and no other human interaction. He needs someone who smiles and laughs occasionally."

"Georgiana, you are going to create a spoiled child who is used to being the center of attention," she said. "Children must learn to amuse themselves. I can see I still have a lot to teach you, and so does Nanny. A lot of work to do on your behalf, but

I am willing to sacrifice my time if this household finally runs the way it was meant to. I hope you will take note of our instruction. It is for your own good, and for your son's."

Why could I not find the courage to tell her what I felt?

A FEW DAYS went by. I didn't hear from Darcy or from Belinda. I knew Darcy could not communicate with me when he was away, but I always worried. In the meantime I kept myself cheerful by visiting my son. We took our walks in his pram. We built towers of blocks together and had fun in his bath. It was delightful. Nanny did her best to make things difficult. When I entered the nursery she always had an excuse. He was still sleeping because he'd had a bad night. It probably wouldn't be wise to put him in the bathtub in this cold weather. A sponge bath was all that was needed and she could do that in a few seconds. However, I persisted. Nanny remained sullen when she saw how eager he was to go to me. Perhaps this would finally make her decide that she'd rather be with her begonias in the Lake District.

Fig showed no signs of wanting to leave. She clearly liked the food and the warmth. I persuaded her to come on walks with James and me and even suggested that she might like to help with the farm animals while Darcy was away.

"Me? Muck out pigs?" she shrieked. "Georgiana, that is why you have farmhands. It is only absolutely clueless people like Binky who insist on helping with the calving and other disgusting matters."

"Aren't you missing your own children?" I asked as she came

for a walk with James and me. "I miss James every moment I'm away from him."

"Miss my children?" she asked. "My dear Georgiana, I am training myself for when Podge has to go away to school. Then I shall not see him for months at a time. And I think you are doing James a disservice by smothering him with affection. It will be such a hard wrench when he goes off to school. Podge is actually looking forward to his next big adventure."

He would be, I thought. If Fig was my mother, I'd be only too happy to get away. At least I'd helped persuade them to put down his name for a good school near us. A school that seemed to be warm and encouraging to its pupils. And he'd come to us at half terms and I'd spoil him.

We came back from our walk to be greeted by Mrs. Holbrook. "You had a telephone call while you were out, my lady. It was Miss Belinda. I have taken down the number and told her you would return her telephone call."

"Thank you, Mrs. Holbrook," I said. "Would you ring for Nanny to come and fetch James? I'll telephone her right away."

It was with some apprehension that I asked the operator to connect me. It was a Knightsbridge number, which presumably meant that Belinda's telephone had been hooked up and she was back in London.

She answered the phone herself. Well, she would with a maid who couldn't understand the caller on the other end.

"Belinda, it's Georgie. You rang?"

"Oh, hello, darling," she said. "I got back to London yesterday and I was going to write to you, but then miraculously the telephone people came this morning and I finally have my phone."

"I hope your maid told you that I had called on you while you were away. I left my card. She said you had gone to your father. Was that right?"

"Yes. I was summoned home to Gloucestershire unexpectedly."

"Your father was ill?" I asked, cautiously.

"Oh, not Daddy. Daddy's fine. No, it was his cousin George's son, Rupert. He died in a climbing accident in Snowdonia. Daddy and George were quite close when they were boys, so Daddy felt we should show solidarity and attend the funeral."

"I'm so sorry," I said.

"It's all right. I hardly knew Rupert. We invited him to my coming-out party when I was a deb, but I think that was the most recent time I saw him. A rather spotty youth, I remember. Rather lacking in conversation and social graces, but apparently he was passionate about climbing. He was training in Snowdonia in preparation for going on an expedition to the Himalayas when his rope broke and he fell hundreds of feet."

"How horrible."

"Yes. Cousin George and his wife, Petunia, were quite cut up about it. So was my father. So I stayed on for a few days while I tried to be the loyal daughter. But now I'm back and I'd love to come down and visit. Is Fig still there?"

"Oh yes," I said. "I don't know how I'm ever going to get rid of her. She likes it here."

"And Nanny?"

"She is too, but I'm working on it. I'm scoring small victories. I'll tell you all when I see you."

"I'll come down tomorrow, then, shall I?"

"And bring Brunhilde with you?"

"Oh yes. I have to keep training her and teaching her English. I think the count she worked for must have been far too forgiving. She didn't even know how to polish shoes properly, or how to clean my pearls."

"Perhaps counts are two a penny in Austria and she's just been in some kind of farmhouse."

"Quite possibly. Oh well, at least she's willing to learn. So I'll see you tomorrow, then. Must fly. I need to look out for some anti-Fig spray."

With that she hung up. I put down the receiver and stared at the telephone for a long moment. Another accident to a young man of good family. Oh dear. Belinda did say that bad things always came in threes. Let's hope that this was the third and all would be well.

Chapter 9

TUESDAY, MARCH 2
EYNSLEIGH

I'm so relieved that Belinda is coming to stay. She'll know how to handle Fig.

Fig was most put out when I informed her that Belinda was coming to stay.

"That's the young woman with the loose morals, is it not? How old is she now? Almost thirty and still not married? I suppose she's good-looking in a cheap sort of way, but what does she propose to do when the bloom starts to fade?" When I didn't answer any of these questions she went on, "You were fortunate, Georgiana. You managed to snap up a husband before it was too late. My mother always said that after twenty-four a woman is doomed to spinsterhood. They become set in their ways and make terrible wives and men know this."

I didn't like to ask her how old she was when she married Binky. Instead I made sure a nice room was prepared for Belinda and looked forward to her coming. It turned out to be a very good day as Darcy also arrived home. He didn't tell me where he had been, but he had a satisfied look on his face of a job well done, and the way he hugged both me and James indicated that he had been through something a little dangerous and was glad to be back safely.

Belinda arrived, with impeccable timing, just as tea was being served. Mrs. Holbrook took Trudi up to unpack while Belinda joined us in the Long Gallery. I noticed Fig eyeing Belinda critically.

"So, Miss Warburton-Stoke, I understand you have been living abroad until recently?"

"Yes, that's right. I have just returned from Paris."

"And what were you doing there? Some sort of work?" I suspected that Fig knew very well what Belinda had been doing, but she liked harping on the fact that Belinda had to work for a living.

"I was designing with Chanel," she said. "You know, the dress designer?" The way she added this was perfect. It implied that the way Fig dressed she might not have heard of designers.

"Ah. I see." She studied the outfit Belinda was wearing: a suit with mannish trousers and an impeccably cut jacket with a lacy blouse beneath it. "One hears that Madame Chanel is . . . how should one say . . . rather too generous with her favors."

"If you mean that she hands out pieces of clothing to her

friends and employees, the answer would be no," Belinda said. "She never forgets that she started from great poverty and she makes her employees pay for every piece, even those with flaws."

"No, not that," Fig said. "I meant her favors toward men. She has never been married, has she? But she always seems to have a protector of sorts."

"Madame Chanel's private life is her own," Belinda said. "As is mine."

Fig gave a little snort and took a large slurp of tea. Belinda and I exchanged a grin.

"All the same, Miss Warburton-Stoke, I'm sure you'd like to be married and settled in a property like this one." Fig was not easily daunted. "Your parents, after all, did pay to send you to a very expensive finishing school and then have you presented at court, all of which could only be with the purpose of finding you a husband."

"True," Belinda said. "And I would certainly marry and settle down if the right man came along."

"You didn't manage to meet a French marquis, then?" Fig continued.

"I did. Several. All charming and rich."

"Then why did you not marry one?"

"Because I was not a suitable bride for them. I was not Catholic and I was not a virgin. They offered me the role of mistress, which I declined."

This remark made Fig blush and she coughed on some cake crumbs. She quickly recovered. "We must help her, Georgiana. Those cousins of yours and Binky's. They are both still unmarried. They have an estate in Scotland, do they not?"

She was referring to Lachlan and Murdoch, two hairy and terrifying Scotsmen in kilts who consumed vast quantities of whiskey and food. I would not have introduced my worst enemy to them.

"Thank you, but Belinda is not that desperate," I replied. "I'm sure she'll meet a perfectly lovely man at the right time."

"But until then how is she going to survive if she is no longer working for Chanel?" She turned back to Belinda. "Will you find yourself a job at Harrods or something?"

Belinda was still smiling sweetly. "Actually I inherited several properties from my grandmother," she said. "I don't need to work. I studied with Chanel because I like designing clothes. I may go down to Cornwall and revamp my grandmother's house. She left a lovely property on the coast there."

"And see Jago?" I asked.

"Who knows."

At this moment we were saved from further interrogation on this subject by Nanny coming in with James. Darcy took him and for the next half hour he was the center of attention.

"He's gorgeous, Georgie," Belinda said as we went up to her room after tea. "Makes me feel a bit broody."

Trudi was nowhere to be seen, but Belinda's clothes were now hanging in the wardrobe.

"It will be interesting to see how she gets along with the rest of the staff," I said. "It should improve her English."

"I hope so," Belinda replied. "I'm tired of having to mime everything I want. It might be easier to take a crash course in German."

"Ask Darcy," I said. "He seems to go to Germany quite a lot these days."

"Does he? What for?"

"Who knows. Things I'd rather not hear about."

"So he is some kind of spy, then? I'd always suspected it."

"I don't ask and he doesn't tell," I replied, "but he does work for the government in some kind of secret capacity."

"How jolly exciting," she said. "That's the sort of thing I'd like to do. I wonder how one gets started."

I looked at her and laughed. "You can't mean that. Spies get shot."

"Not if they're good. I can see myself seducing a foreign general and getting him to reveal all sorts of secrets between the sheets."

"Belinda! You are incorrigible."

"Oh, I do hope so," she said. "I was afraid I was becoming rather boring."

At dinner that night she asked Darcy.

"So tell me how one sets about becoming a spy."

Darcy almost choked into his mock turtle soup. "What a strange thing to ask, Belinda," he said. "How would I know? And why should you want to know?"

"Because I thought it sounded rather interesting," she said. "Something I might like to do."

He was looking amused now. "My dear girl, you have no idea," he said. "Are you good at keeping your mouth shut at all times? Not giving anything away even to your nearest and dearest?"

"Oh, I expect I could if necessary," she said.

"And what about torture?"

"Torture?" Now her eyes flew open. "I've dabbled a bit in S and M. You know, whips and boots and stuff."

"I mean real torture. If you were captured and the enemy wanted to get information out of you, how good would you be at not betraying your associates?" He gave her a long look. "When they came toward you with a red-hot poker or they pulled out your fingernails?"

"Fingernails? Oh gosh. I really like my fingernails. No, I hadn't thought of that aspect. Does that sort of thing happen often?"

Darcy chuckled. "I couldn't say how often, but I would imagine it might be an occupational hazard."

"Then I think I'll stick with remodeling my grandmother's house," Belinda said.

⁂

THE NEXT FEW days were delightful. Belinda and I went into Haywards Heath to do some shopping. We pushed James around the grounds. Fig sulked and glowered and even talked about Binky needing her. Nanny glared when I popped into the nursery unannounced and whisked James away to play with him. It really was most satisfying.

The first batch of letters finally arrived from *The Lady*. I handed them to Belinda. "Read them to me," I said.

She opened the first one.

"'I haven't actually been a nanny but I have helped my sister with her four kiddies and I have to say I'm very good with little kiddies. They like it when I tell them stories. . . .'" She read in an appropriate accent. We looked at each other and shook our heads.

"'Before I left Russia in 1920 I was nurse to the Grand Duchess Olga's children,'" she read in a good Russian accent.

Also discarded.

One had worked in a nursery. One had been a nanny until her weight meant she couldn't climb stairs. I looked at Belinda. All hopeless, no improvement on Nanny Hardbottle, and that was saying something!

"It's a shame your nanny has seen me," Belinda said. "Otherwise I could have pretended to be your new nanny."

I laughed. "One would only have to watch you for five minutes with James to realize you had no idea what you were doing."

"True. And I would hate changing nappies."

"That's the one thing that Nanny gives to poor Maisie to do. Maisie was supposed to be the assistant nursemaid. Only Nanny won't let her near James. Maisie was so good with him too. He adores her."

"Then keep Maisie on as your nanny, and get rid of the other one."

I hesitated. "I intend to keep her on, but she's not up to being the nanny. Her way of speech is that of a country girl, isn't it? James will need to learn how to behave. He'd be teased if he went to school with a strange country accent. I'm going to make sure he spends enough time with Darcy and me, but a properly trained nanny is expected of us and Fig will not leave us in peace until one is settled."

"Let's hope the next post brings something more suitable," Belinda said.

Chapter 10

I'm no nearer to finding a new nanny, but I must say things are a
    lot easier with Belinda here. Now all I have to do is find a
    tactful way to make Fig want to go home.

The morning's post brought no new applications for the nanny
position but a letter from Binky to Fig. She read it while eating
her toast and marmalade, frowning. "Trouble with the boiler
again. That's not good. We paid a fortune to have a new one
installed. Rotten workmanship these days. And Binky is hopeless about such things. Oh, and Podge has had a nasty cold. . . ."

"Perhaps you need to go home," I suggested. "It sounds as if
they need you there."

She hesitated. "Oh, Binky will figure it out. He usually does in the end."

"But what about Podge and his cold?"

"Nanny knows what to do about such things, and I certainly wouldn't want to catch it. You know how delicate my chest is."

So much for motherly love, I thought.

We had just finished breakfast when a telegram was delivered. Since telegrams are associated in my mind with bad news, I held my breath as I opened it.

"Back from Ireland. Popping down to visit. All right? Telephone if I shouldn't come. Zou Zou."

"Zou Zou's coming to visit," I said, beaming.

"That foreign princess person?" Fig asked. She knew perfectly well who Zou Zou was, but she liked reminding the world that Zou Zou was foreign and therefore strange and different. Fig never missed a chance to score a point in her own mind.

"How lovely," I said. "We'll hear all about how your father is doing, Darcy, and about the racehorse they intend to enter in the Grand National."

"I don't suppose the old fool is making any progress in his courtship of Zou Zou," Darcy said. "Too stubborn."

"Perhaps Zou Zou doesn't want to be tied down," I replied. "She likes men to be interested in her but she likes her freedom. I might, if I had oodles of money like her."

"Then I'm glad you were penniless like me when we met," Darcy said. We exchanged a smile and I had that warm feeling inside when he looked at me. I reminded myself how jolly lucky I was to have a husband and baby.

A room was prepared for Zou Zou and she arrived that evening, driving herself in her Aston Martin sports car.

"Wonderful drive down," she said. "The roads were delightfully empty and the little car just whizzed along. I got up to over eighty when I was past Croydon." Her cheeks were pink and her hair, under her silk scarf, was windswept. She looked a picture of health. It struck me how she enjoyed each moment, in contrast to Fig, who looked to find something wrong with everything.

Sherry was served in the drawing room.

"So tell us about Ireland," I said. "How is Darcy's father?"

"Flourishing, I'm glad to say," she said. "He's been working wonders with this horse. We're most hopeful for its chances in the National. You must come up to Aintree to watch. So exciting."

"Isn't that the race where all the horses fall at the high fences and break their necks?" Fig said.

"I'm afraid there is an occasional tragedy," Zou Zou said, eyeing her with distaste. "But it's also a glorious spectacle to watch. Oh, and speaking of tragedies, Darcy, your father asked me to pass along some rather sad news to you. We met a man you both knew when we were in Dublin. Porky Smithers, I think that was his name. Big man. Big voice. Loud laugh. Does that ring a bell?"

Darcy frowned. "I don't think so."

"Apparently his son was at school with you. The son was big like his father and I gather you used to call him Shrimpy as a joke."

Zou Zou looked at Darcy. Recognition spread across Darcy's face. "Shrimpy Smithers. Yes, I remember him. Big bloke. Not good at sports. Sort of quiet and studious."

"Well, he said his son had just died. He suffered from asthma, apparently, and he had an attack and something went wrong with his medication. He had been prescribed something called epinephrine, or something similar, when he had the attack. Apparently he took his normal medicine but it didn't work. He had a seizure and died. So tragic. His father was really cut up about it. Only son . . ."

"When was this?" I asked.

"It had only just happened," she said. "The father told us this was the first time he'd left the house and had to do so because business was piling up."

"Another one," I said.

The other occupants looked up at me. The only sound was the shifting of logs in the fireplace.

"What do you mean, another one?" Fig asked.

"I mean another death of a young man about Darcy's age. This makes number four that we've learned about in the last couple of weeks. First it was the man whose funeral you went to, Zou Zou. Then Belinda and I met Gussie Gormsley, and he said he'd just been to a college friend's funeral. Then you went to your cousin's funeral, Belinda. And now this."

"What are you getting at, Georgie?" Darcy asked. "Accidents happen, and one does tend to hear of them in clusters."

"I said before that this sort of thing comes in threes, and I stick with that," Belinda said. "The other three were daredevils who risked their lives all the time, and fate finally caught up with them. This last one we've just heard about is someone who had a serious illness and for some reason his medicine didn't work when he needed it."

I tried to push back my own thoughts. Darcy was right. Three daredevils had tempted fate one time too many. And a man with a serious illness had succumbed to it. Sad but true.

"So," Fig said, changing the subject. "Have you had your invitations yet?"

"Invitations?" Darcy asked.

"To the coronation, my dears. It's coming up shortly, isn't it? Didn't they say in May? I understood they were keeping the date planned for Edward's coronation, if he hadn't fled to France with that disgusting woman. Anyway, one has to be prepared. I've just written to Binky to tell him to have our coronation robes brought up from storage, cleaned, and make sure there are no moths in them. It wouldn't do to have holes visible at the Abbey."

"I don't suppose we'll be going," I said.

"Not going? Of course you'll be going. You're the new king's cousin as much as you were for the departing king."

"I might be the king's cousin," I said, "but my husband is not a peer at the moment. Only an honorable. I'm currently just plain Mrs. O'Mara."

"Oh, don't be silly. You know that Bertie and Elizabeth are very fond of you. They often speak of you when we're over at Balmoral."

"I don't suppose they personally write out the invitation list," I said.

"Well, Darcy's father will be invited, won't he? I presume he has his coronation robes from the last one, although that was some time ago now."

"I believe my grandfather was still alive when King George was crowned," Darcy said, "and I think I heard that Grandfather wouldn't attend because it was a tricky time in Ireland with the republican movement at its height. So he stayed home out of solidarity with his people."

"Hmph," Fig said, hinting that anyone who sided with Ireland over England was suspect. "And they are still fighting over Northern Ireland. They never let it rest, do they. So would you refuse to go if asked?"

"I made my choice when I chose to become a British citizen," Darcy said. "If we are invited and Georgie wants to attend, then we attend."

"Then I'll have them bring your tiara from the vaults at the same time," Fig said. "It will need to be cleaned and any missing stones replaced. I'll wear the Glen Garry tiara and you can wear the Royal Scottish heather."

This was good as I liked the Scottish heather one much better. Sprigs of heather done in diamonds. Quite dainty and unobtrusive, unlike the bigger Glen Garry tiara with huge diamonds. I found myself hoping that we might be invited after all. It would be fun to be at Westminster Abbey and watch Cousin Bertie and Cousin Elizabeth crowned.

"And you, Princess." Fig turned to Zou Zou. "As a member of foreign royalty, will you be invited to attend?"

"What?" Zou Zou looked up, startled.

Fig repeated the question.

"Oh, I shouldn't think so for a moment," Zou Zou said. "And coronations are not really my cup of tea. London will be completely crazy. Too many people. I'll probably get in my little plane and zip down to the South of France."

Something was bothering Zou Zou. I could see that. She was unnaturally quiet during dinner, and afterward she beckoned me. "Georgie, can I drag you away for a moment? There is something I want to show you."

She took my hand and led me up to her bedroom. I was expecting a new dress or piece of jewelry. Instead she shut the door firmly behind us.

"I need to talk to you," she said. "What you said earlier. Another one. All those accidents and young men dying. You were concerned, weren't you?"

"I suppose I was startled," I said. "It is highly unusual to hear about four young men dying accidentally within a couple of weeks."

"I agree," she said. "I have been uneasy since I attended that young man's funeral." She toyed with the tassel hanging on the bedpost. "Sebastian's mother told me she found it hard to believe. I thought she meant that she found it hard to accept that her son had gone. But perhaps she meant that he was too good a driver to have misjudged that corner." Our eyes met. "You were thinking the same thing, weren't you? I could tell. You had decided that these deaths were suspicious."

I hesitated. "I suppose I was alarmed by the coincidence."

"Yes," she said. "I suppose it had to be just that. Coincidence." She hesitated. "I don't suppose we'll ever know now. . . ."

I WAS GETTING undressed when Darcy came into the bedroom.

"Where did you disappear to?" he asked. "I had to entertain your dreadful sister-in-law."

"I'm sorry, I needed to think," I said. "About those young men who died. And Zou Zou wanted to talk to me. She's also concerned."

"Concerned?"

"Hearing about four young men who had died."

"I agree, it is pretty sad, but . . ."

"You don't find anything strange about it?"

He shook his head. "I agree it's a strange coincidence that we hear about four deaths at the same time. What were you suggesting?"

"I'm not sure. I just feel uneasy," I said.

He shook his head. "They were all accidents, Georgie. Think about it. They were daredevils, weren't they? They did things in which they risked their lives."

"Yes, but four of them. In the space of two weeks . . ."

"You think there is some connection, then?" Darcy asked. He was frowning now.

"I'm wondering if there could be," I said. "First, they were all young men in our sort of social level. Didn't we learn that they were all only sons? All about the same age. Was this Shrimpy person in your year at Downside, Darcy?"

"No. He was in my house, but I was about two years below him."

"So that ties in. They were all around the same age. All

around thirty. And they all died doing something they loved doing, and were good at. Except your schoolmate Shrimpy. We don't know what he was doing when he died, except he had an asthma attack and his medicine didn't work."

Darcy was frowning now. "Are you suggesting that these were not accidents at all, but someone planned them?"

"It seems possible. Zou Zou said she had felt there was something wrong with Sebastian's death. So did his mother." I broke off, toying with this. "I suppose the first thing to find out is whether they knew each other, whether they were in some way connected. I wonder whether the others were at school with you. Sebastian something? Did you have a Sebastian at school with you?"

He was still frowning. "I can't say that I remember one."

"And what was the name of the man that Gussie Gormsley knew? Algie. That was it. Algie Beauchamps. Did you know him?"

"The name is vaguely familiar. Maybe from the time when we were all debs' delights and went to the coming-out parties."

"And Belinda's cousin's son? Rupert. I'm not sure if he was also a Warburton-Stoke. Did you know him?"

"I can't say that I did, but hold on a moment, Georgie. Aren't you reading too much into this? You know what Belinda was saying about accidents coming in threes. You read about a train crash or a plane going down, and then lo and behold you read about another one. So maybe they don't really come in threes, but because you are tuned in to the first, you are more aware of the second."

"But don't you think someone should check on it, just in

case? We should see if the men knew each other, if their families were connected. . . ."

"So you think that there is something furtive about this? A distant relative who would inherit four properties lurking and plotting to get rid of the rightful heirs?" He gave an uneasy chuckle.

"Well, something like that did cross my mind. Some kind of foul play."

"I think that's a big stretch, Georgie."

"Is there any way you could look into this? Find out what you can about the accidents, if the families know each other, if there is any kind of link?"

"Do you not think that the police would have checked if anyone had suspicions about a motorcar missing a bend and going off the road? Would they not have examined the car, or found out if the young man had been drinking? And the other two: losing control of a speedboat, falling while mountain climbing. They are not at all surprising."

"But if they were somehow connected?"

Darcy put a steadying hand on my shoulder. "Oh no, Georgie. Let this lie. This is nothing to do with us. We are very sorry that four chaps have lost their lives, but it's none of our business. Now, come to bed and stop worrying."

Reluctant, I allowed myself to be led across the room. When Darcy put his arms around me I felt the tension melt away.

"It's having Fig here," he said. "You always get riled up when she's around, and I have to confess she is a bit of a pain."

"A bit?" I asked. "Darcy, she drives me round the bend. Whatever we do, whatever we talk about, she finds something to criticize. And she is so rude to the servants I'm afraid they will leave."

"And you're no nearer to finding a replacement nanny yet?"

"No. The first round of applicants were hopeless."

"Then I think the thing to do is to play along with Fig's game. You tell her you realize now that Nanny is wonderful. You're leaving everything to her from now on and you thank Fig for finding you such a treasure and say you couldn't possibly keep her away from her own family for another minute. Binky and her children need her. Castle Rannoch needs her."

"Golly, do you think that will work?" I said. "You know I'm hopeless at lying. Could I really bring myself to say the words 'Nanny is wonderful'?"

"You couldn't bring yourself to lie to send Fig packing?"

"I suppose I could, if necessary. I'll try . . . and just pray that a nice nanny appears out of nowhere and that this one will leave if I sack her."

Chapter 11

I wish Zou Zou hadn't shared her own worry with me. Now I
can't stop thinking about it. If only I can persuade Darcy to
look into the four families and see if there is any
connection. . . .

In the morning, after I had fed James, I went straight down to
the library and took out *Debrett's* and *Burke's Peerage*. They
didn't tell me much other than confirming that Algernon De
Vere Beauchamps had been an only son of a baronet, and Sebastian's father had inherited a peerage. Belinda's cousin did not
have a title but was in *Burke's Landed Gentry*, as were Leopold
Smithers and his son, Leonard. But one was in Derbyshire, one
over in Suffolk, one in Gloucestershire and one in London. So

geographically nothing in common. The one thing in common was age. They were all born around the same time.

At breakfast Zou Zou announced that she thought she should go back to London after all. There were things she should be doing. Belinda perked up instantly and asked for a lift. Much as she loved seeing me and James, she too ought to be getting on with life, settling back into her London house, maybe going down to Cornwall to check out her grandmother's house there. I realized neither of them was a country girl at heart. Life at Eynsleigh was too quiet and boring for them; also enduring Fig was probably more than they wanted to stomach. So I accepted this as gracefully as I could, trying not to think that I would once again be stuck alone with Fig and Nanny.

As we were leaving the breakfast table Zou Zou said brightly, "Why don't you come up to London with us, Georgie? We'll have a girls' night on the town. You can stay with me."

"Oh, I couldn't," I said. "I have a baby, and we have a guest. It would be rude to leave her."

"You also have a perfectly competent nanny. You said yourself that James had lost interest in breastfeeding and you're in the process of weaning him. So, you're free to spread your wings again."

"But what about Fig?"

Zou Zou glanced around to see who might be within hearing before saying, "Darling, if you go, she has no excuse to stay on, does she? It's the perfect solution to getting rid of a poisonous person."

"And if you stay on in London, perhaps we can put out more feelers for a replacement nanny, one you actually like," Belinda added.

I toyed with this. Going up to town with Belinda and Zou Zou sounded wonderful. Finding a way to make Fig leave without having to lie sounded even better.

"Will we all fit into your sports car?" I asked.

"If one of you squeezes into that silly little backseat with my train case on your lap."

"I can always send Trudi on the train with my luggage," Belinda said. "Or I could take the train and let Georgie travel with you if there's not enough room in the motorcar."

"Don't be silly. We'll have fun," Zou Zou said. "We're all slim and lovely, aren't we? We'll squeeze in perfectly, as long as I have enough room to change gear."

"And just hope that Trudi manages to get on the right train and finds her way back to my house," Belinda said.

"It will be good for her," Zou Zou replied. "Let her know what is expected of a maid in this country, and see if she's really up to snuff."

"Yes. Good idea," Belinda said. "She seems all right in some ways, but she didn't have much idea about doing up the back of my dinner dress. As if she had never seen hooks and eyes before!"

I went to find Darcy.

"Would you mind if I went up to London with Zou Zou?" I asked.

He was in his study, gathering papers together. He looked surprised. "But she just got here. And she's going back already?"

"You know Zou Zou. Creature of impulse. So what do you think?"

"Darling, you're a free woman. Do what you want. You don't need my permission."

"But what about James?"

"He has a nanny now and whether you like her or not, she is perfectly competent. It will do you good to see that you are free to come and go again."

"But what about Fig? I can't leave her here with you, can I?"

"God no," he said. "Tell her you have been called away and I might also have to be up in town for a couple of days, so there is no reason for her to stay now that Nanny is settled in."

I was chewing on my lip again. Really I had to get out of girlish habits and be an elegant lady of the manor. "All right, I suppose," I said.

He took my hand and squeezed it. "You can do it," he said. "Be brave."

※

I WENT FIRST up to the nursery. James was sitting on the nursery rug with several stuffed toys around him. He was dressed not in his usual rompers but in a sailor suit with a stiff white collar. He crawled over as soon as he saw me, clutching at my leg. "Mama," he said. He'd just learned to associate this sound with me.

I lifted him into my arms. He wrapped his little arms around my neck. "Mama." His voice broke into a sob, making me decide that I couldn't possibly go away and leave him—ever.

"You see what you've created, my lady," Nanny said, appearing from the night nursery with a stack of folded linens. "He now expects to be picked up and amused the moment he sees you. Children can so easily turn into little dictators if you give them free rein. And I need Master James at this moment to work on our potty training. We're trying it once an hour on the hour. He's doing quite well, aren't you, young man? Wee-wee in the potty like a big boy?"

"Mama Mama." He clung to my neck now.

Oh dear. This was getting complicated. Was I wrong for trying to visit my child during the day? Was I upsetting his routine?

"You have to go with Nanny now, because Mummy is going out for a while," I said.

He started to cry, a very impressive, dramatic wailing. Nanny's look said it all. You've brought this on, the look said. All your fault. She took him from me, very firmly. "None of that silly noise, young man. You'll scare your teddy and your elephant, and we don't want that, do we?"

She nodded that I should go.

"I came up to say that I have to go up to London and will stay overnight. Mr. Darcy will also be away, so James will not be brought down at teatime," I said.

"That's exactly how it should be. I'm so glad we're progressing, my lady," she said. "Come on, Master James. Off we go. And if you're a good boy you can ride the rocking horse later. You like that, don't you?"

James turned to stare at the beautiful rocking horse that stood in the window. I had adored that horse when I was a child. It was far too big for him yet, but I presume Nanny held him on while it went back and forth. Anyway, the crying stopped and I took the opportunity to sneak away. I went down to my bedroom and found Maisie there, putting away clean undies in my dresser drawer.

"Oh good, Maisie, there you are," I said. "I'm going up to London for the night. Would you pack a small suitcase for me?"

"Very good, my lady," she said. "What kind of clothing will you require? Will you need a formal gown for evening?"

"Oh, I don't think so. Just a smart dress will do, in case we go out to eat. And I'll have to wear a warm coat and hat if we are driving in Princess Zamanska's sports car, especially if she keeps the top down."

Maisie nodded. "Right you are, then. Will the duchess be going with you?" The tone was hopeful.

"I suspect the duchess will be leaving now that Mr. Darcy and I will be away."

I saw the relief flood her face. I suspected that being a maid to Fig was not an easy task.

"And Nanny? She will still be here looking after young Jamie?"

"I'm afraid so, for the moment."

"She don't let me near him," Maisie said. "When I go up to the nursery she immediately gives me the pail of dirty nappies and tells me to take them down to be washed. But she don't let me hold him or nothing."

"I'm sorry. I understand how you feel. I know you love James and he loves you. I am trying to sort this out."

"I could take care of him myself, you know. I'm pretty good at it," she said. "We don't need no stuck-up, bossy nanny like her."

"I'm sure you can do a perfectly good job with James, but nannies have to do more than just keep children clean and safe. They have to educate our children on how to behave on social occasions, how to address various grown-ups, proper manners at teatime, all those sort of things that you really can't know about, so that they are ready to go out into society."

"I suppose you're right, my lady," she admitted. "I haven't had much chance to know about how the gentry lives."

"You're doing very well as my maid," I said. "And you were a good nursemaid to James too. So you are appreciated here, Maisie."

"Thank you kindly, your ladyship," she said, and I saw her wipe away a tear. Such a dear girl.

As I came out of my bedroom and was walking down the hall, Zou Zou stepped out, looked around first, then beckoned me.

"A word, if you don't mind."

She waited until I had walked the length of the hall, then pulled me into her bedroom, closing the door behind us. "I came down to Eynsleigh yesterday because I needed cheering up after that funeral. I found it so heart-wrenching that I needed to be with a happy family like yours."

"I'm glad we could help," I said.

"Having said that, I find that I am now more upset than when I set out. It was what you said last night, Georgie. Another one. I can't stop thinking about it."

"I'm sorry. I should have kept quiet and not blurted it out like that."

"No. You were quite right. You voiced out loud what was lurking at the back of my mind. All along I felt that something was not right at that funeral. Sebastian shouldn't have died. I thought at the time that it was just that he was so young and full of life, but the moment you voiced your suspicions I realized that I'd felt the same way. He should not have died because he was a good driver in a good car on a road that he drove every day and knew like the back of his hand."

"So you suspect that someone arranged his death?" I heard my voice shake a little.

"I don't know what to believe, only that I have an uneasy feeling in the pit of my stomach. I want to go back to Derbyshire, Georgie, to put my mind at rest, and I want you to come with me. That was why I invited you up to London."

"Derbyshire? I don't know about that, Zou Zou. We'd be away for days, wouldn't we?"

"We need not stay that long. If we drive fast up the A1 we can make it by tonight. We'd do our nosing around tomorrow and then drive home. I can drive through the night if necessary and you'd be home in a couple of days. Nobody would mind that, would they? James is being looked after. Darcy is going to be away, and you want Fig to go."

"I suppose so," I said. I had an uneasy feeling in the pit of my stomach. I didn't really want to do this, but I couldn't find a way to say no to Zou Zou.

She reached out and took my hand. "I really want you with me, Georgie. You are so good at this sort of thing. Look how you worked out that horrible business at the creepy manor house. You have a knack for getting to the bottom of things."

"I don't know about that." I gave an embarrassed shrug. "I've helped solve a few murders, but I just seem to stumble upon them. I certainly don't go looking for them. And I don't know how I can possibly help with this. I'm not a trained detective. I couldn't examine a motorcar and see if something had been tampered with. I don't know anything about motorcars."

"But you have a good Celtic sixth sense. You'd pick up on something that didn't seem right, I know it."

I stood there, still hesitating. What if James developed a fever, or had a bad dream and needed me? What sort of mother would I be if I wasn't there to comfort him? I knew Nanny would keep him clean and safe, but she certainly wouldn't be good in the hugging and comforting department.

"Four young men died, Georgie," Zou Zou said. "What if there really is a connection? What if none of them were accidents? We have to face the fact that maybe a killer is still on the loose. We have to stop him."

"Golly," I said.

"Then you'll come with me?" She had that sweet, hopeful look on her face that every person in the world finds irresistible.

"All right, if you really need me." I gave a big sigh as she patted my shoulder.

Chapter 12

Why did I ever agree to do this? I am not a trained detective.
What can I possibly learn that might lead us to the truth?
What if it was just an accident? What if they were all
accidents and I am leaping to conclusions?

I went downstairs to find Fig. She was sitting, as usual at this
time, in the morning room with the newspapers spread out
around her.

"Ah, there you are, Georgiana," she said. "I see they are fore-
casting snowstorms in Scotland. Snowstorms when it's now
March—I ask you. Castle Rannoch is probably freezing with
that ridiculous boiler acting up again. I don't know why we no
longer spend our winters at the London house. Actually I do

know. It's the cost of fuel and food. At home we have an abundance of fallen trees and the produce from the home farm to keep us going. But winter in London would be nice. If the herd of Highland cattle finally starts making a profit, then maybe . . ."

She looked almost wistful. I did understand. People like us inherit estates and have to pay enormous death duties, which leave us with no money to run them. Binky was doing his best and he'd have school fees starting next year. I, of course, inherited nothing. I'd had to make my own way relying on my wits and a lot of luck until I met Darcy. He was also pretty much penniless until we were offered this house by my godfather. Without it we'd have been living in a bleak and depressing London flat and I'd have been drying James's nappies on the boiler in the cellar.

"You'd certainly be welcome to stay on here, Fig," I said, "but unfortunately I have to go up to London today. I'm getting a ride with Zou Zou."

"Really? You didn't mention this before. What on earth is so important that you go whizzing off at a moment's notice?"

"It's . . . something Zou Zou is planning," I said, stumbling over the words the way I always do if I'm forced to lie. "Some kind of event she wants help with. You know Zou Zou. She's always involved in some kind of charity function."

"I don't see why she'd need you," Fig said bluntly. "You aren't exactly the fashionable society hostess, are you? And you have no experience in planning big functions. If she needs someone to fetch and carry and hold things for her, she can use her maid."

"I don't know how she wants to use me, but she has invited me and she has always been so jolly generous that I can't really say no. She gave me my trousseau, Fig. She bought me clothes in Paris and she practically furnished James's nursery. She's done an awful lot for me. I'd like to repay her."

"I suppose so," Fig said grudgingly, probably processing the fact that she had given me a ghastly silver stag from Castle Rannoch as my wedding present. Then a cunning little smile crossed her face. "In which case I should definitely stay on here until you get back. Nanny is still not familiar with the house or the grounds if she wants to take James for a walk. And I don't think the other servants have warmed to her yet, for some reason. I should be here to smooth things over. To be the lady of the house until you return."

And escape from the blizzards in Scotland, I thought. I tried not to let my expression show how miffed I was that she hadn't taken the bait. But then I realized it wasn't such a bad idea. I knew Mrs. Holbrook could run the house perfectly smoothly if I was away, but Fig might be useful in dealing with Nanny.

"I should only be away one or two nights," I said. "And Darcy also has business up in town, so you'll probably be dining alone. You'll be all right, won't you? I'll have a word with Mrs. Holbrook and with Pierre. He can cook you anything you fancy."

"I must admit you do have a good chef, Georgie. How lucky you were to snap him up in Paris. Of course, having the money to afford proper food really helps too. We seem to have to wait until a cow needs putting down before we eat meat."

I knew this was an absolute exaggeration as Fig had never stinted herself of food, but I nodded politely.

"Now, if you'll excuse me, I'll see if Maisie has packed me an overnight bag."

Maisie, efficient as usual, had a small suitcase and my train case sitting on my bed. Now that we were going up to Derbyshire, I realized that I'd probably need warmer nightclothes and a wooly jumper. I did a hasty bit of repacking, not nearly as neatly as Maisie had done it. As I came out of my room, I stared up the staircase to the nursery, wanting to hug my son one last time, but realized I shouldn't upset him again. So I went downstairs, fighting back feelings of guilt about leaving him. Belinda was already outside, her luggage stacked on the gravel drive and Trudi standing beside her. As I stood in the front hall Queenie appeared, clearing away the last of the breakfast things.

"I'm glad she's going," she said, looking past me to the scene outside.

"Miss Belinda? Why would you say that?" I frowned at her.

"Not Miss Belinda. 'Er. That Kraut woman. I don't trust her one bit."

I smiled. "That's because she's foreign and doesn't speak much English. I'm sure she's perfectly nice, Queenie."

Queenie shook her head. "There's something shifty about her."

"It's not your place to pass judgment, is it?" I said. "Let Mrs. Holbrook know that I am leaving."

I went out to join them. Belinda was speaking to her maid. "Now, you understand, Trudi. Men at station help with bags, *ja*? You give them a tip."

"Tip?" Trudi looked blankly at her.

"What is it in German?" Belinda scratched her head. "*Trink-geld*. Is that right?"

"Ah, *Trinkgeld. Ja.*" Trudi nodded enthusiastically. "*Wieviel?* How much?"

"Sixpence should be enough. You know sixpence? Little silver coin?" Belinda opened her purse and put a sixpence in Trudi's hand. "I've given you money for train and taxi in London. You see how much to pay for the taxi on the meter at the front. Taxi. London. Shows how much." She did a lot of miming. Clearly having a non-English-speaking maid was exhausting. I wondered how long Trudi would last.

We looked up as a taxi came up the drive. Bags were loaded. Trudi got in, looking rather scared. Off they went.

"I wonder if you'll ever see Trudi or your bags again," I said with a grin. "She may wind up in Brighton, meet a man and decide to stay."

"Don't say that!" Belinda did not smile. "Honestly, Georgie, I can't work out how thick she really is. I'm never sure what she does understand and what she doesn't. I'd hoped that being here with the other servants might have brought her English along, but perhaps they didn't interact with her much. There was probably some suspicion because she speaks German."

"I'm sure that's true. But if she can't make it to London alone with your luggage, then you need to look for another maid, don't you?"

"Absolutely. I'll give her another week or so to see how she improves, but then I'll have to decide if I take her down to Cornwall. Oh, dash it all, Georgie, servants are a confounded nuisance, aren't they? I wish we'd been brought up to fend for ourselves."

"You fended for yourself in Paris and I did quite well on my own in London," I said. "I just wish they'd make clothes that were easier to put on. They always seem to have buttons down the back, which are quite impossible."

"And then taking care of them is such a pain. Most of our gowns can't be washed so you have to know how to clean spots off them. I suspect the servant industry is in cahoots with the clothing makers so that one will always need a maid to get dressed."

We were smiling when Zou Zou came out to join us. She looked stunning as always in her dark mink with a red silk scarf tied over her long black hair.

"Are we ready, my darlings? I've told your chauffeur to bring round my little car."

Maisie came out, carrying a large pigskin suitcase, a train case and a jewelry box. Zou Zou did not believe in traveling light. Exactly on cue Phipps drove up in the sports car. I noticed the top was down. He got out and opened the boot, stacking her big suitcase, my small one and one of the train cases and securing them with leather straps. The other train case and the jewelry box had to go on the minute backseat. Belinda climbed in beside them.

"Will you be all right there?" I asked.

"Oh, don't worry about me," she said. "I've been in much more uncomfortable positions than this in my life." And she laughed. Somehow everything Belinda said had a naughty meaning. She exchanged a glance with Zou Zou.

I went into the house to say good-bye to Darcy.

"So you're off, then," he said. "Right. I'll be going up on the train later today. There is some sort of do I have to attend tonight and then meetings all tomorrow. I'm not sure when I'll be back." He gave me a kiss. "Have fun. Be good."

I went back out to the others. Zou Zou was now in the driver's seat, revving up the motor. I got into the front seat beside her and tied a scarf over my fur hat as a precaution.

"And off we go," Zou Zou said. She released the hand brake and we shot forward, spewing gravel. I was reminded of the time that Belinda bought herself a sports car and wasn't very good at driving it.

"Whatever happened to your car?" I turned to ask Belinda.

"Sold it when I went to Paris," she said. "Made quite a good profit. I suppose I'll have to get another one if I'm to be going back and forth to Cornwall."

I saw a sort of hopeful look on her face. She really did want to get back with Jago. I wondered if that could ever work—he a simple Cornish lad and she a rich society girl, used to clubs and parties. I suppose love conquers all.

Chapter 13

SUNDAY, MARCH 7

ON THE WAY TO INCHCLIFFE HALL, PEAK DISTRICT, DERBYSHIRE

With every mile north I have found myself wishing more and
more that I had never agreed to this harebrained expedition.
How is Zou Zou going to explain our visit? Is it wise to sow
doubts when a couple is already grieving and thus make it
even worse for them? But we can't turn back now.

It wasn't easy to converse during the trip, over the roar of the
engine and the noise of the road. Also it was rather frightening
as Zou Zou drove very fast. I could see that she was a brilliant
driver. All the same I held my breath a few times as she screeched
around lorries, missing oncoming traffic by inches. Luckily, being a Sunday, the traffic was light. We passed people coming out

of church and the sound of bells competed with the roar of the engine. Belinda had been remarkably silent all the while. It wasn't until we pulled up outside Belinda's mews cottage and she got out that she said, "I won't invite you in, if you don't mind. The place is still not quite habitable and I won't have any milk to offer you if you wanted coffee."

"Of course not. We quite understand," Zou Zou said. "And about this evening. I know I suggested a girls' night on the town, but—"

Belinda held up a hand to cut her off. "And about that. I hope you don't mind if I bow out. I'm not feeling too well and I fear a migraine is coming on."

She did look rather green. I suspected that sitting sideways on that tiny rumble seat while Zou Zou drove like a maniac might have made anybody feel sick.

"I'm so sorry, Belinda," Zou Zou said. "Do go and lie down. With any luck your maid will appear in the next hour or so to make you tea."

"Would you like us to get you some milk and supplies now?" I asked.

She shook her head. "Don't worry. I'll telephone Harrods and have them deliver. Much easier."

How nice it must be to have that sort of money, I thought. We hugged and left her.

"I'm glad it worked out that way," Zou Zou said as we drove off. "It would have been horrid to have to let her down if she was looking forward to our evening out. But now we can get going right away. I just need to stop at Eaton Square to let Clotilde know what we're doing and to pick up some warm trousers. The

Peak District can be bleak at this time of year, or at any time of year if you ask me." She let out the clutch and we roared off, startling a nanny pushing a very grand pram.

"I don't do well in the cold," she went on. "Thank God I had to leave Poland. I can't tell you how dreadful the winters were there. One wrapped oneself in furs or stayed in bed. Zigmund seemed to be immune to it and went out hunting wild boar. Horrible. We had so little in common."

In two minutes we were outside her house. I was ushered into the sitting room while Zou Zou shouted instructions to Clotilde. In no time at all she was back, Clotilde close behind her carrying tartan rugs, a thermos and a picnic basket.

"I had Henri make some sandwiches and a flask of consommé, so that we don't have to waste too much time stopping for food," Zou Zou said. I saw that she was now wearing tweed slacks under her long mink. We returned to the car, she bundled me into the tartan rug and off we went.

The less said about the journey, the better. It was long. As we drove north it grew colder, with a bitter wind. At one point it rained and we had to stop to put the hood up. Being a cloth hood, it was still jolly cold inside and the windscreen kept fogging over so that I had to lean across and clear it. After several hours of nonstop driving through smoky Midland towns, we stopped at a lay-by and ate the sandwiches, which were roast beef and pickle, ham and mustard and quite delicious. The consommé was miraculously still hot and warmed my frozen toes. We also popped behind the hedge to heed the call of nature. By five o'clock it was becoming dark. There was little traffic on the road and our headlights strafed the blackness ahead. We left the A road at Chesterfield, a good-sized market town.

"I suppose I had better telephone to warn them we are coming," Zou Zou said.

"They don't know yet?" I heard my voice rise. "What if they are not there?"

"Of course they will be there, darling," she said. "They are in mourning. They are not going to go gallivanting around."

We found a telephone box and some pennies. Zou Zou went in and dialed. I waited, my hands and face freezing as the wind was now harsh. I heard her voice, strained at first but then a laugh, a relaxed tone and the receiver was put down. She came back to the motorcar.

"It was Sebastian's father. I had to tell a little white lie and say I was driving Lady Georgiana to her home in Scotland and I thought I should just stop in to see how Tilly was doing."

"And did he sound pleased or annoyed?"

"Oh, pleased, I think. At least he said Tilly would welcome a bit of cheering up and could I find the way in the dark?"

"Well, it's a relief to know we've come so far and they haven't said go away," I quipped, attempting a little joke to lighten the mood as I suspected we were both equally tired and tense by now.

We took a road heading due west. "Over the top," Zou Zou said, which I didn't find very encouraging. The lit streets of the last small settlement were left behind and we started to climb. This now became quite frightening as there were no lights of any sort and we were zigzagging upward into a mountainous region.

Sometimes steep hillsides reared beside us; sometimes we plunged into groves of trees overhanging the road. Even Zou Zou now seemed tense, leaning forward and peering through the windscreen as the wipers worked frantically.

We came to one horribly sharp bend. Our headlights strafed empty blackness beyond. Zou Zou slowed to a crawl. "I think this was it," she said. "Where the accident took place."

I stared out. A blind curve and a railing that looked as if it had been repaired hastily.

"I can see why a car could go off the road here," I said. "You'd only need a little icy patch. . . ."

"Oh, be quiet," she snapped, quite uncharacteristic of her. Then she corrected herself. "Sorry. It's rather tricky seeing ahead at the moment and I was just thinking the same thing."

We drove higher, passing occasional hamlets where a light peeked from between curtains. Sometimes a light shone from a farmstead far below us. I was glad I couldn't see if there was a sheer drop, but I had become more and more convinced that we were wasting our time and this road could cause a fatal accident at any moment. If a lorry came toward us while we were negotiating one of those bends, if the road was slippery and a sheep stepped out . . . There were endless possibilities. The drive seemed endless. How big was Derbyshire anyway? I had heard about the Peak District but never visited anyone there. The word "peak" gave me visions of Swiss mountains, but surely in England there were only hills.

At long last we came to a village. There was a pub with a sign swinging in the wind. The Nag's Head. Two men were standing outside, smoking long clay pipes. From somewhere we could hear a radio playing music. It all looked so friendly and normal that I almost wept.

"I'd be tempted to pop in for a brandy and ginger," Zou Zou said, "but I'd like to get there before it decides to rain or snow. The weather seems so unpredictable at the moment."

We left the one lit village street behind. The road twisted and turned again, then we approached a pair of wrought iron gates, set in a stone wall.

"Here we are," Zou Zou said. "Inchcliffe Hall. We made it. Would you be an angel and open the gates?"

The wind took my breath away as I got out, wondering how I was going to unlock such imposing gates. But luckily they must have been unlocked for us as the left-hand one swung open easily and the little car drove through. I got in again and we set off down a long driveway bordered by tall trees. I could hear them sighing and groaning in the wind as we passed. At last we saw lights ahead and came upon a formidable gray stone building with turrets at both corners.

"Welcome to Inchcliffe Hall," Zou Zou said. "Not a bad little place. Too out of the way for my taste."

Even as she was speaking the front door opened, light streamed out and two footmen were coming toward the car.

"Welcome, Your Highness," one of them said as they assisted us out. "Please go on in. We'll take care of the motorcar."

He spoke with a strong regional accent, a little like the Yorkshire brogue but with flatter vowels. The other gave a nodding bow to me, not sure who I was or how to address me. I nodded back, then hurried up those front steps as fast as I could. Inside was an entrance hall with a floor of black and white marble squares. A large chandelier hung overhead and on the walls were hunting trophies and various weapons. In one corner was a suit of armor. In fact a typical English country house. It could almost have been Castle Rannoch except it wasn't quite as cold and dreary. A maid was waiting to assist us with our coats.

"Her ladyship is in the drawing room, Your Highness," the maid said. "Would you care to go in or to be taken up to your quarters first?"

"Oh, I think we should go and pay our respects first, don't you, Georgie?" Zou Zou said. "Unless you're dying to spend a penny?"

I was, actually, but I could see it would be rude not to say hello. So we were led into a large room stuffed with unfashionable old furniture. Two greyhound dogs were sprawled across the hearth rug and the mistress of the house was seated in an armchair by the fire, her hands held out toward the glowing logs, and staring at the sparks, lost in contemplation.

"Your ladyship, the guests have arrived." The maid bobbed a little curtsy.

Lady Inchcliffe spun around, startled. So she had been far away in her thoughts. "My goodness, I didn't hear the car. Well, the wind is so noisy tonight, isn't it? Thank goodness you got here safely. I couldn't help worrying. I said to Roy he should have told you not to come and risk the drive up on a night like this . . . not after . . . I mean there are so many places where things can go wrong and if it decided to start to snow . . ."

"We made it with no problem, darling Tilly," Zou Zou said. She crossed the room and wrapped her arms around the other woman. "We had to drive past anyway and I thought it would be quite ungracious and uncharitable of me not to pop in for a brief visit just to see how you were doing."

Lady Inchcliffe looked up, holding out a hand to her friend. "It was most kind of you, and I do appreciate the visit. We've been locked away in our own misery here, as you can imagine. Too much time to think . . . if only . . . what if . . . Oh, those horrid thoughts buzz around my head nonstop." She focused on me, still standing awkwardly in the doorway. "Oh, and you must be Lady Georgiana. Of course you are. I've seen your wedding pictures in *The Tattler* last year . . . or was it two years ago?"

"Almost two years now," I said. "How do you do, Lady Inchcliffe?" I went across and shook hands with her. Her hand felt cold in spite of sitting so close to the fire. Cold and bony and almost dead. She was a thin woman, the type whose clothes hang from her. Her face was lined and hollow, making her look much older than her years.

"Would you like a warm drink? A hot toddy? A sherry? Or would you rather freshen up first? We don't stand on ceremony much here, so we're not dressing for dinner at the moment. And I'm sure you haven't brought evening attire with you anyway."

"I think we'd both like to freshen up," Zou Zou said. "Our hair must look a frightful mess. Absolutely windblown to pieces."

"Ethel will show you to your rooms," she said, looking across to the maid, who still stood in the doorway. "And then come straight down. The others will be joining us right away."

"Others? You have other guests?" Zou Zou asked.

"Not guests. Family members," Tilly Inchcliffe said. "My sister Betty and our niece and nephew. Nigel has been living with us for the past few months, but Betty and Olive came up to see how they could help after . . . the tragedy. Now, don't let me keep you any longer. We eat early in these parts."

We followed the maid up the staircase, along a dark hallway, and were shown into two adjoining rooms. The rooms again were over-furnished, mine taken up almost entirely with an enormous four-poster bed and giant carved wardrobe. My suitcase had already been placed on the bed.

I heard Zou Zou saying, "And the lavatory and bathroom?"

"At the end of the hall, my lady."

I came out and found Zou Zou already heading in that direction. "Thank goodness," she whispered to me. "I don't know about you, but I've been dying to spend a penny for hours."

Chapter 14

We are here. We made it although the drive was quite alarming
to me. Inchcliffe Hall seems a rather gloomy place, even
before the tragedy, I suspect. Dark rooms, long dark halls. I
gather they inherited it this way and haven't changed
anything. I wonder if we might be doing more harm than
good coming here, but Zou Zou wants to put her own mind
at rest, I can tell.

I changed into the good wool frock, tamed my flyaway hair and
put on a little lipstick and powder to cover my windblown
cheeks. Zou Zou, as always, managed to look stunning. She was
wearing black velvet trousers and a silky silver blouse with a
blond mink stole casually around her shoulders. As usual I felt

like a country bumpkin beside her. As we made our way down the stairs we could hear voices coming from the sitting room and entered to find several people already assembled there.

Tilly was still sitting in her armchair, now holding a glass of sherry. Across from her, on the other side of the fireplace, another older woman was sitting on a sofa, rather more coarse-looking with a little too much rouge on her face, contrasting with the black dress she was wearing. I realized then that the party were all wearing black. Of course. I should have thought. Thank heavens my dress was the darkest of bottle greens. It would have been embarrassing to be dressed in bright colors.

"Ah, there you are, ladies. Come in and have a drink." A tall, good-looking man had been standing by the fire. His hair was graying at the temples but he had the look of an outdoor type. He held out his hand to me. "How do you do, Lady Georgiana? Roy Inchcliffe. You've met my wife. This is her sister, Mrs. Polton, and my nephew Nigel and niece Olive. They are here, up from London, to buck up poor Tilly."

Nigel had been standing with his uncle beside the fire. He was a gangly, pimply youth and he shot me what seemed like a hostile glance. Olive was sitting beside her mother on the sofa and she looked up shyly, giving a half smile. The black dress she was wearing looked too big for her and she was uncomfortable in it. Perhaps borrowed from her mother, who was a bigger woman. It was clear that Lady Inchcliffe had married above her original station.

"How do you do?" I said. "It's very good of you to take us in. The princess was so concerned for her friend that we decided to break the journey here."

"You live in Scotland, do you?" Tilly asked. "I thought you had moved south after you married."

"Yes. We live in Sussex. But my family home is still in Scotland and I like to visit from time to time." I could feel my cheeks turning red as always happened if I dared to tell a lie. I think the consequences of lying had been so great under Nanny's rule that I knew I'd never be good at it.

"Your father is the duke?" Betty asked me. "The one who was related to Queen Victoria?"

"No, my father is dead," I said. "My brother is the current duke."

A hush descended. This seemed to be the extent of the small talk.

"So, how about that drink, Roy dear?" Zou Zou asked.

"Oh right. Jolly good. We've sherry or whiskey here, but my wife suggested rum punches for both of you as it's quite chilly tonight."

"That sounds perfect," Zou Zou said, looking across at me for approval. I nodded.

The punches were brought for us while the others stuck to sherry. There were warm sausage rolls. It was all very convivial, but I could sense the air of tension in the room and was glad when the dinner gong sounded. The dining room reminded me of a monastery refectory—long oak table, candles in sconces on the dark wood-paneled walls and half the room bathed in shadow. At table I was placed to the right of our host, although that position should have been Zou Zou's—a princess outranking a mere duke's daughter. But she sat next to Tilly at the other end of the long table and I noticed her placing her hand over Tilly's, patting it.

"I'm sorry we've barged in at such a difficult time for you," I said.

"Not at all. We welcome the diversion, actually," he said. "We've been too wrapped up in our loss, I suppose. My wife is absolutely shattered. She doted on the boy." He gave an embarrassed chuckle. "I say boy, but he was really a man, wasn't he? Should have married and settled down by now. But he never seemed to have found the right girl. I don't think he looked too hard. Too busy enjoying himself, driving those damned motorcars, or popping off to the South of France."

"He didn't have a profession, then?"

"He did not. He started to work with a shipping company after he came down from university but didn't like being shut in an office. About that time I inherited this place. I wanted him up here to teach him the running of the estate, thinking he'd have to take it over someday. It's a big job, you know. Large property, grouse and pheasant shoots, sheep, cows. I had to learn it myself quite quickly. I'd been a city man until my cousin died and I found this had been dumped on me."

"So are you enjoying it? I mean, were you enjoying it until this happened?"

"I suppose so. Quite a challenge for one who wasn't raised in the country. I'm Master of the Hunt, you know. Never hunted in my life before." He laughed, then I could see he must have been quite a jolly man until tragedy struck.

"So Sebastian didn't want to join you up here?"

"He didn't, I'm sure. He liked London life. He was quite the debs' delight when he came down from university. You know how it is. All the eligible young men get invited to all the parties and balls. But I didn't have the funds to keep him having fun in London, without any proper job. I told him he needed to get married and settle down, or come up here to help me. It fell on deaf ears. He showed up from time to time. Pretended to be interested, then went off again, when he received an invitation to drive a car in a rally, or go to some race meeting. Mad about cars he was. Always tinkering, trying innovations. Told me he had dreams of designing and building his own car."

"You said he was tinkering." I formed the sentence carefully. "Is it possible he'd tinkered with his motorcar and that was why something went wrong that night?"

He looked up at me, sharply. "We'll never know, will we. All I can say is that he was good at it. He knew what he was doing. Both the driving and the modifications. He excelled at both. And he knew the road, Lady Georgiana. He'd never have taken that bend too fast. That's why it's so upsetting."

"I hardly like to ask this, but had he been drinking?"

He was still eyeing me. "He'd stopped off at the Nag's Head—that's the pub in the village—for a quick pint, but the landlord says that was all. Just a pint and the boy could hold his liquor. It wasn't even late. About seven when we got the call."

"Did he always do his own work on his motorcar or did he have a garage nearby?"

"Oh no. He wouldn't trust anyone to work on his motorcar except him. She was his pride and joy. I think he loved her more than his family." I saw the sadness engulf his face again, a father who had loved his son and had such high hopes for him.

"I'm sorry," I said. "I shouldn't have brought this up. It's obviously too painful to talk about."

"Yes, it is still a bit raw," he said. "Frankly it's still hard to come to terms with. I keep expecting to hear that annoying toot of his horn as he drives up the driveway."

I decided to move to different questions. "Did you inherit this place from your father?"

"No, from my uncle. He only had daughters."

"And who inherits from you now, after Sebastian . . . ?" I couldn't finish the sentence and felt I might have gone too far.

"My nephew Nigel," he said.

"Oh, I thought he was your wife's sister's son."

"No, Olive is her daughter. Nigel is my brother's child and now my heir."

"Has he been living with you for long?"

"Not living with us. He comes up to visit from time to time. He's planning to study agriculture, so naturally he's keen to get experience to get into the Royal Agriculture College."

This was interesting. So Nigel was now the heir and actually wanted this sort of estate life. Could he have helped to bring about the demise of his cousin?

I glanced across the table and noticed Nigel staring at me. Again I felt the hostility. I moved on. "Did you meet Sebastian's friends? Did he bring them up here much?"

He frowned. "Not really. Sometimes some kind of grubby motorcar chap who was going to be in a rally with him."

"But not friends from London? I was wondering if he knew a chap called Algie Beauchamps?"

"Beauchamps? Not that I know of. Certainly hasn't been to stay here."

"What about Shrimpy Smithers?"

"Shrimpy?" He chuckled. "What ridiculous nicknames these chaps give each other, don't they?" He stopped, putting down his soup spoon beside his bowl. "Why all the questions? Are you normally this inquisitive?"

I turned bright red. "I'm so sorry. I'm being rude. I just wanted to get a feel for who Sebastian was, I suppose. I know Zou Zou is really upset about his death. But I see now, you don't want to talk about it. Forgive me."

"Nothing to forgive," he said. "So tell me a bit about your life. Do you manage an estate like this?"

I told him about Eynsleigh and our experiment with the pigs and the farm. He showed interest and we chatted amiably. Occasionally he turned to address a remark to Zou Zou and I spoke to Olive. She was horribly shy and answered me in one syllable, presumably overawed by my royal past. I did gather she was out of school and she was taking a typing course, hoping to get a job in an office. She liked going out ballroom dancing and they had once been on holiday to France. The food was good, if plain—a thick root vegetable soup, roast lamb and then a baked apple pudding. A glass of red wine was served and then we had coffee in the drawing room.

I could feel tiredness overtaking me and I was uncomfortable at missing James's night feed. I wondered how long it would take before my milk completely dried up. I caught Zou Zou's eye.

"If you don't think it terribly rude," she said, "Lady Georgiana and I have had a long drive and I think our beds are calling us."

Tilly was most solicitous. She arranged for hot-water bottles and asked what we might like for breakfast in the morning. We bade them good night and went up the stairs.

"You were deep in conversation with Lord Inchcliffe," she said. "Did you learn anything?"

"Quite a lot, actually," I said. "Come into my room and I'll tell you."

She followed me. "Goodness, what a chamber of horrors," she said. "I thought mine was bad enough, but this bed!" And she burst out laughing. Her merry laughter broke the unbearable tension I had been feeling. I laughed too.

"Oh, Zou Zou, what on earth are we doing here? We can't do any good, can we?"

She plonked herself down on the bed and gave a couple of experimental pats on the eiderdown. "So tell me what you learned."

"Well," I said. "I learned that Sebastian liked being the man about town and wasn't interested in the running of this place. He was brilliant with cars and worked on his car himself, so not much chance for it to have been tampered with. I asked about friends and mentioned Algie Beauchamps' name, but it didn't mean anything to his father. It didn't seem that any of his friends were bright young things—at least not the ones he brought here." I came to sit on the bed beside her. "Oh, I learned, most interestingly, that Nigel will now inherit."

"Nigel the pimply boy?" she asked. "I tried to engage him in conversation but he was not forthcoming, almost to the point of rudeness."

"He gave me hostile looks too," I said. "So he'd have a good motive for wanting to get rid of his cousin."

"He would," she agreed. "But I don't know where we go from here."

"We've established one thing," I said. "There doesn't immediately seem to be a link between him and one of the other chaps who was killed."

"We don't know that," Zou Zou said. "If he spent some of his time in London, he could have quite a different set of friends from the ones he brought home. And if Algie Beauchamps was involved in speedboats, they quite possibly moved in the same circles."

"But he didn't know Shrimpy Smithers either."

"I don't suppose young men want their fathers to know what they are doing when they are in London," she said. "But we have to conclude they were not old school friends or the names would have rung a bell."

"So what next?" I asked.

She sighed. "I'll have a chat with Tilly in the morning. She is clearly not satisfied that it was entirely an accident . . . or maybe she is just grasping at straws to make herself feel better. And then we should go and visit the scene of the crime, if it really does turn out to be a crime."

"I don't know what we'd hope to see," I said. "But it would be good to have a clear picture. I'm thinking we've come up here on a wild-goose chase."

"Nothing ventured, nothing gained," Zou Zou said.

I found myself marveling that someone who grew up speaking Polish and French should have such a great command of the English language. She spoke too without the trace of an accent. She stood up. "I should go and let you get some sleep. I'm only next door if you are visited by the family ghost during the night . . . or are you quite at home with ghosts?"

"We do have a couple at Castle Rannoch," I said, "but I've never seen one."

There was a fire in the grate and the room was comfortably warm. I undressed and got into bed, finding that a stone-hot-water bottle had been placed between the sheets for me. A hospitable house! I lay awake for a while, feeling the unfamiliar sensation of being in bed alone without Darcy's comforting presence beside me. The wind rattled the windows and sighed down the chimney. The idea of ghosts did cross my mind but I dismissed it, finally drifting off to sleep.

$$\mathcal{C}hapter\ 15$$

Maybe we're getting somewhere, but we have no way of proving it. I'll be so glad to go home. I miss James and Darcy.

I awoke to a gray and blustery dawn as sleet peppered my window. Not a promising start to the day. I dressed warmly and went down to find Tilly sitting with her sister in the breakfast room. They looked so intimate, huddled so close together, that I was about to tiptoe out and walk away. But Tilly looked up and saw me.

"Oh, Lady Georgiana. Please do come in. You'll find breakfast on the sideboard."

I went over and helped myself to porridge and tea, then sat down, far enough away from them to be polite.

"Betty was just saying that she should go home and I was begging her to stay on. I need the support at this moment."

"Of course you do," I said.

"I just wish someone could tell me. . . ." She went on, almost to herself, "Why did he take that corner too fast? He must have taken it too fast or he'd never have lost control."

"Was it perhaps icy that night?" I asked.

"I don't think so. It was chilly. It was damp maybe, but there wasn't a frost. And Sebastian drove in rallies across the Alps. He was used to bad conditions. He knew that corner was dangerous. Everyone did around here. It was known as Dead Man's Drop in some circles. He wasn't in a hurry. He'd been over to Matlock to the main post office. He stopped at the pub for a pint and he was coming home in time for dinner. There was no need. . . ."

She broke off, her voice cracking with emotion.

Betty put a hand on her arm. "There, there, my dear. Don't keep going over it. It's not going to help. We can't bring him back."

"I just think . . ." Tilly said, with a little sob, "I think someone must have caused this. Someone got in his way and made him swerve."

"Deliberately, you mean?" I asked.

"Oh, not intentionally," she said hastily, "but if he got headlights in his face suddenly as he came around the bend. If a car was hugging the middle of the road . . . but then if the other driver saw what happened, surely he'd have gone for help? He wouldn't have just driven away?"

"Unless he was frightened he'd be blamed?" Betty said. "Some people might have panicked."

"Then he'll have this on his conscience the rest of his life."

I digested this. "Presumably not too many cars take this road across the Peak District?"

"Not this road. They'd stick to the main road from Chesterfield to Matlock. No need to come up here if you don't live in these parts or you're a hiker or climber during the daylight hours."

"So a strange car might have been noticed?" I asked.

They were staring at me now, eyeing me warily.

"It might have been, but nobody came forward when there was the inquest. It was ruled death by misadventure. Case closed," Tilly said, the bitterness still in her voice. "There's nothing we can do now."

"I hate to ask this," I said, "but did your son have any enemies?"

"Enemies? Sebastian?"

"Did he owe money to anyone? Have any gambling debts? Crossed anyone involved in criminal activity?"

"Good gracious no," Tilly said. "What a thing to suggest. Sebastian never gambled. As for owing money, he might have done, but if you owe someone money you don't go and kill them, do you? You want them alive to pay it back."

That made sense. We could perhaps talk to his circle of friends in London to get a better idea.

"Did he still have a flat in London or did he live here all the time?" I asked.

She frowned. "His father refused to pay for a London flat. He stayed with friends when he was down there. A chap called Morrison. Tubby Morrison. A fellow car enthusiast. They talked of designing a new car together."

"Would you happen to know where this Tubby Morrison lives?"

"Yes. He has a flat in Cadogan Square. No shortage of money there. American mother." She looked up, frowning at me. "Why ask this? My son is gone. No longer there."

"I'm sorry," I said, flushing. "I had no wish to upset you."

I made a mental note to check on Tubby Morrison and went back to eating my porridge in silence. Zou Zou joined me soon after, coming to sit beside me with a plate laden with eggs, bacon, kidneys. How she stayed so svelte had always been a mystery to me. When Tilly and Betty had finished their breakfast and left the dining room I told Zou Zou what I had just learned.

"Oh, that's an interesting point," she said. "If he had run afoul of a criminal element . . ."

"But if they were in London, would they really have bothered to come up to Derbyshire and lay in wait for him on a steep bend? Wouldn't it be easier to stab him on a dark street?"

"That's true," she said. "It would have to be someone who knew that this drive could be risky. Maybe he had mentioned to someone that the last mile or so was dangerous. Or he had run afoul of someone who lives up here?"

"We'll never know, will we?" I said. "At least we can visit this Tubby person. Sebastian would have been more likely to tell a friend if he was in any trouble."

"We'll do it when we get back to London," she said. "I don't see any point in lingering here any longer, but we should stop in the village and ask questions there. Villagers are always so observant, aren't they? They lead boring lives so they like minding other people's business."

I tried not to smile at the way she had summed up "villagers" with one stroke. Typical aristocrat. If I hadn't had a Cockney grandfather I'm sure I would have been the same. I was about to go up and pack when Nigel came in. He saw us sitting there and almost retreated.

"Don't worry, we're about to go," I said. "We have a long drive ahead of us today."

"Oh, right." He nodded and went over to the sideboard, toying with the bacon as if unwilling to sit while we were still there.

"This whole business must have been very upsetting for you," Zou Zou said. "No wonder you don't want intruders at a time like this."

He went rather pink. "I don't mean to be rude," he said. "It's been beastly. The problem is that Sebastian and I didn't get along. He could be damned rude and critical and he resented me being here. Now I feel guilty. . . ."

"Why is that?" Zou Zou asked.

"Because I wished he'd stay away. He wasn't interested in this place and I was. And yet he'd get to inherit it. And now he's gone. I've got what I wanted and I feel terrible."

"It wasn't your fault," I said. "You can't blame yourself."

He looked away. "We had words before he drove off that day. I wondered if I'd made him angry so he drove faster than usual."

"I thought the accident happened when he was coming back from town," I said. "He'd have had time to cool down."

The thought crossed my mind that Sebastian had been to the post office. Had he picked up a letter that gave him bad news or made him angry? Then I reminded myself that the reason I was here was that I was worried about a connection between four so-called accidents. And as yet we hadn't established any at all. Nigel had a reason to want his cousin out of the way. That was the only fact to go on so far. He felt guilty.

I took a deep breath before asking, "So why do you think you and your cousin did not get along?"

He shrugged. "He was much older than me, and he liked that London scene . . . parties, debs. Not for me, thank you. Also he was potty about motorcars. Anything to do with cars and all that motoring crowd."

"I take it you are not a car enthusiast?" I asked.

He gave an expression of disgust, or was it anger? "I don't know how to drive yet," he said. "I haven't passed my test and I don't own a car. I don't have any money to buy one and I can't see my getting the money in the foreseeable future. Maybe for my twenty-first. . . . But I can't say I'm that bothered."

"Did Sebastian let you help him with his motor when he was here?"

"Sebastian? He wouldn't let anyone near his baby. Besides, I could see no point in lying on a tarpaulin under a car in the wind and rain." He stopped, glared at me, then said, "Look, I see no point in harping on about this. Sebastian is dead. There's nothing we can do." He turned back to the sideboard and purposely heaped food onto a plate. Zou Zou and I left.

"What was that in aid of?" Zou Zou asked. "Grilling poor little Nigel?"

"I suppose it was because he is the only one with any kind of motive for wanting Sebastian out of the way," I said. "But now I don't think he had either the knowledge or the gumption to get rid of his cousin. He wouldn't have known how to tamper with a motor."

We had our bags carried down and gave our thanks and farewells to Tilly. Her husband was already out and about on the estate, we were told. The car was brought around, the bags loaded and off we went. The early morning rain had fortunately blown over, leaving a bitter wind and clouds racing across the sky. I tied my scarf tightly as Zou Zou had put the top down again. Off we went, driving back the way we had come.

Chapter 16

On the way home and then Zou Zou's place

I am left with more questions than answers. It seems that
someone could have planned and carried out an accident at
that sharp bend. But who? Maybe we'll know more when we
meet Sebastian's friend in London today. At least the driving
conditions are better and we won't have to worry about
being in an accident ourselves.

Zou Zou drove at her normal speed, in spite of the wet roads,
until we came to the site of the accident. She pulled into a gateway just before the bend and we got out. By daylight it was even
more alarming. To our left the land rose steeply up a wooded
hillside. On our right the road hugged a steep drop as it went
around a sharp bend, a wooden barrier along the edge. Below

was a sheer wooded slope going down to a stream cascading over boulders in the valley far beneath us. I could see now where the car had crashed through the wooden barrier. It had been flimsy enough not to stop a speeding car and was now patched in what I hoped was a temporary fix. We walked toward it and stood looking down.

"Golly." The word escaped before I remembered I was trying to be grown-up in my choice of vocabulary.

"If this was intentional"—Zou Zou said the words slowly and deliberately—"the spot was chosen perfectly. If a car was coming toward him on the wrong side of the road as he went round this bend, he'd instinctively swerve out of the way and he'd have no chance. He'd have gone straight down."

"Yes," I said. "You can see where the bracken and bushes were disturbed and that patch at the bottom beside the river . . . it's all burned. They must have removed the car."

"Well, they had to get his body, didn't they?" Zou Zou said.

We walked on, listening for oncoming traffic as we'd have had no chance to step out of the way and could likely have caused a second accident. There was nothing more to be seen and we walked back to where we had parked our car.

"A vehicle could have parked here, heard Sebastian coming up from the village, or even seen his headlights coming up in the darkness, then pulled out at the right moment," I said.

"How would the person know it was Sebastian?" Zou Zou asked.

"That's a good point. Maybe the car he drove made a distinctive sound? If you were a driving enthusiast you'd know."

I looked around and noticed the entrance to a footpath,

closer to the bend. Too small to have parked a car, but I walked forward to take a look. It did not necessarily have to be a motor-car that came out at Sebastian. A pedestrian would have made him swerve, although that pedestrian would have been taking a big risk. There was a grassy area before the path rose steeply up the hillside. I examined the ground beneath my feet. Puddles with footprints of what looked like boots. Then I saw two things. "Look." I bent to pick up a cigarette stub.

"Someone was here recently. And see here? A tire mark. Too thick for a bicycle. A motorbike, do you think?"

"You may be right." Zou Zou bent to examine where the grass had been crushed. "So someone could have stationed a motorbike here, waited for Sebastian's car and then pulled out."

"Yes," I agreed. "If the rider climbed a few steps up this path he could see the road and a car approaching. If he knew what Sebastian's car looked like, he'd be ready."

"Not if it was dark," Zou Zou said. "Remember how absolutely black it was last night."

"Oh, right," I said.

"But he could stand here and see the headlights coming, if he knew somehow that Sebastian's would be the next vehicle on the road."

"And if his car had been tampered with . . . brakes or steering sabotaged . . . he'd have gone straight over." We stared at each other. "Now all we need to find out is who might have had a motive."

"This is all surmise," Zou Zou said. "It could have been a police motorbike parked here while they investigated. Or as sim-ple as a farmhand stopped his bike for a smoke. It could have been black ice, as you pointed out, or something that angered or distracted Sebastian to make him take that bend too quickly. Even a sheep on the road."

We walked back to the car and drove on. I was feeling sad and dispirited. I felt that we might never know, that it had, perhaps, been an accident and we had been wasting our time. Zou Zou took the bends carefully as we came down to the village and pulled up beside the Nag's Head.

"We should at least see what the locals have to say," she said.

The pub was not yet open, but women were clustered outside the small village shop. They looked up warily as we approached them. Zou Zou explained that we were friends of the Inchcliffes. So sad about poor Sebastian. Did they see much of him in the village?

They shook heads, shrugging. "He didn't mix with the likes of us," one said. "You posh types all keep to yourselves, don't you?"

"But he did stop off occasionally for a pint at the pub, didn't he?"

"I wouldn't know," another woman said. "Pubs are for men, aren't they? We women are supposed to be home making the dinner."

The others grunted agreement.

"When he came through the village did he always drive fast?" I asked. "I know he loved that motorcar and he took part in rallies."

They looked at each other for confirmation. "I can't say he did. He'd often stop to pick up a paper or a chocolate bar at the shop," one said. "He were always polite enough, mind you. Always said good day and commented on the weather. A nice enough young bloke, wouldn't you say?"

The others agreed. Nice enough in his way.

We walked on. At the far end of the village there was a garage with petrol pumps. We hadn't noticed it on the way there because it was obviously closed for the night. Now a motorcar was being serviced and a couple of men were standing watching and talking. They broke off as we went up to them. Zou Zou said that we were friends of the Inchcliffes and asked if any of them had been called upon to help after the accident.

"Aye, we were," one said. "We were at the pub when some young fellow comes running in and says a car's gone over at Dead Man's Drop. So we all go rushing up there. We were too late, of course. The whole thing was on fire. By the time it were put out the poor chap was fried. I reckon he'd knocked himself unconscious or even been killed by the drop, so he wouldn't have suffered."

"What happened to the car?" I asked. "Someone raised it up?"

"Mick at the garage helped with that, and they brought in a crane from Hathersage. They needed to, for the inquest." One of the men nodded toward the burly chap who was pumping petrol.

"I don't know why they needed an inquest at all," the other man said. "We all know that corner is a death trap. He wouldn't be the first bloke who's gone over."

"Did they come to any conclusions at the inquest, then?" I asked.

They shrugged. "Death by misadventure," one said.

"So they didn't find anything suspicious in the car . . . nobody had tampered with anything?"

Now they were looking at me strangely.

"You're a very inquisitive young woman," one said.

"It's just that Sebastian was my friend," I lied. "He was a brilliant driver. He knew that bend. I can't believe he'd have gone over there."

"You think someone might have . . ." one of the men said, not even finishing the sentence. "Who would do that?"

"I've no idea," I said. "I didn't know he had enemies."

"Aye, he was certainly a likable chap when we saw him up here." He looked at his mate for confirmation.

"Did you happen to see him that night, then?" Zou Zou asked, inserting herself into the conversation.

"He came into the pub and had a pint. He said he'd had to stop to get some petrol so he thought he'd pop in for a quick one before he had to face the family."

"So he did come to the garage here?" This was news.

They nodded. "Reckon he did." They looked across to Mick, who had finished pumping the petrol. "Hey, Mick, that night when young Sebastian was killed. He stopped with you for petrol, didn't he?"

"That's right. He said he should have stopped in Chesterfield because I charged too much. Made a joke of it."

"Was there anybody else at the garage at that time? Or any strangers in the pub?"

They looked at each other, wondering what this meant.

"Can't say I noticed any strangers, did you?"

"There was a car with an elderly couple in it. Going to take the waters at Buxton, so they said. Nice people. Oh, and a young chap stopped by earlier," Mick said. "Scruffy type on a motorbike. He only wanted half a gallon in a can he was carrying in case he ran out when he was up in the peaks. Said he was on a rambling holiday. I told him it were not very favorable weather for rambling. He said he didn't mind getting wet."

"Do you know where he came from?"

"Down south," Mick said. "Yeah. A Londoner for sure. He certainly didn't come back this way, so I reckon he went on over to the west and back down through the potteries."

"I presume the police were called?" Zou Zou said.

"Oh aye. Our local constable had to give a statement at the inquest. Wasn't much to say. Car went over the edge and then caught fire. Victim burned beyond recognition."

"Where would we find this local constable?" Zou Zou asked.

"Police station's right behind the church." The man pointed at the spire, set back from the road. We thanked them and headed in that direction, past a churchyard filled with old gravestones and then up a path to a gray stone cottage with a blue light outside, the only hint that this was a police station. The constable listened to us politely. He'd been most shaken up, he said. Horrible to see that car when it was brought up. The victim burned to a crisp. I shuddered at this description but fought to remain businesslike.

"Was it possible to see if anything in the car had been tampered with?" I asked.

He stared at me. "You mean someone might have done this deliberately? Do you have any information we didn't have at the inquest?"

"Not at all," I said. "It's just that he was such a good driver. I don't think he'd have missed that bend."

"I'm afraid the vehicle was too badly damaged from the fire," he said. "It seems he had a full tank of petrol and he was carrying an extra can of petrol in the boot. Of course that all went up when it crash-landed on the rocks."

He couldn't tell us anything more. We got back into the motorcar and drove on.

"So what do you think?" Zou Zou asked. "What do we actually know? Are we any further along?"

"I've been thinking of a couple of things," I said. "A young chap on a motorbike stopped at the garage and had them put some petrol into a can he was carrying. The policeman said that Sebastian's car had a can of petrol in the trunk. Why, when he'd just filled up? And we saw what could have been a motorcycle tire track and a cigarette butt at that gateway. It could have been all planned. This chap on the motorbike waits until Sebastian goes into the pub, then puts the can of petrol into the trunk, knowing it will explode after the crash and make sure he won't survive. Then he waits until Sebastian's car comes up the hill to the bend. He pulls out, with his headlight shining. Sebastian swerves, goes over the edge."

"It would take meticulous timing," Zou Zou said. "But it's possible. So the question is, who is the chap on the motorbike and why did he want to kill Sebastian?"

Chapter 17

MONDAY, MARCH 8

BACK IN LONDON

I think we've established that Sebastian's death might not be
accidental. Now all we have to do is to link it to the other three.

We came down from the Peak District and drove back to London. The weather was good and we covered the distance in record time, pulling up at Eaton Square just as it was getting dark,
leaving me rather windswept and breathless with Zou Zou's
driving and the top being down.

"I should probably see if I can get home tonight," I said. "I
don't like leaving James for too long."

"Oh, do you have to?" Zou Zou looked disappointed. "I
thought we were just at the beginning of our sleuthing. We have
to visit that Tubby character who was mentioned. He might well

know if Sebastian had had a falling-out with someone who rode a motorbike." She put a hand on my arm. "Come on, darling one. One more night won't be the end of the world for your son. You know he's in safe hands. And we'll have a lovely dinner at my place, just the two of us."

I too was keen to see what Tubby Morrison had to say. I agreed, still battling guilt feelings at being away from James. He was in safe hands, I knew. Maybe not very warm and friendly hands, but at least perfectly safe. And I'd soon find a new nanny and all would be well.

We had a sherry and smoked salmon on brown bread to fortify us, then we drove to Cadogan Square just off Sloane Street in Chelsea. Number seventy-seven was one of those impressive redbrick mansion buildings, so beloved by city dwellers. The doorman gave us the flat number for Tubby Morrison and we took the lift up to the fourth floor.

"Of course he may not be home," Zou Zou said as we rang the bell. "Young single men do go out in the evening."

The door was opened almost instantly by a chubby pink-cheeked man with an innocent childlike face. He looked surprised to see us.

"Hello. Can I help you?" he asked. "Are you looking for someone?"

"Yes, Tubby Morrison. Are you he?" Zou Zou asked.

"I am, but . . ." He looked wary now. He took in Zou Zou's mink and stylish hat. "Are you collecting for some charity? Because you see I'm just about to go out to dinner."

I noticed then that he was wearing full evening dress under his overcoat.

"We won't keep you," Zou Zou said, "but if you have a minute to spare, we'd like to ask you about Sebastian Inchcliffe. I gather you were a good friend of his. He stayed with you when he was in London, didn't he?"

"He did. We had some good fun together," he said. "I was damned sorry to hear about his death. Absolutely gutted to hear about it. Of course one knew that Sebastian took risks. He drove in motor races, for God's sake, and rallies. We were together in a couple of them. That rally across the Alps . . . absolutely terrifying. But he was a terrific driver. He handled those hairpin bends . . . so to hear he'd gone off the road. I mean, who would have thought it." He paused then. "I say, what is this about?"

"I'm Princess Zamanska, a friend of Sebastian's mother," Zou Zou said. "We too have questions about his death and we wondered. . . . Could we just come in for a moment? It's not very comfortable chatting in the hall."

"Oh, all right." He let us in. The flat smelled of cigarette smoke and was not very tidy. Tubby removed a newspaper and scarf from the sofa and bade us sit.

"We won't keep you long," Zou Zou said. "It's just that you knew Sebastian well. We wondered . . . whether he had fallen foul of somebody? Gambling debts? Whether his death might have been intentional."

"Good heavens above." Tubby's innocent-looking face registered surprise. "No, that never crossed my mind. I did wonder if he'd had a drop too much to drink, you know. He did like to knock it back sometimes."

"He only had one pint, so we're told," I said.

Tubby frowned, thinking. "I can't think of anyone who'd

want to do old Seb harm. He was a likable bloke. Got along with everyone. In our field you mix with all sorts."

"We are interested in someone described as a scruffy bloke on a motorcycle," I said. "Does that ring a bell? Someone Sebastian knew?"

He gave a snort. "Motorcycle? Sebastian loathed motorcycles. He called them the scourge of the road. He had an unpleasant encounter with one once and if he had his way they'd be banned from the roads."

"An unpleasant encounter? Recently?"

"God no. Years ago, when we were all doing the debs rounds in London and we were learning to drive. But it put him off them for life." Tubby shifted impatiently. "Look, I suppose I should offer you a drink but I really ought to be going. I'm meeting some fellows and they don't like to be kept waiting."

"Of course." Zou Zou stood up. "It was really good of you to take the time to speak with us, Mr. Morrison."

"I'm not sure I've been of any help, but I suspect a slick road had more to do with old Seb's death than any evil intent."

"Thank you." I stood up too and held out my hand to shake his. Then I remembered. "Do you happen to know a chap called Algie Beauchamps?"

"Name rings a bell," he said. "Oh yes. The speedboat chappie. Trying to break the world speed record when his boat blew up. I read about it."

"But you don't know him personally?"

"I believe I met him once years ago. I think he was at uni with Seb."

"But not one of Sebastian's current friends?" I asked.

"Not that I know of. I think Seb said he was a studious type. Not part of his set."

"What about Rupert Warburton-Stoke? Or Shrimpy Smithers?"

"Don't know those chaps." He pulled out a pocket watch. "Look, must dash. You can find your own way out, can't you?"

He ran ahead of us and jumped into the waiting lift, leaving us to stand there until it returned for us.

"None the wiser," Zou Zou said. "Maybe we are chasing straws and should just leave this alone."

"I suppose you're right," I said. "There doesn't seem to be much connection between Algie and Sebastian, does there? And the Londoner on a motorbike. Would he really have chased Sebastian all the way up to Derbyshire?"

"Let's go and have a bloody good meal and lots of booze to cheer ourselves up," Zou Zou said. She took my arm and steered me from the building.

Zou Zou's chef cooked us a wonderful dinner of poached turbot with parsley sauce, a lamb cutlet and then profiteroles. She apologized for the simplicity of the supper but said we couldn't expect Chef to do more with short notice. Personally I thought it was perfect.

It was also accompanied by champagne, then red wine, then a little brandy, and I fell into a sound sleep, to be woken in the morning by Clotilde bringing in a tea tray adorned with a pink rose. I got up, bathed and breakfasted before Zou Zou appeared, still dressed in a flowing fur-trimmed negligee.

"I really should go home," I said. "Thank you for a lovely time."

"I'd volunteer to run you down to Eynsleigh," she said. Before I could refuse this she went on, "But I really don't think I could face your sister-in-law at the moment. I'm feeling quite fragile. I think reliving that car crash has really upset me. I shall take to my bed for a day or so."

I nodded in understanding.

"But I'll have my chauffeur run you to Victoria."

"Oh, that really isn't necessary," I said. "It's a nice day. I can walk."

"It's no trouble," Zou Zou said, and yanked on a bellpull. "And if you decide to do any more sleuthing, do let me be in on it. It was rather exciting in a way, although rather depressing too. We could go up to Windermere to find out about that boat crash, and then to Wales to see about the climbing accident. What do you say? Just give me a couple of days to revive myself. I'll go to the Turkish baths and be slapped and pummeled by a giant Russian woman, then I'll be good as new."

"I don't think I should go running off again," I said. "It's not right to leave James. . . ."

"Darling, James has to get used to having a nanny. If you show up every two seconds he'll expect to rely on you for everything and that's not right."

The chauffeur brought around the Rolls that Zou Zou used only on official occasions and I was driven in style to Victoria. It had crossed my mind to stop in and see Belinda, to learn if I could get more details on her cousin's accident, but I didn't feel I should ask Zou Zou's chauffeur to change her orders. I got on the train and sat impatiently as backyards turned to suburbs and then to countryside. I cheered up when I saw the lovely spring green of the fields with new lambs bouncing around with abandon. Perhaps I was reading too much into four accidental deaths, I told myself. Perhaps it was none of my business. It did not appear that the men knew each other, at least in recent years. They may have been on the debutant scene in their early twenties, but most chaps of my social class were. No connection since then made it unlikely that their deaths were carried out by one person. One thing nagged at me. These deaths were not like a random stabbing in a dark alleyway. Each person died doing what he liked best and did best. The racing driver crashed his car, the speedboat record setter blew up his boat, the mountain climber fell while climbing. I didn't know details about Shrimpy Smithers, but I wouldn't be surprised to learn that he had died doing something he loved. So either this was the sort of accident you'd expect to happen if you took up reckless pursuits, or it was cleverly orchestrated, meticulously planned. That indicated a vicious, clever and dangerous mind. One thought that had passed through my mind minutes ago still haunted me. The one thing all those men had in common was their age and their class. Sons of peers or gentry. I froze, staring unseeing out the window as the scenery flashed past. . . . What if someone with a chip on his shoulder, a fervent communist maybe, was targeting the sons of peers? And sons of peers also included Darcy.

Chapter 18

Golly, what a mess I've come back to!

Rather than telephoning Phipps from the station to come and get me, I threw frugality to the winds and took a taxi. I sat impatiently, waiting to get home. I didn't think that Darcy would be back from whatever assignment he'd been on and I worried. Was some communist chappie, a scruffy motorcyclist, at this moment planning Darcy's demise? I found myself wondering what Darcy did best. He used to be a first-class rugby player, but he'd put that aside some time ago. You have to be super fit to play rugby, and Darcy enjoyed his food and wine too much. What he enjoyed was being with us, his family, and pottering about the home farm. I couldn't wait to see him and share these thoughts with him. He might think I was crackers but at least he'd been warned. And he had the facility to look into communist sympathizers who were in the sights of MI5.

As I opened the front door I heard raised voices. I stood listening in amazement. My servants knew better than to shout at each other. What on earth was going on? Luckily at that moment Mrs. Holbrook appeared through the door that led down to the kitchen and servants' area. She stopped, horrified, when she saw me.

"Oh, my lady. I'm so sorry. I had no idea you were coming home and I was just trying to make him see sense."

"Make who see sense, Mrs. Holbrook?" I asked, taking off my coat and hanging it on the hall stand.

"Why, Pierre, that's who. He's threatening to quit. To leave us in the lurch."

"Why would he do that? Has my sister-in-law been complaining about his food?"

"Oh no, my lady. He says that he's a chef and he should not be asked to get up to cook breakfast."

"Why would anyone want him to cook breakfast?" I asked. "Surely that's Queenie's job."

Mrs. Holbrook's face turned bright red. "Ah well, you see, her grace, the duchess, gave Queenie the sack yesterday."

"She did what?" My own voice rose enough so that it echoed up the marble staircase.

"I suppose she was within her rights," Mrs. Holbrook said. "Queenie was rude to her."

"What did she say?" I hardly dared to ask.

Mrs. Holbrook's face turned even redder. "She called the duchess a mean-spirited old cow."

I tried not to let my delight show or to applaud this.

"So your sister-in-law sacked her on the spot."

"Where did she go?"

"Back home, I suppose. She left in a hurry."

"Oh dear, Mrs. Holbrook. I suppose I'd better go back up to London to find her."

"Pardon me for saying it, my lady, but are you sure you want her back? She's not the easiest of employees."

"I know that, Mrs. Holbrook, but I do somehow feel responsible for her. She stuck with me when I couldn't afford to pay her, and she saved my life. She was jolly brave. And she does cook quite well."

"I'll give you that. She's a dab hand with cakes and biscuits, and even Pierre didn't mind her helping him in the kitchen, which says something."

"Then we'll have to get her back, won't we? But first I have to go and see my baby. I've missed him terribly. I hope he's been all right?"

"Good as gold, according to Nanny," Mrs. Holbrook said. I couldn't tell from her expression whether she thought this was the truth or a good thing.

"Please tell Pierre that I will be down to see him and I will make everything right," I said. I gave her an encouraging smile and went up the stairs. I had only reached the first landing when who should be coming toward me but Fig herself.

"Georgiana, you're back," she said. "I suppose you had a rare old good time wining and dining with that so-called princess."

"She is a princess, Fig, and as such should take precedence over you. And yes, we achieved quite a lot. I need to have a chat with you if you'll go down to the sitting room, but first I have to see my son."

She actually put out a hand to stop me. "This would not be a good time," she said. "I spoke to Nanny not too long ago and she was about to put him down for his morning nap. If you ask me, Nanny is working wonders in such a short time. She now has him on a perfect schedule and he's even responding to potty training. Just what we wanted. I knew she'd be the right choice."

I fought back my desire to push her down the staircase. I'm not normally a violent person but Fig makes my hackles rise every time we converse. She apparently didn't see the color flooding to my cheeks. "I knew as soon as I came here that all this household needed was some discipline," she went on. "Babies in the drawing room, lying on the floor with the dogs. I mean, we are not Saxon peasants, Georgiana. And as for your servants, I had to sack one of them for absolute insolence. That girl Queenie. She had the nerve to call me 'missus' instead of 'your grace.' I corrected her on it at once but then she did it again. 'Bob's yer uncle, missus,' she said, and then she added, 'Lady Georgie don't mind how I talk to her, but then she's a proper lady, not a mean-spirited old . . .'" She broke off, unable to describe herself as an old cow.

I pressed my lips together, determined not to smile. "She was my servant, in my household, Fig. You had no authority to sack her. How would you feel if I came to visit and sacked Hamilton?"

She looked surprised at this. "Nobody would ever want to

sack Hamilton," she said. "He is a treasure of a butler, as you very well know."

"I was just giving you a comparison," I said. "Coming into someone else's house and bossing around their servants. It's just not done, Fig."

"Someone had to do it," she said. "That girl was hopeless, Georgiana. I said it from the first. You should never have taken her on, and having done so, you should have corrected her faults and turned her into a proper servant. You are too weak, that's your trouble. You need to find some backbone. Your servants walk all over you, especially that disgusting girl. You're well rid of her. You'll thank me for it." While I was trying to form the right response to this in my head, she went on, "I blame it on your background, of course. Hopeless father, off wasting his money on the Riviera, and that mother, sleeping with one man after another. No wonder you had no guidance in your forma- tive years."

I could feel anger bubbling up inside me, but Fig went on, oblivious to this, "You should have let those older and wiser guide you when you had the chance. You do, after all, come from the royal family, on your father's side, but I'm afraid it's that mother of yours from whom you have inherited too many traits. And that awful common grandfather. If you had allowed yourself to be molded and instructed, you'd have married at the correct level to some European prince, and not been stuck with a commoner."

That was enough. She could insult Queenie. She could trash my servants, but she was not going to say anything about my family and definitely not my husband.

"My husband is the son of an Irish baron," I said. "He will

one day inherit this title. And what's more I wouldn't have cared if he was the son of a dustman. I happen to love him and he loves me and that's all that matters." I took a step toward her. "This is the final straw, Fig. You come as a guest, uninvited, I might add, to my house, you send me a nanny I didn't want and don't like, then you upset my servants, you sack one of them and now you insult my family and my husband. I've been polite to you for years, and let you walk all over me, criticize everything I do, and I've held my tongue because I happen to love my brother and your children. But you have crossed the line. I'm going to have to ask you to pack your bags and leave right now. Go home to poor Binky, although God knows he doesn't deserve a miserable cow like you."

Her face turned ashen white. "I have never been spoken to like this in my life. How dare you, Georgiana, speaking to your betters in this way."

"I do dare, Fig. It's about time somebody dared," I said. "Poor Binky won't. He's too softhearted, but it hurts me to hear the way you talk to him as if he's a slow-minded child. And as for being my better, do I need to remind you that I'm the king's cousin and you are not? You are the one who married above your station." I gave a triumphant little smile.

"Well," she said. "Well, really. I try to do my best for you and that is the gratitude I get. Just like your common mother. I shall go now. Have your girl pack my bags and have your chauffeur bring round the motorcar for me. Oh, and make sure you telephone Binky to let him know he has to send the chauffeur to meet the train. It will have to be the night train, I suppose. So inconvenient. I won't get a sleeping car at this late stage."

When I said nothing, she turned on her heel and flounced back to her bedroom. I watched her go, not knowing whether to burst out laughing or be terrified. I might have cut off all connection to my family, I realized. Binky was extremely loyal. He would probably take her side. Then I asked myself if it was any great loss that we didn't have Fig descending on us every few months, usually when it was too cold and miserable in Scotland. I went down the hall and into my own bedroom. My face in the mirror was still bright pink. I stared at myself, unable to believe what I had done.

"I've actually done it," I said to the person in the mirror. "I finally told Fig what I thought of her." And I gave a nervous little laugh of triumph. Then I took off my hat, put a brush through my hair and went down to give my remaining servants instructions and to appease Pierre.

Chapter 19

I can't believe what I just did. But then I can't believe what Fig
had the nerve to do either. Perhaps I am becoming the lady
of the manor after all.

Fig left the house with a face like thunder. I watched from an
upper window as she almost threw herself into the car. After I
had talked to Pierre and promised him I would bring back
Queenie, I met Mrs. Holbrook coming out of the dining room.

"Oh, my lady," she said. "What a to-do. I've never seen the
like of it. Her grace stormed out of here. If looks could kill we'd
all be lying in pine boxes by now. What did you say to her?"

"I told her she had no right to interfere with my servants, let
alone sack one of them. She was then rude about my upbringing

and my family, telling me I had had no proper guidance. Then she made the mistake of telling me I had married a commoner. That was it, Mrs. Holbrook. I could put up with her insulting me, but she's not going to insult my husband or my family. I told her to pack her bags and leave. You should have seen how white her face turned."

She laid a hand on my arm. "Good for you, my lady. That's what she needed. I have to say that in this instance Queenie was right. She was a mean-spirited old cow, even if she was your relative."

"Only by marriage, Mrs. Holbrook," I said with a grin. "So the question is now, what do I do about Queenie? I suppose I'd better go back up to London and rescue her."

Mrs. Holbrook's face grew solemn. "Are you sure you want her back, my lady? I know she's not a bad little cook and she gets along all right with Pierre, who isn't the easiest to please. But she's also quite a bit of trouble, isn't she? She breaks things, she does not behave in a manner fitting to a great house of this sort and she is embarrassing on a regular basis." She paused. "I wondered if this might be a good opportunity to let her go without you seeming to be the one who had done the deed."

I was tempted, I confess. Queenie was a liability. I knew that. It was all right most of the time she was kept in the kitchen, apart from the occasional fire or knocked-over dish. But when she came out, when she burst into the living room to bring in tea, for example, one never knew what she was going to say or do to distinguished guests. If Their Majesties chose to visit one day . . . The thought made my blood run cold. But then I thought of Queenie, her loyalty, her big smile and "whatcher, missus." I remembered when she had saved Darcy and me at his father's Irish castle and I knew I couldn't do it.

"The trouble is that I feel responsible for her. Who would employ her, Mrs. Holbrook?"

"That's true enough, your ladyship," she said. "She wouldn't last two minutes in a normal household. But you can't keep a lame duck all your life. You're not a charity."

"I know, but she does bake rather well. Her cakes and puddings are quite delicious. And she was awfully ill last year when she was poisoned by the ghastly man."

Mrs. Holbrook looked at me solemnly. "I can tell you want to get her back. Well, if you will take my advice, you should not go looking for her for a couple of days. Give her time to think about it, to appreciate what she had here and maybe what she did wrong. If you turn up now, then she'll think she's won and you know how uppity she can be."

"Good point," I said. "I'll give her time to realize she does not want to be stuck at home and maybe to find how hard it would be to get another situation without a reference. Then I'll show up as her rescuer, offering her one last chance. That might work well."

"Although knowing Queenie, I doubt it," Mrs. Holbrook said.

We both laughed.

Having got rid of one nuisance, I thought I should use that newfound courage to tackle another. I'd go and give Nanny her notice. James didn't need a nanny that badly that I couldn't do without one until I found a suitable replacement. Maisie would love to have the chance to take care of him, and he adored

Maisie. As I walked through the front hall I noticed that some letters had come in my absence, including another package from *The Lady*. This was maybe a gift from heaven. I went into Darcy's study, sat down and opened them. The first was a woman who had looked after her own kids; they had flown the coop and she missed them. Her husband had died. She'd like to become a nanny. Signed "Florrie Robinson (Mrs. now widow) from Putney." Probably not the right sort of person I was looking for, with no proper training or experience in an upper-class home. Another was a French au pair who wanted to stay on in England. No, too young and inexperienced. But the third. "I have been a nanny for two families. I now wish to obtain a new position." She left me a telephone number. I asked the exchange to ring it for me and a voice answered. Yes, she was Daphne Hawks.

"Who was your last position with?" I asked.

"Major and Mrs. Duffy in Dorset," she said.

"I would want to ask them for a reference," I said. "How long ago was this and why did you leave?"

"I didn't want to," she said. She sounded quite pleasant, and my hopes rose. "It was sort of forced upon me."

"Why was this?"

There was a long pause. "I suppose you'll find out the truth," she said. "I went to jail for five years."

"Golly." The word just slipped out. "What for?"

"Receiving stolen goods. My boyfriend was a bad lot. I didn't know until too late."

I couldn't find what to say. If she was indeed the innocent receiver of stolen goods, then she had been wrongly punished and I couldn't judge her.

"You don't have to worry," she said. "I know what I did wrong. I was just stupid. It won't happen again. Come on, missus. Give me a chance."

I hesitated. "I would need to discuss this with my husband and he's away at the moment," I said. "I will be in touch later."

Then I hung up. I felt horribly conflicted as I walked away. She might be a sweet naïve girl who had been taken advantage of by a slick criminal type, but what if she wasn't? She had been to prison and paid her dues to society, so wouldn't it be a good gesture on my part to give her another chance? Then I decided for once I would defer to my husband. He was a man of the world and he was wise. I'd do whatever he said.

After this I felt rather exhausted. Too many upsetting things had happened at once, and all coming after what had been a most unnerving time in Derbyshire. Now the worry that Darcy might be on somebody's assassination list would not go away. I wondered when he'd come home. I wanted to see him, to know he was safe, to feel his arms around me. Then I thought I needed to see James, to hug my darling son. That would make me feel better.

As I went up the stairs I reconsidered having a confrontation with Nanny. I didn't know if I could face a second one in one day, and in many ways Nanny was scarier than Fig. So I steeled myself and took a deep breath as I went up the second flight of stairs. I opened the nursery door and found Nanny sitting there, glaring at me. She rose as I came in.

"I have come to see my son," I said in what I hoped was a commanding voice. I wasn't very good at commanding voices.

"Master James has not yet awoken from his morning nap,"

she said coldly. "It would be unwise to awaken him and thus throw off the schedule to which he is now accustomed."

Oh dear. It was going to be another confrontation.

"Look, Nanny," I said. "You are hired to look after my child. I'm sure you are good at what you do and that he is safe and well cared for. However, the fact remains that you are my employee and this is my son. So I will come to visit him whenever I wish, and at times it will disturb his schedule. Too bad. You'll have to get used to it if you wish to stay in this household."

"That is just the point, isn't it?" she said. "Your sister-in-law, her grace, the duchess, came and told me what you had said to her this morning. I was appalled, let me tell you. Flabbergasted that anyone would speak to a duchess this way."

"And I was equally appalled that she had had the nerve to sack one of my servants in my absence," I said. "After she had foisted a nanny on me whom I did not choose and frankly do not want."

There was a frosty silence. Nanny stood there, fixing me with what was probably the iciest stare I have ever received. Frankly I felt she might actually be a Gorgon and I'd be turned to stone. "I rather fear you have made my choice for me," she said. "I considered this long and hard after her grace told me of your behavior. I would not dream of staying in a household where I am not wanted and appreciated," she said. "I shall be giving my notice starting immediately. I shall collect my wages and go this very day."

"Oh dear," I said. "My sister-in-law had agreed to pay your wages for the first six months. And she has just left. You'll have to write to her in Scotland." Then I went through to the night nursery. James had woken up, hearing raised voices. He had hauled himself up, clinging onto the side of his cot. He saw me and his face lit up in a huge smile. "Up, Mama," he said.

I scooped him up into my arms. "It's all right, my darling," I said. "From now on it's going to be all right."

Chapter 20

TUESDAY, MARCH 9

EYNSLEIGH

Things can only look up from here, can't they? Now all I need is
a new nanny and my husband to come home. Oh, and to
find out who is killing the sons of peers.

After luncheon, which thankfully the newly appeased Pierre
cooked, having been promised that I would return Queenie in a
couple of days, I went to take a little nap. It had been an exhausting morning. Nanny had departed in a taxi, also with a
face like thunder. I had found Maisie and told her that she was
in charge of the nursery for the immediate future until a new
and nice nanny could be found. She positively beamed at me.
"Oh yes, my lady. I've missed the little chap so much. I'll take
good care of him, don't you worry. Can I go up and see him

now?" And she bounded up the stairs. So at least one person was happy in our household.

I awoke refreshed and sat at my bedroom window with a sheet of notepaper on my lap. I wrote down the names of the four men who had died. Then what I knew about them. Not much. All around the same age. Different parts of the country. Might have known each other when they were attending debutant dos in London but seemingly not since. So if someone had planned to kill them, why those four? Were there others I didn't know about? I'd have to ask Darcy to look into this. Had someone been systematically killing sons of aristocrats for some time—presumably after they turned twenty-one and could therefore inherit? If so, that would explain why these men were around thirty and not younger. Perhaps they were far down a list. Otherwise, why not kill them the moment they turned twenty-one? Was there some kind of organization like the IRA or the Communist Party that was behind this? Organized crime? But surely not that, as their crimes were for personal benefit— kidnappings for ransom, not senseless murders.

I got up, washed my face and then brought James down to the sitting room. Mrs. Holbrook served tea and biscuits. "No cake, I'm afraid, my lady," she said. "No Queenie to bake it today."

I could see I'd be making a sacrifice if I waited a few days to retrieve Queenie, but I agreed with Mrs. H that she did need to be taught a lesson. Would she be grateful enough, when I went to find her, that she'd be a reformed character and try to please? Probably not, but it was a nice thought.

I had just finished tea when the dogs started barking. I put James down on the rug and went to see what was wrong. Then I realized that the barks sounded joyful. And I heard a familiar deep voice. "Down, you crazy mutts. You're getting hair all over my suit."

"Darcy!" I called and ran toward him. "Oh, I am so glad to see you. I've been worried about you." I flung my arms around him. He hugged me back, laughing.

"I wasn't anywhere dangerous," he said. "Just a conference in Edinburgh, discussing the potential Nazi threat. I had to report on my recent observations."

"And do you see them as a threat?"

"Definitely," he said. "Hitler has expansionist plans. He doesn't want to be outdone by Mussolini either. I see them both as a threat and I think we should be ready."

"To fight them, you mean? Another war?"

"Possibly. Let's hope Hitler's own people see the folly of this before it's too late."

"Golly, so many things to worry about," I said.

"I don't think you should be worried," he said, stroking my back tenderly. "You should be enjoying life with me and James."

"I left James in the sitting room," I said, realizing the implications of this. "I'd better go back to him before he gets into trouble. Come on in."

"James is allowed in the sitting room and it's not four o'clock?" he teased.

"Nanny is no more," I said.

"You killed her?" He looked amused.

"She has departed in fury," I said. "I was intending to sack her, but she resigned. It was wonderful, Darcy. In one day I got rid of Fig and Nanny. I am so proud of myself."

We came into the sitting room in time to see James had pulled himself up against a side table and was reaching for a vase of dried flowers on it. Darcy scooped him up. "This," he said, "is why we need a nanny. This child is too mobile these days."

James giggled as Darcy swung him around.

Darcy seemed to have taken in what I said. "You got rid of Fig and Nanny?" He sounded surprised.

"I did. I can't believe I actually did it, but they were both awful, Darcy. They both bossed me around and finally I'd had enough. When I came back today I found that Fig had sacked Queenie and Pierre was threatening to leave. I confronted Fig and she said some awfully rude things to me." I recounted word for word what she had said.

"That woman has damned cheek," Darcy said. "I don't know why she thinks she has been appointed to judge others, and why she ever took it upon herself to sack another person's servant."

"I know," I said. "When she insulted you, that was the last straw. I told her to pack her bags and leave. She stormed out. I may have broken contact with my brother, but I couldn't let her go on any more."

"Oh, I don't think you'll have spoiled your relationship with Binky," he said. "I bet he's secretly glad that you spoke to her the way he'd like to but is too much of a coward."

I had to smile at this. James squirmed to get down from Darcy's lap, then dragged himself across to the fire, needing to be grabbed again. I did see Darcy's point that someone now needed to watch him all the time. I set James down on my knee and let him ride horsey, horsey.

"And then you gave Nanny the boot too?" he asked.

"When I told her that I was the employer and that I would come to see my child when I wanted to, she resigned."

"So now we need a new nanny?"

"Maisie will do perfectly until I can find a good one. Speaking of which, I did have an application today. She'd been in two households before and she sounded all right. The only thing against her was that she'd been in prison for five years."

"Crikey," he said. "No, thank you. We are not a rehabilitation center."

"She claims she was innocent. She had a boyfriend who was a bad lot and foisted stolen goods on her."

Darcy gave me a pitying look. "And you think she didn't know they were stolen? Come on, Georgie. If he's a man at her level of society and he hands her a diamond bracelet to look after, do you think she didn't wonder where it came from?"

"I suppose so," I said.

"And in my profession I can't risk hiring anybody with a dubious background. Who knows what they might find in my study? What's more, we have had enough of lame ducks with Queenie. Speaking of whom, I don't suppose you want her back, do you?"

"I don't know if I want her, but I feel obliged to rehire her. She's quite a good cook, and Pierre does need an assistant."

He nodded. "So quite a lot has happened since I went away."

"It has."

"Did you have a good time with Zou Zou? You went up to London with her, didn't you?"

"Actually," I said, "we went up to Derbyshire."

"Derbyshire? What on earth for?"

I described our journey and filled him in on the details of what we might have learned.

He listened politely, then said, "It could all be coincidental, Georgie. You haven't found anything that links these men together, have you?"   ·

"One thing occurred to me on the way home," I said. "One thing that does link them together. They are all sons of aristocrats, or at least of gentry. Only sons. Sons and heirs. What if someone, either a fanatic or a mad person, has decided to kill off the sons of the aristocracy? Perhaps a dedicated communist, or even the IRA?"

He looked at me, long and hard, not saying anything.

"That's why I was worried about you," I said. "You might be on their list."

"Georgie," he said softly, "I think you are taking this a bit too far. We know of four young men who were killed. Tragic accidents, but at least the first three were doing something dangerous. The sort of thing that came with the risk of an accident. And they just happened to die at the same time. That's all we know."

"But you could check, couldn't you? You know people who have access to this type of information. We could see if there have been other cases recently we didn't know about, other sons of the aristocracy who have had so-called tragic accidents."

"Don't you think we might have heard about it?" he asked. "We move in the same circles, after all. I'd be in London and someone would say, 'Did you hear about the Duke of whatsit's son?' Or it would have been reported in the papers."

"All right. Maybe they are just starting. Starting near the bottom and working up to dukes."

Darcy laughed at this.

"It's not funny, Darcy. You might well be next. You could at least ask for me."

He thought about this. "Yes," he said. "I suppose I do know people who could check this sort of thing. I suppose I could ask them, if that would ease your mind."

"But you don't believe it, personally? You don't think it's a possibility?"

"I think it's highly unlikely. For one thing, if some sort of group was carrying this out, they would usually brag about it. Let us know who they are and what they are achieving."

"And if it's one man, someone deranged? Working in secret? Someone who hates aristocrats?"

"Then I would say he would finally slip up. And again, such individuals are often cocky. They want the world to know how clever they have been."

"But you will ask for me? Please?"

He smiled. "I will ask for you. And I hope you are wrong."

"Thank you, darling." I planted a kiss on his cheek. James objected to being squashed and tried to get down again. I stood up. "I should probably take him back to the nursery," I said. "It was much easier when he lay on a blanket and smiled at us."

"You wait until he walks and climbs," Darcy said. "When I was growing up I was always falling out of trees and skinning knees."

"All right. I agree. A new nanny," I said. I kissed James. "Let's go and see Maisie."

I got as far as the door, then something else occurred to me. "Do we know where Smithers lives?"

"No idea," he said.

"Is there any way we could find out?" I paused, thinking. "Don't you have a directory of old boys from your school?"

"Probably somewhere," he said. "But that would only list his parents' address from eleven years ago."

"That would be useful, wouldn't it? People don't move that often. Can you look for it, please?"

A brief frown passed over his face. "Georgie, we can't barge in on people I don't know, right after their son has died."

"And if their son was one of a chain of murders? Might it not be important then?"

James wriggled in my arms, calling, "Dada!" Perhaps he was picking up my tension.

"He had asthma, Georgie. His medicine didn't work properly. I don't see how that could be attributed to a possible murder. If you told Scotland Yard, they'd laugh at you."

"And if someone had tampered with his medicine? What then?"

He gave me a half smile, half frown. "You are very persistent, you know. And so passionate about this."

"Partly because I feel in my heart that something was not right with those deaths and partly because I'm scared that you might be on someone's list. So will you find out the parents' address for me and we can go and talk to them if they are not in the Shetland Islands?"

He got up and gave an exaggerated sigh. "I suppose so." Then he chuckled as he went toward his study while I carried a protesting James up the stairs.

Chapter 21

I'm waiting anxiously to hear what Darcy has found out. In a
way I hope he's right and we are talking about accidents. No,
actually I hope Zou Zou and I are wrong because if we are
right it means an evil person is systematically killing. Then I
could stop trying to think what could possibly be going on.

Darcy had, after much rooting through old trunks and boxes,
found the school directory and located the Smitherses' address.
They had an estate in Ireland but also a London house in Chelsea. There was just a chance that they might be living there at
the moment and I begged Darcy to visit when he went up to
London, just in case. Reluctantly he agreed.

"What am I supposed to say to them?" he asked.

"You're the man who is involved in some kind of international intrigue and you can't ask a simple question?" I gave a derisive snort. "I don't know how you manage with foreign spies. Perhaps I should come along on your next assignment."

"Georgie, what I meant was this is a delicate subject. If his parents are there and they are grieving a lost son, I can't suggest to them that murder might be a possibility."

"Of course not," I said. "You say you were in London on business and had just heard from your father about their son's tragic death and you wanted to offer your condolences in person. Then tell them you have memories about poor Shrimpy having problems with his asthma while you were in school together. You were sorry to learn that it had still plagued him." I gave a small, triumphant nod. "They might well offer more information on the circumstances of his death. Then you could ask if there had already been a funeral and did any of his old pals come: Algie Beauchamps? Rupert Warburton-Stoke? Sebastian Inchcliffe? And see if you get any reaction to any of those names. If you do, then my hunch may well be correct and it is more than just four men, but sons of aristocrats."

"The Smitherses were hardly aristocrats," he said. "Lots of money but no title."

"Actually I don't think Belinda's cousin is an aristocrat either," I said.

"So you have disproved your theory yourself," he said, looking annoyingly smug.

"You are not taking this seriously," I said. "You really don't believe anything I have told you."

"I'm trying to be open-minded, Georgie," he said. "But

believing that someone is bumping off heirs to a title, one by one, is a bit hard to swallow."

"Then let's hope we disprove it before it's your turn," I retorted.

⁂

THE NEXT DAY I waited impatiently for Darcy to return from London. I still felt uneasy. If he came back and said that Shrimpy Smithers's death was not suspicious and there were no other men who had been killed in so-called accidents, then I could breathe a sigh of relief. I took James in his pram and the dogs for a long walk, down to the farm, where James was delighted to see the chickens and pigs again. The pigs, I regret to say, were now large and fat and would soon be going off to market. Such is the cruel life of a farmer. I did realize this was why we were raising them and I had to say they were no longer adorable, but I still felt guilty. As I watched James's excited face I couldn't help thinking about those young men who died. All only sons. What if something happened to James one day? It was too painful to think about. Suddenly the wind seemed icy cold. I pushed him hastily back toward the comfort and warmth of the house.

When I arrived I was met by Mrs. Holbrook. "You had a telephone call, my lady," she said.

"From Mr. Darcy?"

"No, my lady. From your friend Miss Belinda."

"Oh, thank you, Mrs. Holbrook," I said. "I'll just take James up to the nursery and then I'll ring her back."

"Maisie is in the servants' hall. I'll go and fetch her for you," she said. "No need for you to go up all those stairs." And off she went, leaving me thinking that I should appreciate the easy life I have. Other mothers have to look after their own children while they clean their own house and cook meals for their husbands. I suppose knowing my grandfather has made me realize what a privileged position I am in. I don't suppose such thoughts ever occur to Fig. She takes it all for granted. Thinking of Fig was not a good idea. I went hot under the collar. Had she arrived home and told Binky how rude I had been to her? And how had he reacted? What if I never saw them again? But it needed to be done, I told myself. She had been insufferable to me for too long.

I broke off these thoughts as Maisie came running down the hallway toward me. "Here I am, your ladyship," she said, breathlessly. "I'm sorry. I just popped down for a cup of tea."

"You don't need to apologize, Maisie," I said. "You are entitled to time to yourself."

"And as for you, you little horror," she said, playfully, lifting James from his pram, "let's go up and see your toys, shall we?"

He went quite happily. I took off my coat, hung it up and then put in a call to Belinda. Her maid answered. "Residence of Miss Varbutton-Schtoke," she said.

When I asked to speak to her she replied, "Moment, *bitte*. I go tell her. *Ja?*" For a moment I was reminded of a Bavarian princess I once had to look after—a princess who turned out to be something she was not. Almost immediately Belinda picked up the phone.

"Hello, Georgie, how are you? How was your evening with Zou Zou? Did you go somewhere fabulous?"

"We went up to Derbyshire, actually."

"Derbyshire?" She said it as if I had said Alaska or Siberia. "What on earth for?"

"We were looking into the death of Sebastian Inchcliffe. You know, the one who drove his car off the road. She wasn't satisfied that it was an accident and now that we've seen the site and talked to the people involved, I'm not either."

"Oh gosh," she said. "When Zou Zou passed along a message from Darcy's father about some chap Darcy knew dying, you said, 'Another one.' I wondered what you meant then. Did you really suspect that these accidents had something in common?"

"And you said bad things come in threes. But the last one made four. Darcy is going to speak to this chap Shrimpy's parents today."

"Georgie, do you really think there is something odd about all these deaths? Not just daredevils doing something stupid and tempting fate one time too many?"

"I may be wrong," I said. "I admit I can't find anything that ties the various chaps together so far. But another awful thought came to me. I was wondering whether some madman, or some kind of extremist movement, was killing the sons of the British upper class, one by one. Making it look like accidents."

"Oh God," she said. "That would be awful. I do hope you're wrong."

"So do I," I said, "because Darcy would be on that list. He's going to ask people in London, who can check on that sort of thing, to see if there have been cases before, and if it's been going on for some time."

"I see," she said. "You know, I wouldn't have believed it for a minute, but my father's cousin George came up to town yesterday and took me out to dinner with one of the chaps who'd been climbing with Rupert. He said he'd been really shaken up about it, because Rupert was a meticulously careful climber and would have double-checked his equipment before he started out."

"The rope broke, you said?"

"That's right. Rupert was the best of them, and the steadiest, so he went up first. Then the cloud closed in and they couldn't see him above them because he'd disappeared into the cloud, but suddenly they heard a cry and watched him plunging down. The rope should have held him but it didn't."

"So somebody could have sabotaged the rope," I said. "After he had checked it."

"But how and when?" Belinda said. "They were staying at a mountain lodge. Only climbers stay there. How would a potential killer know where they were and what they planned to do, and which ropes were theirs?"

"I suppose if the cloud had come down, someone could have been waiting above in the cloud to give him a push."

"That would have to be another mountain climber," she said, then corrected herself. "Although not necessarily. I don't know if you've been to the mountains of North Wales. There are steep rock faces in Snowdonia, but also plenty of walking paths on the less steep slopes. Perhaps there was a path that somehow went above where they were climbing."

"Did Rupert's friend say exactly where they were climbing?"

"No," she said. "I should have asked him but it never crossed my mind at the time."

"You don't have his phone number, do you?" I asked.

"No, I don't usually go around asking strange men for their numbers, not unless they are devastatingly handsome, and this one wasn't." She paused, then corrected herself. "Not bad-looking. Very tall and fit. But the strong, silent type, I fear. Didn't say much."

"It's a pity we can't go and see for ourselves," I said.

"But we can." Belinda perked up instantly. "What I telephoned to tell you was that I bought a new motorcar today. A little MG just like Zou Zou's. It's so natty, Georgie. You'll love it. You could meet me in London and we could drive to North Wales together."

"It hardly seems worth it if we don't know where we're going."

"I know they stayed at a well-known lodge where climbers always stay. That should be easy enough to locate." She paused. "And I suppose I could get Charles whatsit's telephone number from Cousin George. But if I asked him he might get the wrong end of the stick and think I'm interested, which I'm absolutely not. He's a nice enough chap but not my type, you know."

"I do think it might be worthwhile to speak to Charles whatsit. Do you actually know his name, by the way?"

"It's Wetherham, or Woolsingham or Westerham."

"That's a lot of use."

"I'll find out from Cousin George."

"Look, Belinda," I said. "You don't have to get involved in this if you don't want to. You said you weren't close to your cousin."

"But I want to get involved," Belinda said. "My cousin was

family and family means everything, doesn't it? And besides, it's exciting and my life has definitely been lacking excitement lately. And if I do decide to be a spy—not the sort who gets fingernails pulled out, of course—this will be good training."

I had to laugh. "You're incorrigible. But I'd certainly be happier investigating with you. So you'll telephone Cousin George. You could make up some story about a mountaineering friend who was curious exactly where the accident happened. Oh, and you could also ask him if he knows any of the other chaps who died: Sebastian Inchcliffe, Algie Beauchamps and Shrimpy Smithers. See if you get a reaction to any of those names."

"I suppose I could invite him to meet me for a drink this evening," she said, not sounding too convinced. "One can learn so much more from watching someone's face." She paused, considering. "I suppose he's not that bad-looking, if a little shy and reticent."

"You might even ask him if he is worried that foul play could have been involved and whether Rupert had any enemies."

"I'd have to phrase that very carefully," she said. "What if it was one of the other chaps they were climbing with?"

"Then Charles would have his suspicions."

"All right. So I'll do my Mata Hari act of getting information out of him today and we'll head for Wales tomorrow, then."

Reality was creeping into my thoughts.

"Hold on a moment, Belinda," I said. "I've been thinking. I have a baby. I can't go rushing off every few minutes."

"You can leave him with Nanny, can't you? You're not still breastfeeding."

"I've more or less stopped," I said. "Or rather James has lost interest. I suppose I could leave him if I had a nanny, but she left."

"How did you manage that?" She sounded delighted.

"It was after I told Fig to go home, and then told Nanny that I would come to visit my son whenever I felt like it. She said she couldn't stay another minute in such a household, and off she went. It was the best moment of my life."

"You told Fig to go home? Good for you, Georgie. It was about time you put Fig in her place. And you actually dealt with that nanny. I'm so impressed."

"I know," I replied. "I was rather impressed with myself."

"But now you're without a nanny, I suppose."

"Maisie is going to fill in until I find a suitable one."

"Well, you can leave him with Maisie, can't you?"

I paused, considering this. "She is awfully good with him, but what if something goes wrong? What if he falls and hurts himself or he becomes ill?"

"That could happen even if he had the best of nannies," Belinda said. "You can't stay home all your life just in case your child might need you. He's quite safe in the nursery, isn't he? And Darcy is around. And Mrs. Holbrook. And we'll telephone at regular intervals just to check on him."

"Well," I said slowly, "if I were only away one night. Would that be possible, do you think?"

"London to North Wales is a whole day's drive. There are no major roads once one crosses the border. Come to think of it, it would be quicker to take the train. There's a good line to Bangor, I seem to remember. We could do that." She sounded enthusiastic. "And then hire a taxi to drive us around. Gosh, this is going to be exciting."

"How long does the train take?"

"At a guess four or five hours?" She broke off, then went on excitedly, "Actually I've got another idea. Cousin George lives in Shrewsbury. That's on the Welsh border, almost on the way. We'll take the train to Shrewsbury. We could stay with him and borrow his car. And he'd know the exact location."

"You don't think it would be too upsetting for him if he finds out we're here to check on how his son died?"

"Wouldn't you want to know the truth if you were he? And if we can find out anything at all that would help us track down a killer, then he'd be all for it."

"Maybe," I said. "I don't know if I'd want to find out the truth if it were my child. It can't bring Rupert back, can it?"

"We'll figure it out on the way there," Belinda said.

"I think that's a bad idea," I said. "I don't think we should barge in on your father's cousin or ask to borrow his motorcar."

"We could say we were doing a walking holiday for a few days," Belinda suggested.

"No!" I said. "Come on, Belinda. You don't think he'd find it upsetting if you said you were going walking exactly where his son was killed? I think your first idea was the right one. Your cousin won't be able to supply us with any more details about where his son was killed, and probably won't know much about his friends. He was a grown man, after all. He didn't live with his parents, did he?"

"No, he was working as a solicitor in Bristol."

"Not married?"

"No, too keen on going off on expeditions like your Sir Hubert."

"Yes, it does hamper a love life," I said. "Sir Hubert still regrets that he lost my mother, but then he wasn't around to adore her. You know what she's like."

"All right. So we won't visit my cousin. We'll hire a car in Wales. Come up to town tomorrow and we'll take an early train."

"What do you mean by early?"

"Oh, you know, ten-ish?"

"I can manage that," I said, trying not to smile. Belinda had never been an early riser. "But I'll have to check with Darcy first. If he comes back with important news, we may find that Scotland Yard has taken over our investigation."

"That would be good, wouldn't it?" Belinda said. "After I had talked to Rupert's friend I felt so angry. I hadn't believed it when you insinuated that the four deaths were linked in some way and there was something suspicious about them, but then doubts started to creep in."

"Yes," I said. "It was just too much of a coincidence that we actually know four men who died within a week or so of each other."

"Well, you've been a good detective before, Georgie," she said. "If anyone can get to the bottom of this, you can."

"Oh, I don't know about that," I said. "I think most of the cases I have stumbled upon have been solved more by luck than anything else."

"Nonsense. Look how you caught that woman in Cornwall."

"Not in time," I said.

"You did all you could. So you'll telephone me when you've checked with Darcy, and in the meantime I'll look at the railway timetable to see what time an express goes north. Oh, and I'll wheedle information out of Charles whatsit."

"All right," I said. "We should wear stout shoes and bring rain gear. It always rains in Wales, doesn't it?"

"It doesn't sound very appealing now," Belinda said. "But we have to if we're going to find the truth."

I stood, wrapped in thought as I put down the receiver. Was it wrong of me to leave James for a couple of days again? Would he be safe? I knew he'd be happy as he loved Maisie, but was she competent to know what to do if he ran a fever? It would all depend on if Darcy was going to be home. And what could we actually discover in North Wales? There would hardly be a knife left by the murderer on the rock above where Rupert fell. Still I sensed that Belinda wanted closure the way Zou Zou had. Neither could believe that someone so competent had died in an accident. I had to do everything I could to find out the truth. Maybe Darcy would know more when he came home.

Chapter 22

I'm dying to know what Darcy found out. Of course, I'd rather
not know if somebody has been systematically killing the
sons of peers. No, that's wrong. I'd rather know that Darcy
was forewarned and thus taking care.

Darcy came home just before dinner.

"Oh, I'm so glad to see you," I said, standing up to em-
brace him.

"That's what you said yesterday." He gave me a warm kiss.
"I'm glad you appreciate my company every time I come through
the front door."

"I'm glad to see you tonight because I've been dying to find out what you learned and to see if we're further ahead with the investigation."

He shook his head. "Sorry to disappoint you," he said, "but I'm afraid you've been barking up the wrong tree. There is no instance on record of upper-class young men dying in accidents, at least as far as Scotland Yard could see. And I went to the Smitherses'. Quite embarrassing, actually. I felt like a horrible intruder. And it's clear to me that he does not belong in the same category as the other three. He'd had asthma all his life, as I told you, and for once his medicine didn't work. Really sad but not what you could describe as an accident."

"Did you ask at all about the other chaps, to see if he was connected to any of them?"

He shook his head. "His father didn't seem to react to any of the names. He said that Leonard, which I learned was Shrimpy's real name, had lost touch with his university friends after they came down from Cambridge. Apparently he married almost immediately after graduation and they had two little children. He was the model suburban father. The sad thing was that his wife was killed just over a year ago. She was French and it seems she stepped out into the street looking the wrong way and was hit by a bus."

"Oh, how horrible. So those children have lost both their parents."

"They have," Darcy said. "Lucky for them they have gone to live with Shrimpy's older sister, who has two kids of her own. So they'll be well looked after. But it's never the same, is it?"

"Of course not," I said. "So what was Shrimpy doing when this asthma attack came on?"

"Strangely enough, he was swimming," Darcy said. "As I told you he was always a bit portly at school and under Monique's cooking he'd put on quite a lot more weight. So the doctor told him this extra weight was making his asthma worse and he should exercise. He started swimming and it turned out he was quite good at it. He was actually training to do an open water swim across a lake. He was in the water when the attack came on. Brought on by the water being too cold, they think. He had his inhaler at the side, within reach. He used it, had a seizure and drowned before he could call for help. His father said it's not uncommon that the medicine doesn't always work."

"They did an autopsy on him?" I asked.

"Georgie, he drowned. Water in his lungs. Tragic but not suspicious."

"So we don't know if the medicine had been tampered with."

Darcy frowned. "I think we put this one aside, Georgie. In fact maybe it's time to admit the deaths were a horrible coincidence, and nothing more. The men don't seem to have known each other. They didn't move in the same circles. They weren't doing the same sort of things. Let it go, Georgie. It's clearly getting you down."

"Not quite yet," I said. "Belinda wants me to go with her to North Wales. She met her cousin's climbing partner, who said that Rupert had always been meticulous about his equipment and was a clever but cautious climber, which is why they always let him go first. This man couldn't believe that Rupert fell in the first place and that the rope broke."

"And what do you think you might find out in Snowdonia?" Darcy asked.

"I think it might be useful to find out how and where the equipment was stored and who else was staying at the climbing lodge."

"You don't think the local police might have examined the rope and looked into that sort of thing?"

"Maybe," I said. "But probably they accepted it as a climbing accident."

"You're quite happy to go running off again, so soon after you couldn't leave James for two seconds?" He sounded peeved now.

"No, I'm not at all happy," I said. "But I feel I've had a little experience with this sort of thing and I might be useful at spotting something. Sometimes it's the smallest of clues—" I broke off. "Which reminds me. There was a cigarette butt I picked up in Derbyshire where it looks as if a motorbike was parked. Is there any way of finding out who smoked it?"

Darcy laughed. "Fingerprints on a cigarette butt? I'm afraid not. The type of cigarette might be telling if it was unusual."

"I'll go and get it," I said. I went upstairs to retrieve my purse. The butt was still in it, wrapped in my handkerchief. I brought it down to Darcy. He looked at it, sniffed and said, "It's a Woodbine, I think. Cheap cigarette. The sort of thing that working-class people smoke."

"So the scruffy chap on the motorbike who sounded as if he came from London might have smoked it?"

"He might."

"So we're getting somewhere. Almost proof that he did wait for Sebastian's car."

"Not even close," Darcy said. "Any local laborer would have smoked Woodbines. It was probably a local farm boy who stopped there to have a quick smoke before getting back to work. And it could have been there for any amount of time."

"You're being so negative," I said.

"I'm trying to approach this in a purely factual way. I haven't heard anything yet that would make me think these cases are linked. Or that they were anything but accidents." He eyed me critically. "Why is this so important to you? I thought you were glad to get out of the house when Fig and Nanny were there, but now . . ."

I shrugged. "It's important because if there is a murderer he needs to be stopped, and nobody is taking this seriously except me. If you don't want to take me seriously, I'll keep pressing on until I can convince you," I said. "Are you going to be around for the next couple of days?"

"I may be in and out."

"But you're not disappearing on an assignment?"

"Not as far as I know."

"Then I feel better about leaving James for one night, if you're here."

"As if I'd know what to do if a baby vomited," Darcy said.

"You could go for a doctor if necessary," I said. "And I'll telephone as soon as I get to North Wales—if telephone lines actually work that far."

He reached out and stroked my cheek. "Actually I'm glad you're getting out and about," he said. "You've been a devoted mother so far but it's good to realize you are a person as well as a mother."

"I've enjoyed every moment of being with him," I said. "And

I intend to stay a big part of his life, even when we find another nanny."

"Are we making any progress about that?" he asked.

"You didn't want the one applicant who might have been suitable."

"You mean the ex-convict one? Who had a criminal boy-friend?"

"She might have been a victim, Darcy," I pointed out. "She sounded nice."

"And if the boyfriend and his criminal pals decided to make use of her again, and we found we were harboring stolen goods?"

"I suppose you're right," I said.

"You know your trouble." He looked at me fondly. "You are too softhearted."

"Is that a bad thing?"

"Not at all." He blew me a kiss as he went off to his study.

I went up to the nursery to tell Maisie that I would be gone and did she think she could cope alone?

"Oh yes, my lady," she said. "So you're not taking a maid?"

"I am not," I said. "And if I were I'd be out of luck. You're looking after James and Queenie has gone."

"I don't think she was much use as a maid, was she?" Maisie said, giving me a cheeky grin. "She didn't have much clue about pressing clothes."

I had to smile. "You're right."

Her face took on a worried look. "Don't get me wrong, my lady. I liked being your maid, but I'm glad that I can devote every minute to Master James. I'll love that and so will he. So don't you worry one bit. I won't let him out of my sight and I'll listen for him all night."

"You are such a sweet girl, Maisie," I said. "We are very lucky to have you."

"Thank you, my lady. You're so good to me. I really appreciate it."

I thought she was about to cry or hug me or both, so I beat a hasty retreat. I went to find Mrs. Holbrook to tell her I would be away. She looked uneasy.

"Are you going to find Queenie?" she asked. "And bring her back? Chef is complaining again about the extra work. He says he needs an assistant cook or he will leave. You know how dramatic he is."

"Oh yes. Queenie. I'd almost forgotten," I said. "It's only been two days, hasn't it? Let her stew a little longer and start to get worried."

"Good idea," Mrs. Holbrooke said. "That girl is too full of herself, in more ways than one, if you get my point." She walked off, chuckling. And I went down to soothe Pierre's ruffled feathers. Were all chefs so temperamental? I wondered. But then I realized I held the trump card. When he complained about extra work and that it could not go on, I sweetly reminded him that I had saved him from the gallows. He should never forget it. At that he went a little pale and said that I was right, of course, and he was everlastingly grateful. But he would be so much happier if I found him an assistant.

"Do you want Queenie back?" I asked, cautiously. "Or should we be looking elsewhere?"

He hesitated. "This Queenie," he said. "She is annoying. She makes cow eyes at me. But on the other hand she is a good helper. She does what I show her. And she bakes well. And I am used to her now. I would have to get used to another girl. That would be disagreeable."

These complicated thoughts fluttered around my head when I went upstairs to pack an overnight bag. I had to learn to do this myself, now that Maisie was occupied with James. Perhaps it would be nice to have a proper nanny so that Maisie could become my maid again, at least for part of the time. I remembered when Queenie had been my maid. The shoe she had lost on my wedding day. The velvet ironed the wrong way. The fact that she could never wake up in time to bring my morning tea and when she did it was slopped in the saucer. Yes, she had been an utter disaster. So did I really want her back? I could advertise and get a good, efficient undercook. No more drama in the household. No more Queenie bursting in with no sense of decorum, saying, "Whatcher, missus."

It was tempting. But then I had to remind myself that Pierre wanted her back, and above all else I did not want to lose such a brilliant chef. I also realized that she'd never get another job and if she did, she'd never hold on to it. So she'd be stuck, living at home with her parents, maybe working scrubbing floors or in a factory. And I did like her cakes, and her jam roly-poly. So I had to have her back, if only to show Fig that she wasn't going to boss me around.

I'll give her until I get back from North Wales, I told myself. By then she should be truly contrite and worried and maybe she'll learn to be more humble and accommodating.

Chapter 23

I'm heading off again, this time to North Wales. I'm glad we're going by train and Belinda isn't driving. I remember the last time she had a sports car. We only just managed not to go over a cliff. But I can't think why I agreed to come along with her. I really don't want to scale a peak looking for clues.

I met Belinda at Euston Station in time for the ten-o'clock express train.

"I see you didn't bring Trudi," I commented as the train pulled out of the station. Belinda had arrived in a taxi just in time to leap on board.

"No point in that," she said. "I don't need a maid for one night. She'd just be an inconvenience to take around with us."

"How is she working out?" I asked. "Are you happy with her?"

"I can't say I'm overjoyed," she said. "She makes me morning tea but, my dear, it's so pale it's like drinking dishwater. She doesn't seem to think it's her job to do housekeeping, which I suppose is fair enough, and she's not actually brilliant as a maid. I have to ask her to do things which she should do naturally. I shouldn't have to say, 'Would you polish my shoes?' She should notice that they have some mud on them. I don't know what the family who had her before expected. So I'm not sure about keeping her. Maybe I don't know anything about Austrians. In some ways she seems like a simple peasant girl but in others she's quite sophisticated. And I heard her using my telephone and speaking to someone in German. I suppose it may have been another maid who is in London, but that's not quite right, is it? I mean, do your servants use your telephone?"

"Absolutely not," I said. "They wouldn't dream of it. I don't think they'd know how to, except Mrs. Holbrook, of course. She answers when somebody rings me up."

"I don't think I'd know how to use the phone in Austria," Belinda said. "As a matter of fact I'm beginning to think that I should dispense with the personal maid and get a cook, housekeeper instead. She can do the washing and mending, can't she, and I took care of my own wardrobe when I was living in Paris."

"I'm doing without my personal maid at the moment," I said. "Maisie is looking after James until I find a new nanny. I seem to manage quite well, except for those dresses with buttons down the back. Why do people make dresses that way?"

"It makes sure they keep maids in business," Belinda said. She leaned closer to me. There were two other occupants in the compartment, an elderly clergyman and a woman who might have been his wife, both reading newspapers. "So did Darcy find out anything of note?"

I shook my head. "He didn't. No young noblemen have died in spectacular fashion and Shrimpy Smithers died because he had an asthma attack when he was swimming. Darcy thinks this whole thing is a wild-goose chase. But he's humoring me. So did you meet Charles whatsit, and find out what his surname is?"

"It's Abernathy," she said.

I burst out laughing. "Not exactly close to Woolsingham or Wetherham."

"All right. So I got it wrong." She glared. "And, yes, we had quite a pleasant drink together. Without Cousin George there he was much more chatty and actually quite amusing. I may see him again. I did touch upon the possibility of foul play and he seemed interested but also perplexed. His comment was 'Who would want to hurt old Rupert? He was the most harmless chap in the universe. Everyone liked him.'"

"Well, that's interesting," I said. "And what about the other names? Did you ask him about them?"

"He knew about Algie Beauchamps because he'd read about the explosion in the newspaper, but he didn't think any of them were Rupert's friends. He said they might have been at university together, but these days he only mixed with the mountaineering fraternity."

"So we're none the wiser, really."

The train sped along, reaching Chester in excellent time. We changed platforms and were soon heading west toward the

Welsh border and the mountains of Snowdonia. It was a brilliantly fine day. When I caught my first glimpse of the mountains, I saw that the tops were dusted with snow that sparkled in the sunlight.

"What a spectacular view," I said. "It reminds me of home."

"Of course, one forgets, you grew up in that sort of landscape, darling," Belinda said, peering out of the train window beside me.

"Only wilder, I expect. There aren't many places more remote and rugged than Lake Rannoch."

"You don't miss Castle Rannoch, do you?"

I looked at her and laughed. "And the freezing-cold wind coming down the chimneys and Fig telling me what a burden I am to the family? No, I don't miss it at all."

The train line now ran along near the edge of the sea—the Irish Sea, I supposed. There were whitecaps in the brisk wind and clouds raced across the sky. We stopped at a couple of seaside towns whose names I could not pronounce and about three o'clock the train arrived at Bangor Station. As we went along the platform toward the exit my ear picked up unfamiliar sounds. People were speaking Welsh. It came as a shock to realize there were parts of Britain where English was not the main language. I knew, in theory, that some Scots spoke Gaelic, but not where I lived. Belinda noticed this too.

"I hope we can make ourselves understood," she said.

"I presume everyone learns English in school." I glanced across as a woman said something and her companions burst out laughing. I had the embarrassing feeling they were saying something about us, but I couldn't think what it could be.

There were several taxicabs waiting outside the station. Belinda selected the one that looked the most reliable and least ancient and went over to talk with the driver while I stayed with our bags (Belinda had brought a bigger one than me). I saw much hand gesturing going on, the way one would converse in Italy, but eventually she came over.

"I think he'll do. I asked him how much to hire him for the rest of the day and he gave me quite a reasonable figure. I mentioned that there might be some mountain passes involved and he said you couldn't get far in this part of the world without going up a mountain. Has a good sense of humor apparently."

As we were talking the man came over to us, picked up both our bags and deposited them in the luggage area of the taxi. We took off, rattling over the cobbled streets of Bangor. It seemed to be quite a substantial town and we passed the university before leaving the streets of terraced town houses behind. Almost immediately the road entered a pass, mountains reared on either side and we started to climb.

"So where is it exactly that you wanted to go?" the taxi driver asked, turning back to us as the road swung around a bend and we both grabbed onto the seat back.

"We would like to go to the place where the climbers stay," Belinda said. "I can't pronounce it, but it is supposedly well-known."

"Pen-y-Gwyrd, you mean?" The words tumbled out easily from his tongue. "The mountain lodge at the top of the pass? That's where most of them stay."

"If someone wanted to tackle something called Bilberry Terrace on a mountain called Lliwedd? I'm not sure how it's pronounced," Belinda asked.

He looked back again to us, then had to swerve hastily to avoid a sheep in the road. "You're not thinking of climbing on Lliwedd, are you? You must be bloody mad. I wouldn't advise that to most men. Certainly not to delicate-looking women like yourselves. But you can't be climbers. Not at this time of year, and you've no equipment with you."

"No, we're not climbers," Belinda said.

"Bloody stupid, if you ask me," he said. "It's usually raining and you never know when the rain will turn to snow. There was a young chap died climbing at that very spot not too long ago. We read about it in the papers. And supposedly an experienced climber he was too."

"That was my cousin," Belinda said. "He was an experienced climber. He was training for the Himalayas."

"I'm sorry to hear that, my lovely. Even the best can make a mistake," the taxi driver said. "And the conditions here can get very wet and slippery, you know. That rock face on Lliwedd, you miss one handhold and you're plunging down a thousand feet."

"We were told it was an accident but we're not sure about that."

"What do you mean? Someone helped him to fall?"

"It's possible," Belinda said. "I don't know how we'd ever prove it wasn't an accident, but I needed to see for myself. I've brought this lady with me who is a well-known detective."

I saw him examining me with interest in his mirror and tried to look like a well-known detective, rather than someone who was feeling quite carsick with the constant bends in the road.

"Really?" He looked back again. "Another Miss Marple, are you? Who would have thought it? You look quite normal to me."

"She's exaggerating," I said, hoping he'd keep looking at the road, which was now winding in most dramatic fashion. "I've been involved in a few . . . uh . . . cases." I was going to say "murders" but I didn't want him to turn back to look at me again.

"And why do you think this poor man's death was anything but an accident?" he asked. "People die when climbing around here quite regularly. The rock faces are sheer and it's usually raining so they are slippery too. And English people come here, ill prepared, you know. They think that Wales is just like another part of England. Little gentle hills. Nothing dangerous. You watch them walking up Snowdon, wearing their shorts and summer gear, and suddenly the cloud comes down, they lose their way and they are stuck overnight and they freeze to death."

"My cousin fell because his rope broke," Belinda said. "The family is just not satisfied, so we hope someone will be able to provide us with some answers."

"And they send a couple of slips of girls to do the work for them?" He gave an annoying chuckle. "Are there no men in your family, then?"

"No men who could do this as well as us," Belinda said, coldly.

He was still chuckling to himself, clearly not believing that we would be of any use to anyone. We were now entering the high country. Mountains rose on both sides, not the steep peaks that I knew of Switzerland but more like the mountains of Scotland I was familiar with. I wondered where the actual climbing took place because the slopes we passed had sheep grazing high on them. We came to a small village, just a few cottages, a chapel and a couple of shops.

"This is Capel Curig," the taxi driver said. "And now we go into the mountains proper."

He took a road going off to the right. Peaks rose to one side. Bright ribbons of water tumbled down steep sides.

"That's Glydr Fawr," he said, waving one hand while steering with the other. "That's a tricky mountain, I've heard."

The countryside was now bleak. There was grass and rocks and an occasional windblown pine tree. We passed a small lake and a river coming from it. Before us were higher mountains, the one in the middle with its top dusted with snow.

"That's Yr Wyddfa, that you English call Snowdon," the taxi driver said. "And we'll soon come to one of the paths that people take up the mountain. Not the easiest one, mind you. It's several miles of hard uphill. Not that I've done it myself. I'm no outdoorsman. Personally I think it's bloody stupid to walk seven miles uphill when there is a perfectly good railway up the mountain. But I tip my hat to those who do." He slowed down. "Ah now, see ahead. That building at the crossroads? That's the place you're looking for."

It was a simple low building made of local gray stone, unimpressive, not what one could call a hotel. The taxi pulled up in the forecourt. "Now, are you ladies wanting me to wait for you while you go inside and ask your questions? And will you need driving around a bit more and then back to Bangor?"

Belinda looked at me. "I think we should spend the night," she said. "That way we'll have more people to talk to. Would you mind coming back for us in the morning?"

"If you're going to pay me, I'll come back anytime you want," the man said. "There's not many outside visitors at this time of year, so I welcome the work."

"We should leave about nine," I said, "if we want to get back to London in good time."

"The express goes at nine thirty," he said. "That's what you want to catch. I'll come for you about eight thirty, then. Change in Chester and you'll be back in London in no time. Although why anybody would want to live there is beyond me. All that smoke and noise. I like it here with good clean air."

He got out, came around and opened the door for us. As I got out the wind hit me full in the face. It was strong and icy cold, reminding me of home and why I was glad I didn't live there anymore. Belinda paid him, then he carried our bags into the lodge. There was a small reception area, all done in dark wood. The driver gave a good thump to the bell on the front counter and a man came out. He looked, well, outdoorsy. Lots of color in his cheeks, and wearing a heavy knitted dark blue jumper.

"Hello, ladies," he said. "And what can I do for you?"

"Do you have a room for the night?" Belinda asked.

"Just the one night? Passing through, are you?"

"That's right," Belinda said. "So you have a room?"

"At this time of year you can take your pick," he said. "There aren't too many climbers foolhardy enough to brave the ascents when it might still snow on them. You're not climbers yourselves, then?"

"We are not," Belinda said firmly. "But I have family members who are, one of whom just stayed here."

"Really? What was his name?"

"Rupert Warburton-Stoke," Belinda said.

His expression changed. "Oh. The young bloke who was killed?"

"I'm his cousin," Belinda said. "Belinda Warburton-Stoke."

"I'm so sorry. I actually knew him. He'd been up here climbing many times. I'd say he was a skilled mountaineer. Knew what he was doing. It was just bad luck, like all of us have sometimes."

"Maybe," Belinda said.

"So what exactly are you doing here?" the man asked.

"Trying to find out what really happened," Belinda said.

Chapter 24

THURSDAY, MARCH 11

IN A LODGE ON A MOUNTAIN IN THE BLEAKEST PART OF NORTH WALES

I'm not sure why we are here. What did we hope to find out? I'm
certainly not about to go and take a look at Bilberry Terrace
(which sounds like somewhere to sit and have a cup of tea,
but it's not). It would involve several miles of trekking up to
the climbing bit. Then one of the hardest climbs in Britain.

We found our room. It faced away from the road and we looked
out at a rocky slope on which some hardy sheep were huddled
against a dry stone wall. It was basic in the extreme, the sort of
room that hardy mountain-climbing men would want: two narrow beds, some hooks on the wall and a bathroom at the end of
the passage. In true Castle Rannoch fashion, the bathroom win-

dow was open, letting in the howling gale. When I came back to the room Belinda had changed into wool trousers, a large Icelandic jumper and a cashmere scarf. I put on the warmest clothes I had brought with me, realizing as I dressed that I was not going to be warm enough. But when we went down to the bar we found a roaring fire and the room pleasantly warm. It was, again, a manly room, paneled in dark oak with dark wood tables and benches. I noticed that climbers had carved their initials into beams on the ceiling, as if wanting to prove that they had been alive and well, in case the worst happened. It was too early for a drink, so we ordered a pot of tea and some sandwiches. They were beef and ham, with plenty of pickles, and we both tucked in as if we hadn't eaten for months.

When we had almost finished, the man who had been at the front desk came in to ask if everything was all right. We thanked him and he pulled up a bench to sit with us. "You say you've come here to find out what happened to your cousin, is it?" he asked. I noticed now that his voice had a definite Welsh lilt to it. "I don't know how you'd find out any more than we already know. He was climbing on Lliwedd. That's one of the mountains that joins Snowdon itself. Part of the Horseshoe, you know."

"Horseshoe?" I asked.

"That's what climbers call the ring of mountains around Snowdon. You go up Lliwedd, then around to the actual peak of Snowdon, then across Crib Goch and down the other side. It's not for the fainthearted, I can tell you."

"It's funny," I said. "But from what we've seen, the mountains aren't steep at all. Not like Switzerland."

"Ah," he said. "They look tame enough, walking country.

But each of them has some sheer faces with the toughest climbing you'll find. Take Lliwedd, now. It's got some really tricky climbs. You need to be experienced to tackle it at the best of times and I remember the weather wasn't good when your cousin was attempting it. It was rain, turning to snow, but your cousin and his friends said they were training for the Himalayas and snow was to be expected."

He was staring out past us, into the fire, then got up and put on another large log, sending up a shower of sparks.

"The first we heard of it was that evening when the other men came back and told us what had happened. He said your cousin was the lead man, going up first, but tied to the others. When they were near the top the cloud came down the way it often does. They couldn't see him. Suddenly they heard a shout and he came falling past them. The rope should have held, but it didn't."

"Did anybody check the rope afterward?" I asked. "To see if it might have been tampered with?"

He looked shocked. "Tampered with? Is that what you are thinking? Who would want to do that?"

"I don't know," Belinda said. "But his friend Charles Abernathy says that Rupert was always very fussy about his equipment, checking and rechecking it."

"He was with a group of friends," the man said. "Men who knew each other well and clearly enjoyed each other's company."

"Where was the equipment stored while they were here?" I asked. "Did they keep it in their rooms?"

"Oh no. We've an area for equipment at the back, next to where they store their muddy boots and wet oilskins."

"So anyone could access it?"

He frowned now. "I suppose so. But only people who are staying here. You can't get to it from the outside."

"Who else was staying here at the same time?" I asked.

"In my recollection they were the only party climbing that day." He paused. "Wait a minute. There was one young fellow who just came for the night. He said he had business in Caernarfon and while he was in the area he was scoping out routes he might take for a walking holiday in the summer."

"Where was he from, do you think?" I asked.

"Somewhere in the south of England, I'm pretty sure. He sounded to me like a Londoner but I'm not good at foreign accents."

"So his speech wasn't that of a cultured person?"

"I'd say not. Not like yours anyway. A bit rough-and-ready, if you get my meaning. Not the normal type we see here. He didn't look to me much like a walker. People from London don't often go in for climbing and scrambling, do they, now?"

"What did he look like?" I was sitting up straight now, my whole body alert.

"Not much to look at. Skinny chap, a bit unkempt, if you get me. He was wearing one of those leather jackets you wear on a motorcycle."

"So he came on a motorcycle, then?"

"Must have done. I didn't see it, personally, but I think I heard him mention it when he was chatting with some of the other men. He asked them questions about how hard the climbs were. One of them was quite cutting, I remember. He said, 'You wouldn't last two minutes wearing gear like that.' And the young bloke laughed and said he wasn't attempting to tackle one himself. He was just curious."

"What was his name?" I asked.

"I'd have to go and look." The man got up, went out to the reception area, then returned. "He signed the book as Albert Smith."

"Smith?" I said. "I bet that wasn't his real name."

"You know who he is, then?"

"I have some idea."

"So what might his real name be?"

"We don't know that, I'm afraid," I said. "It's just that the description matches."

"And you think he might be responsible for this lady's cousin's fall?"

"Again it might be pure coincidence, but I believe this same chap might have caused the death of another friend of ours."

"You don't say." He shook his head in disbelief.

"He might have tampered with the rope," Belinda said, "but Rupert was a good climber. He wouldn't have lost his grip unless somebody pushed him, and the chap you describe would hardly have climbed up the rock face and waited for them."

"That's true enough," the man said. "But the strange thing is that the Miner's Track, one of the routes around the Snowdon Horseshoe I told you about, goes up and over Lliwedd. So it would be possible that someone who wasn't a climber could get near the top of that face without doing any climbing himself."

"And wait there in the mist. Maybe drop a rock onto Rupert," I said.

We stared at each other, each of us picturing the scene.

"Did the man leave an address when he registered at the hotel?"

The man shook his head. "He only wrote Tottenham, London. No street address."

"It won't be easy to find him. Tottenham, London, is a big place and it might not even be a true address," I said. "But now at least we have confirmation that a similar-looking man appeared in Derbyshire just before our other friend's car went off a sharp bend."

The man looked really worried now. "Do you have any idea who he is and why he might be doing this?"

"No idea at all. That's the trouble," I said. "These men are all quite posh, around the same age, but didn't seem to know each other."

"That's a pretty puzzle for you," he said.

"I don't suppose the rope was brought back here?" Belinda asked.

"It wasn't. If it broke, the top part may well be hanging there on the mountainside, for all I know."

"Well, we're not climbing a mountain to retrieve it," Belinda said.

"And I don't know how you'd prove that anyone messed with it." He was still frowning. "All you'd need to do would be to cut through a few strands, do it so it wasn't obvious. If your cousin had checked his equipment the night before, he'd just have picked up the coil of rope, slung it over his shoulder and off he'd go. None the wiser."

I shivered and looked at Belinda. "We have to find this man before it's too late."

Belinda nodded. I could see the wheels turning in her head. "He said he was working in Caernarfon. Did he mention where?"

The man shook his head. "I'm sorry, but I didn't really chat with him. I heard him talking with the others when I brought in their dinner."

"You have to ask Charles Abernathy," I said. "He might be able to give us the vital clue to finding this chap. Anyway, it will be a good excuse to see him again."

"Shut up." She gave me a warning look.

Chapter 25

COMING HOME FROM NORTH WALES

Heading back home. Everything we learn makes me feel more
anxious. This is obviously a clever person who works things
out in meticulous detail. A madman, maybe? Or a foreign
agent? But he sounds like a Londoner. I don't know where
we go from here. We just need one thing that ties all the
deaths together. I'm now wondering if I should go up to the
Lake District and find out if a scruffy motorbike rider was
seen where Algie's boat was kept.

The next morning we awoke to a new dusting of snow and the
promise of more to come. The taxi arrived for us as promised and
we caught the train back to London. On the way back we devised
our plan. Belinda would arrange to meet Charles Abernathy

again and see if the elusive motorbike rider gave away any details of himself that we could follow up. I could think of things I should be doing, like chatting to Gussie Gormsley again and finding out exactly who was at Algie's funeral and what connection they all had. Instead I was going to go home to check on my son. I had wanted to telephone Darcy the evening before just to make sure that James was all right, but the telephone service at the lodge did not manage to be connected for a trunk call to far-off England. So I worried all the way home, my brain conjuring up scenarios in which James fell out of his crib, on his head, was rushed to hospital, or suddenly developed measles.

I arrived home just as it was getting dark and found a peaceful domestic scene. Darcy had James down in the drawing room, playing with him on the rug by the fire. He was pretending to be a bear and creeping up after James, who responded with a great roar of laughter. They looked up when I came in, both clearly pleased to see me but not with looks of desperate, heartbreaking longing.

"Mama!" James crawled toward me. He was actually crawling rather well now.

"As you can see, all is well here," Darcy said as I dropped to my knees beside them. James crawled into my arms and I hugged him so fiercely that he wanted down again.

"Your son is thriving. We've had a good time, apart from only getting cold scrambled eggs for breakfast this morning as Pierre complained he would not cook disgusting kidneys and it was about time we learned to like croissants."

"Oh dear," I said. "I'd better go and retrieve Queenie, I suppose. I suspect she'll be insufferable when she learns that Pierre wants her back and can't function without her."

"I wouldn't put it that way, if I were you. Tell her we have decided, out of the goodness of our hearts, to give her a second chance."

"Good idea," I said. "I suppose I'd better go tomorrow. Unless you're going to be in London anyway."

A look of horror crossed his face. "You should go. She's fond of you," he said.

"I suppose she is, in her way. We've been through a lot together, like that time in Transylvania."

He nodded, then asked, "So tell me about your visit to Wales. Could you understand a word anyone said?"

"Everybody we met spoke English," I said. "No problem at all. And we found out important details too."

"About the death of Belinda's cousin?"

"Yes," I said. "I think we now have proof that even you couldn't ignore."

"Go on." He reached out to retrieve James, who was heading for the fire irons.

"Well, it seems the only person staying at the hotel, other than Rupert's group, was a young man wearing a motorcycle jacket who matches the description of the one seen at the garage in Derbyshire before Sebastian Inchcliffe drove his car off the road. What's more, he gave an address from Tottenham, London, and he wasn't a climber, and it was horrible weather, so what was he doing there? And what's more, that particular climb is up a rock face on a mountain that has a footpath going above it. So a non-climber could hike up there and wait for the right moment. Maybe give Rupert a push, drop a rock on his hand and make him let go. . . ."

Darcy was listening intently while James squirmed to get away from Darcy's hold on him.

"And what's more," I went on, "the equipment at the hotel was stored in a room that anyone staying there could access. So this mystery motorbike rider could easily have cut through strands of the rope and nobody would have noticed."

"I see," he said. "It does sound pretty convincing, I agree."

"So you finally admit that I was not having feminine hysterics by seeing a link between these cases?" I asked, trying to keep the note of triumph out of my voice.

"Georgie, I would never have accused you of hysterics," he said. "And I have to say that you have made sound deductions in the past, so perhaps I was wrong in not believing in this one earlier."

"Thank you," I said. "So perhaps I can now have your thoughts on where to go from here."

"You said you have this chap's address, so we can hand this over to the police and they can look into him."

I grimaced. "Unfortunately he gave his name as Smith and his only address as Tottenham, London. Obviously an assumed name and not much to go on."

"As you say, not much to go on. We can't cruise around Tottenham hoping to see a scruffy chap on a motorbike."

"Tottenham might not even be correct. I'm sure Smith wasn't," I said. "The really perplexing thing to ask is why. What motive could someone have for planning such meticulously prepared accidents? The man must have known an awful lot about each of his victims."

Darcy nodded. "Perhaps there are more we don't know

about. Others where the accident didn't actually work. If Rupert had managed to grab another rock. If Sebastian had swerved out of harm's way at the last moment, we'd never have heard about them."

"It's so puzzling," I said. "Why would anyone want to do this?"

"It had to be personal," Darcy said. "Or passionate in some way. If he was an avowed communist and wanted to get rid of the ruling class . . ."

"But then why not place a bomb in the House of Lords?" I asked. "He seems to be selecting victims all around the same age."

Darcy nodded.

"Which means you also qualify," I said. "Please be careful."

"I don't plan to climb any mountains soon," he said.

"So what do you think I should do next?" I asked. "I could go up to the Lake District and see if anyone noticed a motorbike rider about the time the boat blew up with Algie Beauchamps in it."

"I think that would be a waste of time and money and energy," he said. "If he was practicing for a speed record there would be all sorts of people up there to watch—press and public. A bloke from London wouldn't have stood out, unless he was seen tinkering with the boat, in which case someone would have reported this."

"That's true," I said. "Ah well, I have more pressing tasks, the first of which is to go and find Queenie. I can't say I'm looking forward to that, but if we don't want cold eggs every morning, I'd better do it."

I picked up James. "Were you a good boy for Maisie?" I asked. "Did you miss your mama?"

James wriggled to be put down.

"So much for pining for me." I gave Darcy a pained grin. "Come on, Mr. James. Let's take you up for your dinner. What delicious luxury is it tonight? Strained beets? Semolina mush?"

I carried him out of the room. I had only got as far as the front hall when Mrs. Holbrook came hurrying toward me. "Oh, my lady. You had a telephone call about an hour ago. From a Lady Hockney."

"Lady Hockney?" The name was certainly familiar, but only from the society columns.

"I told her I expected you back shortly and said you would return her telephone call," Mrs. Holbrook said.

"Thank you, Mrs. Holbrook. Did she say what it was about?" I could not imagine why Lady Hockney would want to telephone me. We certainly didn't move in the same glamorous circles.

"She did not."

"Then I'd better ring her right away. Would you please have Maisie take James upstairs and feed him?"

"Of course, my lady. Come along, Master James." She took him from me. "Let's go and find Maisie, shall we?"

"Maymay," he said, looking for her.

I waved and watched him go before I picked up the receiver and gave the operator the Mayfair number. A butler answered and I asked to speak to Lady Hockney. After a long pause she came to the telephone.

"Am I speaking to Lady Georgiana?" came a crisp and plummy voice.

"This is she."

"Lady Hockney here," she said. "I am calling you about your former cook. She has applied for the position of head chef at my London house, and rather than ask her to send me a reference I thought it would be much simpler to speak to you. The telephone is a wonderful device, is it not? Makes everything simpler."

"Yes, it does." I stammered the words. "My former cook has applied to be head chef?"

"That's right. So I wondered what you had to say about her and whether you thought she was up for the job. She says she could serve French food and had catered a dinner party of fifty."

My innate honesty wrestled with betraying Queenie, but my vision of her as head chef in one of the swankest houses in London, serving toad-in-the-hole and spotted dick to the aristocracy, won out.

"What exactly would she be asked to do?" I asked, stalling as I composed what I was going to say about Queenie.

"We are usually around six people. My husband and I, our two unmarried children and my mother and her companion, but we entertain on a regular basis in London so dinner parties for twelve are not uncommon. And my husband has a very discerning palate. He was educated on the Continent, you know."

That was enough for me. "I'm sorry, but I'm afraid my former cook would be quite unsuitable for you. She has exaggerated her capabilities. She is a good plain cook and does bake quite well; however, she worked under my head chef who is French. She would not be able to handle a kitchen alone or to serve you the sort of food you'd expect."

"I see." The voice was frosty now. "May I ask why she left your employment? She says she wanted more of a challenge in a posh household. I have to say her writing and her spelling were not impressive.”

“She was let go because she was impertinent to a guest,” I said. “She is a Cockney girl who sometimes pushes the boundaries of her station.”

“I see,” she repeated. “Well, Lady Georgiana, I am so glad that I spoke to you. You have saved me from what might have been an embarrassing interview with the girl. I shall write to her immediately and tell her that she would not be suitable in any way for my household.”

“I’m afraid so,” I said.

“I thank you for your honesty,” she said. “Good day to you.”

As I put back the receiver I felt terribly conflicted. I had just stopped Queenie from bettering herself. And yet I knew I had done the right thing. I just pictured her trying to prepare the sort of food that Pierre served to us with his wonderfully delicate touch. There was nothing about Queenie that was delicate. And I doubted if she had actually learned to make any of the dishes that Pierre cooked. Perhaps I was wrong, I thought. Perhaps she had been practicing and she might be able to cook them now. But she was still Queenie. She’d still say “whatcher, missus” to Lady Hockney and be impertinent to guests. She was never going to learn.

I decided to wait another day, until she had received Lady Hockney’s reply, before I went to rescue Queenie.

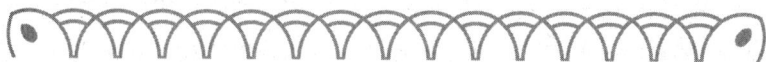

Chapter 26

I have never felt so confused. We now have slivers of evidence
that somebody helped Sebastian and Rupert to their deaths.
We have a vague description. We have Tottenham. And yet I
have no idea where to go from here. I suppose I am not much
of a detective after all. But then if I were at Scotland Yard I
could send out men all over Tottenham to look for the
motorcyclist. I could send a team up to Wales to find out
which train he came on. I could send men up on the track
that passed over the top of the rock face where Rupert
fell to see if there was evidence left of someone having
waited there. And maybe try to retrieve the rope that
broke. But I was just me, with a family and a baby to take
care of.

I waited until Monday before I took the early train up to London. Maisie was delighted to be in charge of James again.

"If I take over as his nursemaid," she said, "I don't think I can do a good job as your personal maid as well. Do you mind?"

"Of course not," I replied. "Right now it's more important that you look after the baby. When we get the situation sorted out we can decide how much time you spend with each of us."

"Sorted out?" She looked worried.

"He will need a proper nanny at some point, Maisie. I did tell you that. You take wonderful loving care of him, but you can't educate him to be a young man who knows how to behave in society. That's what a good nanny does."

Her brow wrinkled. "I suppose you're right, my lady. But I can keep helping out, can't I? I do so enjoy my time with him. He's a lovely little chap."

"Of course we'll make sure that you continue to help with him," I said. "And not just changing dirty nappies."

She grinned. "If that old woman had had her way he'd have been done with nappies by the time he was a year old."

I reflected on this as the train carried me to Waterloo Station. Such a nice girl. So willing. And I was about to retrieve a girl who was obstinate and sometimes rude and had caused more disasters than the average person in a lifetime. And yet I smiled to myself as I took the District Line of the Underground out to where Queenie's family lived in the East End of London. I came out to a smoky haze hanging over the Thames. It was a dockland area with chimneys belching smoke in every direction. Granddad lived just a little farther out, but I still worried about his bad chest when I saw weather like this. Perhaps I'd pop in on him today and bring him back with me. That thought cheered me up as I found Queenie's street and checked the house numbers.

It was a sad little back street of terraced houses, no front gardens and with a huge gasometer behind it. I knocked on the door and it was opened by a large man wearing an apron, his shirtsleeves rolled up.

"Yeah?" he asked in a growly, belligerent tone. "We don't need no charity here."

"I am Lady Georgiana, Queenie's former employer," I said. "Do I have the right house? Is Queenie here?"

"She is, but you just leave her alone," he said. "You've already upset her enough, throwing her out after she's served you all this time."

"Mr. Hepplewhite," I said. "Your daughter was rude to a duchess. She called her a mean old cow."

I saw his mouth twitch, trying not to smile.

"Yeah, well, I suppose that weren't right," he said.

"It wasn't," I said. "This particular duchess can be very annoying and I have to refrain from telling her what I think of her. But a servant must never speak to a guest unless spoken to. There are rules, Mr. Hepplewhite."

"Yeah. You're right," he said. "I told her she was bloody silly to lose such a plum job. She'd found her place with cooking, I reckon. She told us you loved her cakes. And that Frenchie bloke, he were ever so grateful she was helping him."

"She has turned into a good cook, that's true," I said. "Look, may I come in? It's not right to be talking on the doorstep."

"Come on in, then," he said. "We've not been lighting the fire in the front parlor on account of the price of coal. And the one in the back parlor has been smoking something terrible. We need that chimney cleaned but the sweep ain't been around for a while."

He opened the door fully and led me into a dark and narrow hallway. "I can't take you into the kitchen," he said. "That wouldn't be right for a lady of your standing. So I hope you don't mind the cold room."

He opened the first door we came to and I stepped into a parlor with furniture covered in dust sheets. He pulled one off a mock Chippendale sofa and bade me sit. "Sorry the wife's out," he said. "She's working down the factory. I got laid off from my job so someone has to bring in the money." Then he was clearly embarrassed by what he had told me. "I'll go and find Queenie," he said. "She was hanging out the washing, although knowing her, half of it has fallen in the mud by now." He gave me a knowing look. "She tends to be a bit clumsy, don't she? Doesn't get it from me, I can tell you."

With that he left. I sat, looking at the china dogs on the mantelpiece, the painting, a copy of *The Monarch of the Glen*, on the wall. It was a room probably identical to most of the others on the street. It was horribly cold and I was glad I was wearing a coat with a fur collar and gloves. Luckily I didn't have to wait long before I heard the familiar thumping of an approaching Queenie. She burst in, her cheeks red with cold from having been outside.

"'Ello, my lady," she said. "What are you doing here?"

I noticed that she had addressed me properly, not as "missus," proving that she had known all the time how to do it.

"I've come to see you, Queenie," I said. "Just to check on you. I was not pleased to find that you had been dismissed while I was away. I felt that was not the correct way to do things. Nevertheless, her grace was quite right to dismiss you for rudeness. No servant may speak to her employer in that fashion. I hope you realize that."

"Yeah, well, she said some right nasty things to me first," Queenie said, sticking out her chin defiantly. "But you're right. I shouldn't have spoke back to her. But she got right up my nose with the way she was talking to me."

"I'm afraid a servant may have to put up with employers who are not always polite," I said. "You were very lucky with Mr. Darcy and me. We have always been very tolerant concerning your various mishaps and failings."

"So what are you doing here?" she asked, hands on hips and still with a belligerent look on her face. "You don't come all this way up to the Smoke for nothing."

"I was on my way to visit my grandfather," I said, "and wanted to make sure you were all right."

"Me? Yeah. I'm doing all right. Going to find a better job, now I've got experience. That's what I'll be doing. Head cook. That's what I'm going to be."

"That's good news," I said.

"Yeah. I've already sent out quite a few applications. From what I've seen in the papers, lots of people are looking for good-quality cooks."

"And have you had any responses yet?"

"Yeah. You heard of Lady Hockney, I suppose."

"Of course I have. She's a leader in high society."

"Well." Queenie gave me a smug grin. "She just wrote to me, she did."

"Lady Hockney has offered you a job?" I knew full well she hadn't.

"Well, no, not exactly. She thought head chef might be a bit much for me, seeing how much she entertains, but she wrote a nice letter back. She might want me as assistant cook in Mayfair."

I paused before I said, "So you would not want your old job back, I take it?"

Queenie had the sort of face that showed every emotion. It perked up instantly. "So you're missing me, then. I knew you would." She couldn't help grinning. "I told my old dad, you just wait. They'll come crawling back when they see how much they need me."

"Queenie," I said, but she went on.

"That Pierre. I knew he couldn't do without me. He fancies me, that's what he does."

Nothing could have been further from the truth of how Pierre felt about Queenie.

"Queenie," I said, more firmly this time. "If we offer you your old job back, it would only be because Mr. Darcy and I are prepared to give you a second chance, because of your loyalty and bravery in the past. That is all. So I don't want you thinking you are indispensable. In fact Pierre was talking about bringing a young woman over from France to be his assistant. She comes highly recommended."

Queenie's expression became guarded. "Garn," she said (which is how Cockneys say "go on"). "She couldn't do no better than me. He couldn't like her better than me, could he?" And the first hint of doubt crept into her voice. "You think I cook quite well, don't you, missus . . . I mean my lady? You like my cakes and puddings?"

"Yes, Queenie. I do think you bake well. But your attitude will have to change if I accept you back. No more speaking out of turn. Kitchen staff are supposed to stay silent when out of the kitchen, especially not chatting with guests. Is that clear?"

"I suppose so," she mumbled.

"So I take it you do want to come back, rather than waiting to see if Lady Hockney offers you a job as assistant in her household?"

"Well, if you put it that way, yeah, I sort of like being in your house. You and me, we've shared some good moments, ain't we? And I like working with Pierre. So I suppose I'll say yes. I'll come back."

I didn't quite like the way this was swinging in her favor. "You realize, Queenie, that you will be on probation if you come back. On your best behavior. If you put a foot wrong, if you speak rudely to one of my houseguests, then you'll be out on your ear and no more second chances. And no reference."

She stood, eyeing me up and down for a moment. I thought she might refuse, but then she nodded. "Bob's yer uncle, missus," she said.

Chapter 27

MONDAY, MARCH 15

UP IN LONDON

I think we are getting somewhere at last.

I was so close to my grandfather's house that I couldn't pass up
the chance to see him. As well as being worried about him in the
current smoggy air conditions, I wanted to use his experience of
years in the police force. I felt quite excited when I exited the
train and walked up the hill to his street. As I turned the corner
I saw a figure walking ahead of me. Slightly stooped, walking
slowly and carrying a large shopping bag. I hurried to catch up
with him.

"Now, what are you doing carrying a heavy bag like that?" I
asked, trying to take it from him. He reacted in a startled manner before he realized it was me.

"You scared the daylights out of me, you silly ha'peth," he said. "I thought you were some kind of robber, wanting my groceries."

"Oh, Granddad." I kissed the top of his balding head. "I'm sorry. I shouldn't have attacked from behind."

"You wouldn't have done in my younger days," he said. "I'd have had you flat on your back. Of course, I wouldn't have been carrying groceries in me younger days."

"Here, let me carry the bag." I tried to take it from him.

"It's only a few more yards and I'm not quite old and feeble yet," he said.

"It's not good for your chest to be out in this weather," I said. "Doesn't Packer's deliver if you ask them?"

"I'm not asking for delivery unless I'm sick and in bed," he said. "It's not right. I've got two perfectly good legs to walk to the shops. Besides, I enjoy my chats with Mr. Packer. And I usually see people I know when I'm out and about."

He was lonely. I knew that. But he didn't feel comfortable at my great big house.

I put my arm on his. "I do wish you'd come back and stay with us. Fig has gone, you'll be pleased to know. We're all alone."

"I can't do that. I've just bought food for the next week," he said.

"Some of it will keep."

We reached his front door. He put down the bag and fished for his key. We went inside. It felt rather cold to me.

"You're not keeping the place warm enough," I said.

"Yeah, well, coal don't grow on trees, you know," he said. "Besides, I'm usually in the kitchen, which is always toasty warm."

He led me there and put on the kettle. I helped him put the groceries away while the kettle boiled.

"So what are you doing up here?" he asked. "Come to check on your old granddad or did you have something else that brought you up to the Smoke?"

"I've just been to see Queenie's family," I said, and told him the whole story.

I saw his lips twitch when I said that Queenie had called Fig a mean old cow.

"And you came up here to offer her her old job back?" he asked. "Was that wise?"

"Oh, Granddad, who else would employ her?" I said.

"That Irish couple seemed to like her."

"Yes, they did. But their aged butler finally retired and they've a new young servant girl who is looking after them."

"I see. Well, I hope Queenie won't get too uppity that you came begging."

"I made it quite clear that I was giving her a second chance out of the goodness of my heart," I said. "I told her she was on probation."

"It won't sink in," he said as the water boiled and he poured it into the teapot. "That girl don't want to learn. Still, I have to admit she bakes a good maid of honor."

"She does bake well," I said. "We'll just have to see."

He put a cup of tea in front of me, together with the biscuit barrel.

"I do wish you'd come back with me," I said. "The air is horrible this close to London. And damp this close to the Thames. Not good for you, you know. We're all alone at Eynsleigh. I told you Fig has gone." And I related the rest of the story. This time he allowed a smile to cross his face. "You said that? Well, good for you. She's been lording it over you for too long, bossing everyone around. If only that husband of hers had put her in her place years ago she might have turned out different."

"Anyway, she's gone. And who knows, we may never see her again. So will you come?"

"I've just bought all these groceries. I ain't wasting nothing. You know me. Waste not, want not."

"Then come in a few days, when you've eaten the eggs and milk."

"I'll think about it," he said.

"I actually came to see you not just to find out how you are. I wanted to pick your brains."

He laughed. "Ain't much left up there, after all these years."

"Go on. You're as sharp as ever," I said. "And this is a police matter. A crime, or rather a series of crimes."

He sipped his tea while I laid the whole case out in front of him. "So what do you think?" I asked. "Do you think I'm overreacting or are these deaths really linked in some way?"

He looked at me steadily. "When I was in police work, if I had a feeling, deep down, that wouldn't go away, I was usually right. So if this hunch keeps gnawing at you, I'd say that you'd probably got it right."

I touched his hand. "Thank you," I said. "We do have the motorcyclist linked to two of the accidents, but I can't find any other way to link them."

"They didn't know each other? You said they were all posh. Didn't they go to the same school? They didn't move in the same circles? Belong to the same rugby club? And they didn't have one friend in common?"

"Not for some time as far as we can tell. I think they were all part of what they called the debs' delights when they left university—you know, the eligible young men invited to all the debs' balls. They would have bumped into each other then, but since have gone their separate ways."

"They all went to university, then? Which university?" he asked, eyeing me sharply.

"I don't know. Golly. Wait a minute. Sebastian was at Cambridge, I believe. So was Algie Beauchamps. What if they were all at Cambridge?" Then I shook my head. "But that's silly. It's a big university. It doesn't mean that they knew each other. And if something had happened while they were at Cambridge, nobody would have waited this long."

"You may well find that the motive goes back that far," he said. "If something bad happened at Cambridge, if someone had been tricked, or betrayed in some way, and it's been festering in someone's head all this time, revenge is sometimes slow to come to the boil. Perhaps another student felt cheated or they played a prank on him . . . and now he blames this for messing up his life. . . ."

"Golly," I said again. "Why didn't we think of that before? I suppose because when we mentioned the names of the other men they didn't seem to register with their families. But if they were all fellow students, then perhaps they lost touch after university." Then another thought came to me. "But wait. This doesn't make sense because the motorcycle rider is described as being scruffy lower-class from London. So he would have had nothing to do with them at Cambridge. Also younger than them, I think."

"All the same," Granddad said, "it might make sense to check out the last time we know they were all in the same place. See if they were friends in those days. See if anything happened."

"Yes," I said. "I'll see if I can get Darcy to drive me to Cambridge. But first, while I'm in London, I'll go and talk to Gussie Gormsley."

"Gussie?" Granddad grinned. "A girl? A lady of the streets?"

"No. His name is Augustus. He's always known as Gussie, and he went to the funeral of one of the men because they were at Cambridge together. He would know if anything had happened while they were there."

"Right." Granddad nodded. "You're getting to be a good little detective. You'll be giving that Marple woman a run for her money."

"Oh no," I said. "I met the writer, Agatha Christie, last summer, and she's awfully nice. We got along well and she helped me with that strange business at the poison garden. I think she's very clever."

"And I think it takes a lot to beat my granddaughter," he said.

"There is another possibility." I put down my teacup. "You said what did they have in common? And they were posh. It did occur to me that someone was killing them because they were posh, someone who resented the upper classes. But Darcy has checked with people in London who know how to find out about these things, and they have found no previous evidence of this. So maybe he's just started; these are the first few he's trying out, which is very worrying because Darcy is around their age."

Granddad's look was grave. "If that really is the case, you'd have no way of tracing this bloke, unless he sent a threatening letter or was caught red-handed."

"There's been no mention of a letter," I said. "I presume someone has been through the belongings of the men who died, but maybe not. I'll pass that along to my friend Belinda. Her cousin's parents could search through his things."

"I think you should check up on Cambridge first, because if it's what you just said, then you're really fishing in the dark until the person slips up. They always do in the end, of course. They leave some kind of clue, or what they planned doesn't work how they wanted it to."

"Right," I said. "I'll go to speak to Gussie and see what he might know." I stood up. "I should be off, then. Promise me you'll come and stay very soon. As soon as you've finished those eggs!"

He stood up, chuckling. "All right. As long as that sister-in-law of yours isn't coming back."

"With any luck," I said, "the answer to that will be 'Never.'"

Chapter 28

MONDAY, MARCH 15
UP IN LONDON

I'm feeling quite excited. It's as if the door is opened just a crack
but enough to let light in. I do hope that Gussie can give me
the connection we've been looking for.

I took the District Line back to Central London and telephoned
Belinda from a box at Victoria Station.

"Sorry to bother you," I said, "but do you have Gussie
Gormsley's telephone number? Didn't he give it to you when we
met the other day?"

"Darling, you must be feeling desperate to want a fling with
Gussie," she said.

"You know I'm a one-man woman," I said with mock sever-
ity. "I'm hoping he can fill in one of the missing pieces in the

puzzle. Didn't you tell me that your cousin Rupert went to Cambridge?"

"He did. He was the brainy one in the family, apparently. Although nobody thought of giving me the chance to see if I could get into a university. I had my season, which was jolly expensive, but I was supposed to have found my husband by the end of it and thus be off my parents' hands."

"I know," I said. "It did feel like a cattle market, didn't it? But anyway, Rupert went to Cambridge. So did Sebastian Inchcliffe. Now I have to find out if the others did and if Gussie knew them at Cambridge and if anything bad happened while they were there."

"Cambridge?" she said. "That's a long time ago, isn't it? Are you saying that something that happened while they were undergrads is just now having repercussions? I find that hard to believe."

"It seems to be the only connection we've got, if they all attended," I said. "Anyway, it's worth pursuing. Otherwise we are not much further along than when we started. Looking for a scruffy bloke on a motorbike in London. Not exactly the easiest of tasks."

"Hold on a second while I find my little book for Gussie's number," she said.

There was a clunk as she put the receiver down and much rustling and a minor swear word. Then: "Oh, here it is. Let me see. Here you go, Mayfair 2236."

"Thank you. Brilliant," I said. "So are you still planning to go down to Cornwall?"

"Maybe." She hesitated. "Frankly I'm not sure about seeing Jago again. We really did seem to get along so well, but . . . he hasn't written to me. I get the feeling that he senses the class difference is a problem."

"You won't know until you go and speak to him," I said.

"You're right. But in the meantime Charles Abernathy has invited me to dinner. At Rules, darling. Very traditional and correct."

"You'd better study up on climbing terminology," I replied.

"As long as he doesn't expect me to follow him up a mountain with pitons or crampons or whatever they are."

We were both chuckling as I put down the telephone. I picked it up again immediately and dialed Gussie's number. It was answered by a voice I didn't recognize. "Gormsley residence, who may I say is calling?"

"This is Lady Georgiana O'Mara," I said. "Telephoning for Mr. Gormsley. Is he at home?"

"Let me ascertain whether he is free to talk to you, my lady," said the exaggeratedly posh voice. "Please remain on the line and I shall return momentarily."

I heard voices in the background, then a voice said, "What ho, Georgie. What a pleasant surprise."

"Sorry to trouble you, Gussie, but do you have a moment for a chat? It's quite important."

"As long as you're not asking me to subscribe to your local church roof fund. I'm rather low on cash at the moment."

"I'm only asking for information."

"Are you in London?"

"I am. At Victoria Station."

"Then grab a taxi and come over. It's 21 Derby Street. I'll have Montmorency make us some coffee."

"Who?"

"My new valet. You wait till you see him. You won't believe your eyes. Straight out of the Regency era, I suspect. But so good at creating cocktails and mending things."

My own feeling was that Gussie himself belonged to a bygone era, a time when people of our class had enough money to live comfortably, wasting their lives while others waited on them. I knew that Gussie's father was some sort of newspaper tycoon and he would inherit buckets of cash one day. I also knew that he had tried to get too fresh with me on more than one occasion. I was glad there was now a valet in residence.

I found a cab outside the station and in a couple of seconds it had whisked me around Hyde Park Corner, up Park Lane, then turned onto Curzon Street and right on Derby, where it pulled up outside a tall, thin town house of dark brownstone with light yellow trim. I had expected a bachelor like Gussie to live in a modern block of flats, as Sebastian's friend had done, and stood outside, looking for his name on a bank of bells. But there was only one impressive knocker in the shape of a lion's head. I knocked. It was opened by someone who could not be anyone else but Montmorency. Tall, lugubrious, thinning hair combed over a bald spot, immaculately attired in black suit and white starched collar. He gave a deferential bow when he saw me.

"Lady Georgiana?" he asked. "Please do enter. The master is expecting you in the sitting room. May I take your coat?"

He helped me off with it, then led me through to a

comfortable-looking room with overstuffed chairs and sofas that contrasted with the modern artwork on the walls. Gussie was sprawled in one of these chairs. I noticed there was no fireplace, but the room was delightfully warm. Ah. Radiators. What I dreamed of.

Gussie sprang to his feet as I came in. "Georgie. What a nice surprise. You can bring the coffee now, Monty, old chap."

"I take it you require biscuits too, Mr. Gormsley? Chocolate biscuits?"

"Oh, you managed to find those French biscuits that I do so love. You're a wizard, Monty."

"I do my best to please, sir." He gave a bow and almost backed out of the room.

"Take a pew, old bean." Gussie grinned as he motioned me to take a seat. "I call him Monty because I know it riles him. He likes his full name."

"Where did you find him?" I asked. "Did you lure him from royalty?"

He was still smiling. "Close. My father was doing business with a certain noble family who must be nameless. The owner of the castle died, leaving no heir, and his wife no longer wanted to be responsible for the running of such a large estate. So Father agreed to take it off her hands. And poor old Montmorency had been valet to his lordship. So Father snapped him up too, because he had wanted someone to be keeping an eye on me. I couldn't turn down a free valet, could I?"

"Probably not," I said. "How were you managing before he came?"

"I believe you came to my former flat at St. James Mansions," he said. "We let it go after that tragedy with poor old Tubby Tewkesbury. Father also acquired this house and is letting me live in it. He's pushing hard for me to settle down and produce enough heirs to enjoy the fortune. So a respectable address is the first step."

"It's very nice," I said. I looked up as Montmorency came in, bearing a tray with a white cloth, a silver coffeepot and two dainty cups. He served coffee, put a plate of chocolate biscuits between us and departed. I thought of Queenie, slopping coffee in the saucers and probably grabbing one of the chocolate biscuits herself. And I sighed. Still, would I really want a perfect servant? Nanny Hardbottle had been one in many ways and I couldn't wait to get rid of her.

"So, Georgie," Gussie said. "What did you want to see me about so urgently?"

"First of all, Gussie, were you at Cambridge?"

"Yes," he said, eyeing me warily. "But don't ask about my degree. I did not do too well. The pater has not forgiven me, but I wasn't the best student and found PPE horribly boring."

"I wanted to ask about the chap whose funeral you went to. Algie Beauchamps? He was at Cambridge with you?"

"Yes. Same college, but we weren't actually friends. He was one of the swots who studied all the time. I just went to his funeral out of respect, you know."

"Which college?" I asked.

"Trinity. Biggest and best in Cambridge." He paused. "At least that's what they told us."

"So it's a big college. You wouldn't know everybody?"

"True."

"Did you know someone called Sebastian Inchcliffe? Was he at college with you?"

"Inchcliffe? Yes. That name does ring a bell. Fairly humble background, right?"

"His mother's family was. They've now inherited a title and property."

"Good for Inchcliffe."

"Not so good. He was killed in a motor accident, around the same time as Algie."

"Oh, bad luck."

"Only I'm not sure it was bad luck," I said. "What about Rupert Warburton-Stoke?"

"What about him?"

"Did you know him?"

"I remembered the name when I met Belinda, but I can't put a face to it. Another of the studious lot in Blue Boar Court. That was their dorm. Rather nice. Better than mine . . . room under a roof that leaked."

"And what about Shrimpy Smithers?"

He frowned, thinking. "Shrimpy? I don't remember a Shrimpy at Trinity. But there was a Smithers. Big bloke. Leonard Smithers, I believe."

"That's him." My heart was racing now. "They were all at Trinity."

"I say, what's this about, then?"

"All four of these men have died recently in accidents. But some of us aren't happy that the deaths were accidental. We worry that someone had arranged their deaths to look like accidents. Sebastian's car went over the edge when he was an accomplished driver. Algie's boat exploded. Rupert fell while climbing in Wales and the rope didn't hold him, and Smithers had an asthma attack while swimming and his medicine didn't work."

"Good God." Gussie was staring at me.

"I've been trying to find any connection between them. No recent ones. They are not apparently friends any longer. They moved in different circles. But they were all at Trinity. So tell me, Gussie, did anything strange or untoward happen while you were at Trinity? Any horrible prank that went wrong? Any accident there?"

Gussie shrugged. "Pranks were part of college life, weren't they? We were always pranking each other and our tutors. But they were harmless unless you got caught at two a.m. with a bucket of cold water over you when you opened your door." He picked up his cup and took a swig of coffee. "Let me get this straight, Georgie. Are you suggesting that someone in college with us was so outraged by a prank that they started killing fellow students almost ten years later?"

"It does seem rather far-fetched," I said. "But this is the first real connection I've found between them."

"And may one ask why you are looking into this? Are you connected to one of these families?"

"No, I'm not, but first of all my friend Princess Zamanska asked me to look into Sebastian's death because it didn't feel right to her, then we met you and heard about Algie, and then Belinda asked me to come with her to Wales to find out more about Rupert's death. It all seemed too much of a coincidence that four young men of the same age, the same social class and now I know the same university should die in strange accidents at the same time."

"I agree," he said.

"When you went to Algie's funeral, you didn't hear anyone expressing an opinion about his accident, did you? Anyone saying that there was something fishy about it?"

"No. But it wouldn't have been the done thing at a funeral, would it? And besides, it was only family and old college friends who were there. None of the mechanics who worked on his boat who might have known more. I'm afraid it was assumed that what he was doing was dashed risky business and not unusual for a boat to explode."

"That's just the problem," I said. "If someone is orchestrating these accidents he's very clever because all of them could be seen as something to be expected. A car goes over the side of a ravine on a very sharp bend. The driver drives racing cars. Maybe he took it too quickly. A motorboat explodes because the driver is pushing it too hard, or there was a spark and petrol was leaking. A mountain climber loses his grip on a wet rock face and the rope wasn't good enough to hold him. And Smithers with asthma—well, perhaps he should never have attempted to take up swimming with his condition."

"So perhaps they all were accidents," Gussie said. "These things do seem to come in clusters, don't they?"

"Except a man of similar description was at the site of two of them. We know that."

"Another of our Trinity lot, you think? Someone getting revenge on old college mates?"

I shook my head. "I don't think so. He was described as a scruffy Londoner."

Gussie had to smile. "Not too many scruffy Londoners at Trinity. If there were, he'd have been teased like billy-o."

"Oh," I said. "Maybe there's the motive. He went to Cambridge on a scholarship. He was treated differently because he was lower-class. Perhaps all you chaps fell on your feet after university and he hasn't managed to get a good job because of his upbringing and accent. And finally it's all spilled over and he's taking revenge."

"I can't think of anyone who fits your description in my year," Gussie said. "There were several grammar school boys, but they were civilized-enough chaps, even if they did have regional accents, shall we say? I remember one chap from 'Up North.' We did tease him a bit. But he went on to become a barrister and I gather he's doing brilliantly."

I finished my coffee. "I think I have to get Darcy to take me to Cambridge," I said. "There must be something. . . ."

"Good luck," he said. "So how is old Darcy? Enjoying domestication?"

"Absolutely thriving on it. Loves being a dad."

"Of course. You've produced the heir. Well done." He grinned. "I suppose if old Darcy can be snagged and settle down, I should really think about doing it. I say, Belinda's a spiffing girl, isn't she? Lots of fun. Has she got anyone in mind? Do you think she might be interested in a chap like me?"

"Belinda is never short of admirers," I said tactfully, "and I actually believe she does have someone in mind."

"She wouldn't be lured by a very comfortable life, would she?

Lots of lovely money to spend, house on the Riviera if she wanted it?" He had a sweet, hopeful look on his face that made me realize that men also felt insecure and worried about ever finding a marriage partner.

"I'm afraid she's quite well-off," I said. "Her grandmother left her several properties."

"Oh damn. This whole marriage business gets harder as one gets older. A couple of the chaps met someone while they were at college and married right after, lucky devils. They didn't even have to go through the debs' cattle market." He paused, thinking. "That Smithers fellow was one of those. I went to his stag night."

"And he'd lived a happy, blameless life ever since," I said, "until his wife was killed a year ago, and then he died."

"Funny how some families have more than their share of bad luck, isn't it?" he said.

I got up to go and Gussie escorted me to the front door. Monty appeared as if by magic, with my overcoat.

"If anything strikes you about your time at Cambridge that might be relevant to this case, do ring me up and let me know," I said. I fished into my handbag. "Here's my card."

"Eynsleigh Manor. You've fallen on your feet, haven't you?"

"I have," I said. "Both with my husband and with where we live. It belongs to Sir Hubert Anstruther and I'm his only heir. So I'm invited to live there. It's perfect—apart from no central heating."

He chuckled at this. "Give my regards to old Darcy, won't you? And if you can think of a girl who might be desperate enough to want old Gussie, do send her my way."

I headed toward Piccadilly, where I could catch the nearest tube to my station. As I stood waiting to cross the street, a thought shot into my head. Shrimpy Smithers's wife had been killed when she stepped out into traffic because she was French and looked the wrong way. But she had been in England for years when this happened. From my own experience at school in Switzerland, I had found it only took a few weeks before one got used to the traffic being on the wrong side of the road. I felt a chill down my spine. She hadn't looked the wrong way. Someone had pushed her.

Chapter 29

This latest revelation has confirmed to me that I am on the
right path. They were not accidents. Someone had planned
to kill four men. In Smithers's case someone had wanted
to punish him so badly that they had killed his wife first.
I wonder now whether the others had experienced bad
things happening to their family first. This indicates to
me that the killer is a real sadist. Not content to have
them out of the way but wanting them to suffer.
Something really terrible must have happened to him,
presumably at university, to make him so angry that
he hit back in this way. But why now? Why wait all
this time?

I arrived home to find that Darcy was out for the day.

"He asked me to tell you that he had meetings in London, my lady," Mrs. Holbrook said.

"But he'll be home tonight?"

"He didn't say anything about that."

"Then I expect he'll be home," I said.

"Did you manage to see Queenie?" she asked.

"I certainly did. I think she's very grateful to come back, but you know how she is. She tried to act as if she was doing us a favor and that we were really desperate to have her back."

"I do hope you put her straight."

"I attempted to. I told her she was on probation and one little slipup and she'd be out with no reference. I think that sobered her a bit."

"That girl." Mrs. Holbrook shook her head. "I hope we're doing the right thing by bringing her back here."

I hoped so too. I paced around a bit, trying to quell the turmoil I was feeling. It was really frustrating when I was dying to tell Darcy what I had found out and suggest that we go to Cambridge as soon as possible. But I was able to put worries aside the moment I went up to James and he held out his chubby little arms to me. I told Maisie she could have the rest of the day off. She perked up instantly and said she'd pop over to see her mum, who was poorly again. I brought James down from the nursery to play with him in the sitting room. He was growing into such a lovely little chap, so curious, such fun. The dogs joined us and I watched as all three romped on the hearth rug, James tumbling with them and getting lots of doggy kisses. I felt a great wave of gratitude and my thoughts went to Sebastian's mother.

How could I ever bear it if something happened to my son? How did my grandfather bear it when he got the telegram that Uncle Jimmy, for whom James was named, had been killed in the Great War? At this moment I didn't even want my son to go to school one day, certainly not boarding school at seven. Maybe by the time he was thirteen I'd feel differently. Maybe he'd have several brothers by that time and I'd be glad to pack them all off. I laughed, and tickled James so that he laughed too.

We had tea. I took James back to the nursery and fed him his supper and gave him his bath, then tucked him into his cot and sang to him. It was all so sweet that I reconsidered ever getting a nanny. Maisie and I could manage well between us, couldn't we?

Darcy did not come back until I was about to go in to dinner.

"Sorry, old thing," he said, giving me a quick peck on the cheek, "I got held up in meetings. The last one was with the prime minister and one can hardly say 'I have to get home to my wife, so do shut up.'"

I smiled. "What on earth did the prime minister want with you?"

"With me, nothing, but with my boss at the Home Office, and I was there to supply the details. Updates on Nazi Germany, actually."

"Oh, I see. So I don't suppose you'd have time to drive me anywhere tomorrow?"

"Tomorrow? Sorry, no. If you can wait till the weekend I'll be free. Where do you need to go?"

"Cambridge," I said.

"Cambridge? What for?"

I told him everything I had found out. It was the last statement about Shrimpy's wife that made him really interested. "You know, that did cross my mind at the time, but one could hardly say something. Of course she wouldn't have looked the wrong way if she'd lived in London for several years." He looked thoughtful. "So you think that whoever carried out these murders had a trial run with family members first?"

"I wondered if he was so full of rage or revenge that he wanted to punish the men before he actually killed them."

"That does sound like a maniac, doesn't it?" he said. "Maybe you should write out what we know and I'll hand it over to Scotland Yard to see if they want to look into it. I certainly don't want a man like the one you've described finding out you're on his tail."

"How would he know?" I said. "And anyway, if we get that final clue that points to who he might be, of course I'll back off. I don't want to find my car goes off the road someday, or someone tries to harm my family." Even as I said this I found myself in a quandary. Was I taking a risk by pursuing this inquiry? Might I be putting Darcy in danger? And if the killer did have some kind of list of aristocrats whom he planned to kill, might Darcy now be added to it? At least he hadn't been to Cambridge, and that did seem to be the linking factor. I decided I couldn't stop now. I'd be careful, but I had to go to Cambridge and find out.

"I can take the car if you don't need it," I said.

"And have Phipps drive you?"

"I'll drive myself," I said. "Between you and me, I'm a better driver than Phipps. He gets nervous on major roads."

"He does," Darcy agreed. "But I'm not sure I'm happy with you driving all the way to Cambridge. You'll have to cross London."

"I can take the North Circular Road, can't I? And avoid all the city traffic."

"You could, but all the heavy lorries travel that way."

I swallowed, thinking of driving with heavy lorries, but I was not going to show any fear. "I can do it. And if I leave very early in the morning I can be back before it gets dark."

"Wishful thinking," Darcy said. "Why don't you wait until Saturday and then I can drive you?"

Again I was tempted. But I shook my head. "No, I want this thing solved. What if you get a call on Friday that you're needed in Scotland or Sweden?"

Darcy was frowning. "Look, old thing, I'm not happy with you driving all that way. If you must go to Cambridge by yourself, and I can't see why it can't wait, then I'll drive you up to London in the morning—I have to go anyway—and you take the train. It's much quicker and safer than driving on roads you don't know."

"Trains cost money," I said.

"Your safety is worth more to me than anything," he said, making me feel that warm glow. "Now, let's eat. I'm starving. It's been a long, boring day."

"Speaking of eating," I said as we took our places at the dining table, "I saw Queenie today and she'll be coming back to us."

"I don't think I can honestly say that I'm about to dance for joy," Darcy said. "But I suppose you're doing the right thing. As you've said, who else would ever hire her?"

"And at least we'll get proper breakfasts again. I have a great craving for bacon and kidneys."

He looked startled. "You're not pregnant again, are you?"

I was startled too. "Golly, I hope not. I don't think so."

"You never know," Darcy said.

That night I lay in bed thinking about this. What if I was pregnant again? Last time my morning sickness had been so bad that my movements had been severely hampered for several months. And what about the nursery? Maisie was doing a stellar job of looking after James, but two babies? I'd need that nanny.

Chapter 30

I'm excited about today. I really feel that we're getting to the
truth at last. Something must have happened in Cambridge
all those years ago.

Darcy woke me early. The first streaks of gray dawn were appearing on the eastern horizon. I grunted, ready to fall back to sleep.

"Aren't you planning to come up to London with me?" he
asked.

"Oh yes." I had not slept well and fallen into a deep sleep
only in the early hours. I sat up and fished for my slippers. We
dressed and went downstairs, where there was no sign of Pierre,
but Mrs. Holbrook kindly made us a cup of tea.

"You can grab a roll at the station," Darcy said, eager to be off.

I put on my warm overcoat, knowing that the eastern side of the country was often colder than we were in Sussex, and a small fur hat (a pass-on from my mother). I just wished I was as tiny and petite as she was because she did have lovely clothes, all too small for me, except the hat.

Darcy, as always, drove smoothly and fast, negotiating the narrow, windy lanes until we joined the major road leading from Portsmouth to London. When I saw the amount of early morning traffic I was secretly glad that I had been persuaded not to drive. It didn't seem to faze Darcy, and we drove over Westminster Bridge in time to hear Big Ben strike nine. Fifteen minutes later I was at King's Cross, then on a train bound for Cambridge. It only stopped a few times and we arrived in Cambridge before eleven. Brilliant!

I asked for directions and then set off, down Station Road and then along Hills Road to the college. It was a good long walk but I enjoyed that feeling of a university town: students with gowns flying out behind them going past on bikes, gaggles of students walking together, deep in conversation, their arms loaded with books. And I tried to suppress the pang of jealousy that this was never offered to me. Of course I wouldn't have got in, with the scant education I was given. I knew a lot about walking with a book on my head and where to seat a bishop at a dinner table, but precious little about things that could be useful in life.

I came at last to Trinity and stood, gaping a little, admiring that impressive forecourt with its ancient butter-yellow buildings, its chapel on one side and a central gateway. Gussie had said it was the biggest college and it was certainly large. Suddenly I felt overwhelmed. Where did I start? What could I say?

I headed for that entrance, passing droves of students, all males, who looked at me with interest. As I stepped into the gloom I found a porter's office. The porter, ever watchful, spotted a young woman about to sneak into a men's college.

"Where might you be going, miss?" he asked.

"I'm sorry, I need to speak to someone about a man who was a student here a few years ago. Who would know such things and how do I find them?"

"What subject was he studying? His tutor would remember him best, I expect."

"I'm afraid I don't know."

"Is he applying for a position and needs a reference?"

"Not exactly," I said. "Actually it's several students in the same year." I didn't want to tell him any more. "I need to find out where I can trace them now."

"The master's secretary would have admissions lists, but your best bet is the bursar. He always has his nose to the ground and probably knows students better than any of the Fellows."

"Thank you. Could you please direct me to the bursar's office?"

"I'm not allowed to let a young woman wander into the college alone," he said. "If you hang on a minute and let me lock up, I'll take you there myself."

He did so with much formality, then I followed him, coming out into a most magnificent courtyard, so large it almost took my breath away (and I've been to most royal palaces). I tried not to let the porter know I was impressed, but when he said, "I bet you've never seen naught like this, eh?" I felt obliged to reply, "Actually I'm related to the king and I've been to Buckingham Palace on many occasions, but this does rival the palaces."

He nodded as if I'd said the right thing. "And what might be your name, then, miss?"

"It's Lady Georgiana Rannoch," I said, forgetting that I was now Mrs. O'Mara.

His demeanor changed. "Well, my lady, the bursar's office is here, over in New Court. Come along."

We crossed the great court, passed through an archway and found ourselves in another courtyard. The porter opened a door for me and I found myself in a very ordinary-looking office with a typewriter clattering away. A gray-haired woman looked up as we entered.

"Lady Georgiana wishes a word with the bursar, Mrs. Stevenson," the porter said. "She's checking up on some young men who were students here." He gave me a little bow. "A pleasure meeting you, my lady."

As soon as he had gone I told the woman what I wanted. "We don't need to trouble the bursar," she said. "I have all the lists of undergrads right here. Which year were they?"

"I think they would have been admitted twelve years ago," I said, doing rapid math. "Or maybe eleven."

"Let's see, then." She went over to a filing cabinet and riffled around before producing a booklet. "Now. The names you wanted?"

"Inchcliffe," I said. "Sebastian Inchcliffe."

She flicked through it with swift efficiency. "Yes, here he is. London address. Studied classics."

I asked for the other three, then I said, "This is an odd question, but have you been here for a while?"

She laughed. "If you count twenty years as a while, then yes."

"Would you know if there was any type of scandal about that year? Whether anyone was sent down for behaving badly or cheating? Anyone who broke the law in any way?"

She looked at me strangely now. "Not that I can recall," she said. She flicked through the pages. "There were some young men who took their studies less seriously than others. Silly pranks. Drinking. Climbing in late, you know. Maybe came up before a magistrate for borrowing someone's car. But I can't recall. . . ." She stared at me. "Why do you wish to know this?"

I decided to come clean. "I have reason to believe that someone has recently been killing men who were all at Trinity in the same year and staging their deaths to look like accidents. However, we can't find anything that links them since their college days. So I thought there might be something that happened while they were here that has driven one of their classmates over the edge, so to speak."

"Gracious me." She looked startled.

"You can't think of anyone who was a clear outsider? A scholarship boy who had a difficult time, perhaps?"

"I don't think that Herbert Heslop had too easy a time of it," she said. "From a coal-mining family, you know. A bit rough around the edges."

"Would you know where he is now?"

"I certainly would. He studied law and is now a practicing barrister in London. A rising star, they say."

"Oh, I see." The same young man that Gussie had mentioned.

I tried another tack. "You can't remember an incident involving anyone from the town? Someone filing a complaint against college boys?"

She laughed at this. "My dear, townspeople are always complaining. Our students are too loud, leave beer bottles on the street, drive noisy motorcars, don't pay their bills. It's always the same, and probably with good cause. We give them a severe talking-to and make them pay their debts."

As she was saying this I wondered if there had been another type of complaint. One I hadn't considered before. A student seducing a young girl from the town, maybe getting her in the family way. I couldn't quite see why this would make anyone seek revenge right now, but it was worth considering. I tried to phrase it delicately. "I'm wondering about a scandal with a young lady. Unwanted attention to a girl from the town, or . . ."

She gave a sad smile. "That does happen from time to time, but there's not one that I can recall at this moment. Besides, that would have concerned just one young man, not four of them, God forbid."

"I suppose not." I did not want to consider the possibility of that. Instead I tried to think of other questions to ask. "The students themselves. Nobody had an accident while they were here?"

"Just the usual sort of thing. Someone falls while trying to climb in a window and breaks an ankle."

"But nothing serious? Life-threatening?"

"Not while they were here. I did hear of one student who died right after his graduation. That was some sort of accident." She frowned, flipping through the pages again. "Ben Waverley," she said. "That's right. And you know what? He roomed with the Smithers boy his first year."

"Ben Waverley?" I stared at her. "Would you know where he lived?"

"His address during his college days was with his parents in Scotland." She consulted her list. "I can write it down for you, if you like." She tore a piece of paper from a pad and started writing, looking up in the middle. "Might I ask what is your connection to these young men? Are they family members? Is this not a job for the police?"

"Not family members," I said, "but family members or connections to close friends who have asked me to find out more. Nobody would believe that any of the deaths were more than accidents, you see. But none of the accidents made sense. I have been trying to find a link between them, and so far have come up empty, apart from the one fact that they were all at Trinity. So I had hoped you'd point to something while they were here."

"I'm sorry to disappoint you," she said.

"You have given me one item to pursue," I said. "Ben Waverley roomed with Leonard Smithers. It may be a complete shot in the dark, but I can talk to the Smithers family. They live in London and my husband already visited them."

"Ah, so you are married," she said. I realized I had not removed my gloves.

"Yes. I'm now Mrs. Darcy O'Mara." Then I added, in case she thought my husband was beneath me socially, "He's the heir to Lord Kilhenny in Ireland."

"How very nice," she said. "Congratulations. In fact I have

followed news of your family with interest—the king's abdication, of course, but also the rather more colorful life of your mother."

"Yes, indeed," I said. "I am quite the opposite. Happy to be a married lady with a baby."

"I wonder if their lifestyle ever brought them happiness," she said. "I wonder if the new duke of Windsor will find happiness with that woman."

"I shouldn't think so," I said. "I happen to know 'that woman' quite well and I think she had set her sights on being queen. She will now be seriously disappointed."

"There is a saying about making your bed and lying on it, isn't there?" She smiled at me again. I thanked her then and made my exit, also thanking the porter, who was now involved with a student who had lost his keys. I didn't linger but hurried straight back to the station and the next train going back to King's Cross.

Chapter 31

AT THE SMITHERS RESIDENCE, IN LONDON

I'm glad I went to Cambridge, or I'd never have thought of
calling on the Smitherses.

Mr. and Mrs. Smithers lived in a fine house in Hampstead. Everything about it spoke of money and good taste. The manicured
grounds, the Bentley parked in the driveway. It struck me how
sad it must be to have all this and to lose your only son. I rang
their bell and the door was opened by a maid. I had decided, on
the train, that it would be important to speak with Mrs. Smithers.
Darcy, being a man, had chatted with Shrimpy's father. Men
never seem to know as much about their children's lives as
women do and never seem to ask the right questions. I hoped
Mrs. Smithers might know more.

"Might I ask what this is about, my lady?" the maid said, when I handed her my calling card.

"My husband spoke with Mr. Smithers the other day, but there are a couple of things he failed to ask. It is rather important, concerning Mr. Leonard's death."

Her expression grew grave. "Of course. I'll go and find her. She's up in the nursery. The grandchildren are staying at the moment. Please allow me to escort you to the sitting room." She led me into a lovely room, upholstered in neutral-colored silks, with a carpet of greens and browns on the floor and a painting of a Mediterranean scene on the wall over the fireplace. There were vases of daffodils and mimosas on various tables. The fire was gas, not logs, but the room was nice and warm. I sat in one of the armchairs and waited. I heard flustered conversation, then Mrs. Smithers came in. She was wearing a cashmere jumper and matching skirt but she looked harassed.

"Lady Georgiana?" She held out her hand but there was no smile on her face.

"How do you do, Mrs. Smithers? I'm so sorry to trouble you," I said.

"What is this about? Something to do with my son?" She perched on the edge of the chair opposite me.

"First let me say how sorry I am for your loss," I said. "And I'm not sure that I should have come, but I wanted to know if you were familiar with Ben Waverley, who was at Trinity with your son."

Now she did look surprised. "Ben Waverley?" She snapped out the words. "What on earth are you bringing that up for now? At this time? Do you think I haven't suffered enough with- out reminding me of that tragedy?"

"I'm sorry," I said. "I just wanted to confirm that your son was friends with Ben."

"They were college roommates his first year," she said. "And good friends. He was going to be Leonard's best man, you know."

"Was going to be?" I asked.

"You don't know?" She was glaring at me now. "He was killed at Leonard's stag night party. Run over by a motorcycle on their way home."

"I didn't know," I said. I heard my voice shaking a little. "Run over by a motorcycle, you said?"

"After the formal party they did the sort of things silly young men do on stag nights. They went to some disreputable places in the East End, which was quite out of character for Leonard—for most of them, I think. They were walking back to the nearest tube station at two in the morning when a motorbike came fly- ing around the corner, ran into them and knocked Ben over. It ran over his neck and he died instantly."

"How terrible," I said. "Was the driver apprehended?"

"Oh yes. There was a lengthy trial," she said. "Our barrister tried to show that it was a deliberate act . . . that the rider had a resentment of the upper class, but the jury wouldn't go along with that. He only got manslaughter. But at least that was twelve years behind bars. That should be enough to teach him a lesson."

"So he's still in prison?" I asked.

"He must be. It's only eight years since his death. But why

do you want to know about this now? What has it to do with my son?"

"Because I think your son's death might not have been an accident," I said hesitantly. "Tell me, were any of the other men who were walking back with Ben and Leonard possibly Sebastian Inchcliffe, Algie Beauchamps?"

Her gaze was now suspicious. "I believe they were," she said. "None of them Leonard's really close friends, he wasn't the sort who was very social, but he'd invited a lot of Trinity men to his stag party."

"Then I have to say that my suspicion is true," I said. "I believe that this man is no longer in prison but is now killing the other Trinity men who put him there."

"But that's . . . unbelievable," she said.

"Those men I mentioned have all died in the last few weeks, all in so-called accidents," I said. "And a motorcycle was observed at the scene of at least two of them. All of them were killed doing something they loved most."

There was a long silence, punctuated only by the sound of someone playing a child's piano, far up above us. "But he's in prison," she said at last.

"He could have been released early for good behavior," I said. "Do you remember his name?"

"Of course. One never forgets sitting in a courtroom, staring at him. He was Stanley Jones. Some sort of clerk from somewhere in South London. Charlton, I believe."

"Now we finally have something to go on," I said.

"You believe this Stanley Jones murdered my son?"

"I think it's highly possible. Did anyone think to check his medication after his death? What if it had been tampered with?"

"Tampered with?"

"What sort of medication was it?"

"An inhaler for his asthma. That's what he used in emergency situations."

"Was he in a swimming bath at the time?"

"No. He was training for a big open water swim, so he was swimming in a lake near Uxbridge."

"Was he there alone?"

"With his coach. The coach was standing on some kind of dock, timing him. Lenny was on the far side of this lake when he went into difficulties. His coach saw him swim to the shore and grab what looked like his inhaler, then before he could do anything Lenny slipped beneath the surface. The water was quite murky and it took them a long time to find him, by which time he was dead of course. His lungs filled with water and the verdict was death by drowning, which it was."

"I wonder if the coach saw anybody."

"I'm afraid there's a public footpath. People walk their dogs all the time. And there are bushes. It would be all too easy to substitute an inhaler or tamper with it." She shook her head. "I find it so hard to believe. This man has carried a grudge all this time and is now killing all the boys who were with Leonard and Ben?"

"How many were there?" I asked.

"Four others. There were six of them altogether, including Leonard and Ben."

I felt the color draining from my face. "That means there is one still alive, unless this Jones person has already got to him." I leaned closer to her. "We have Inchcliffe, Beauchamps, Warburton-Stoke, Ben Waverley and your son. Do you happen to remember the last man's name?"

She had to think long and hard. "Yes, I think I do. Deveraux. William Deveraux. I didn't know him personally. I didn't really know any of them apart from Ben." She paused, thinking. "If what you say is true, what can anyone do?"

"Find out where Mr. Jones is living now and apprehend him. Also find out where William Deveraux lives and warn him."

"Presumably we have to involve the police. This is definitely a police matter."

"Yes, it is. If we can get them to believe what I've told you. I think they will now. My husband is at the Home Office and has plenty of contacts, so I will hand this over to him. Unfortunately I think it will be a challenge to find the right Mr. Jones. Not exactly an uncommon name. But he did give an address in Tottenham. And the prison may have an address for him."

She reached out now and took my hand. "Do what you can, Lady Georgiana. If someone killed my son, I want him punished."

"I'll do my best," I said. "I'll go straight home and put my husband on the case." I stood up and started toward the door.

"Yes." She nodded, then grabbed my sleeve. "It might be wise not to mention this to my husband until we're sure. He does get so wound up about things. And Lenny's death has hit him very hard. Hit both of us so hard. First Monique and now him, and those poor children with no parents. My daughter and

I are doing our best to see they get a happy home and a good education, but it's not the same, is it?"

I didn't like to tell her what I also suspected, that Leonard's wife's death was not accidental either. I bade her good-bye and made my way back to Victoria Station.

Chapter 32

TUESDAY, MARCH 16

BACK AT EYNSLEIGH

Finally we have something to work on. Now all we have to do is apprehend Stanley Jones and warn William Deveraux.

The train down to Haywards Heath seemed to take forever. I squirmed impatiently in my seat. I couldn't wait to tell Darcy what I had learned. To be truthful I couldn't wait to show Darcy that I had been right all along and I had now pretty much solved this mystery. I didn't telephone Phipps to come and pick me up from the station but took a taxi. It was an extravagance but I simply couldn't wait. Of course the taxi I chose was ancient and driven by a similarly ancient man, so we took the bends at ten miles an hour while I had to bite my lip to stop me from yelling "Faster, faster!"

When we arrived in the forecourt at Eynsleigh I ran up the front steps and burst into the foyer. "Darcy?" I called.

A door opened but it was Mrs. Holbrook, not Darcy, who appeared.

"Oh, my lady, I'm afraid Mr. O'Mara is not home yet," she said. "He did telephone to say he might be very late and for you to dine without him."

I thought of all the swear words I'd like to mutter but restrained myself.

"We did, however, have a new arrival today," Mrs. Holbrook went on. "You'll be quite surprised."

Oh golly. My first thought was that it was my grandfather, but then I remembered he'd said not before the end of the week. Sir Hubert, home from wherever he had been? Then not so pleasant thoughts overtook. Please not Fig again, I found myself praying. Not a new nanny sent from Fig.

"Don't keep me in suspense," I said.

She smiled. "It was none other than the prodigal returning. Queenie, bold as brass. She knocked at the front door—the front door, mind you—and said that Lady Georgiana had begged her to come back and she couldn't let her ladyship down, so she turned down all the other offers and here she is."

"Awful cheek," I said. "I told her she could have her old job back but she was on probation."

"The girl is incorrigible," Mrs. Holbrook said. "She went straight down to the kitchen and almost flung herself into Pierre's arms. He was chopping vegetables at the time and she's very lucky she didn't get sliced. And you won't believe what else.

She said she now wants to wear a white chef's jacket like Pierre wears. She says only skivvies wear aprons."

I sighed. "I'll deal with her in the morning, Mrs. Holbrook. Right now I'm too tired for much except a hot bath and my dinner. Oh, and a visit to my son."

I went up to the nursery and found James sitting on Maisie's lap while she rocked him and sang to him, his thumb in his mouth, his eyes closed. It was such a sweet picture I was unprepared for the wave of jealousy I felt. He was happy on Maisie's lap. Falling asleep in her arms. I knew that I should be grateful that my son was so well loved and looked after, but a stupid voice whispered that I should be doing that, not Maisie.

Maisie tried to get up, then remembered James on her lap.

"Oh, I'm sorry, my lady," she said. "He's had a bad day. He's teething again and his little gums are hurting him so I was rocking him to sleep."

"That's absolutely fine, Maisie. I'm so glad you're looking after him so well," I said.

James didn't stir at the sound of my voice.

"I should put him in his crib before he wakes up again," she whispered, stood up and carried him through to the night nursery. Feeling stupid and superfluous, I went to my bedroom, changed into suitable attire for dinner, although not the long dress that would have been expected in most noble houses, then went down for a sherry before the meal. I ate Pierre's delicious fish in a rich sauce followed by a meringue lighter than air but found it hard to taste either. I think I was emotionally overwhelmed by the past few days . . . the trip to Wales, then Cambridge and finally meeting Shrimpy's mother and learning the truth. But now we knew, I told myself. We knew why those men died. We'd find out where Stanley Jones was imprisoned and where he was now and he'd be rearrested.

Darcy finally came home about ten, just as I was going up to bed.

"Oh, you're back," he said. "I wondered if you'd stay the night in Cambridge."

"No, I found out all I needed to," I said.

"And?"

"And I now know why those four men died, who killed them and why."

To say he looked astonished was an understatement. His eyes opened wide. His jaw dropped open. It was most satisfying. I then recounted the whole story.

"Crikey," he said when I had finished. "So you think it's this man, Stanley Jones, who is now out of prison and taking revenge on those men who put him away?"

"It has to be," I said. "All four were walking down that street after Shrimpy's stag party. Except . . . one of them is still alive. We have to see him and warn him."

"Do you know his name?"

"William Deveraux, so Mrs. Smithers said."

He nodded, digesting this. "William Deveraux. I think I've met him. He's a banker, isn't he? Quite a big deal in the city. But what we have to do first is to find out where Stanley Jones was imprisoned and when and why he was released. I'll get someone onto it tomorrow."

I felt a wave of relief. Someone else would now take over the case. They would find Stanley Jones and all would be well. I got undressed and slept soundly for the first time in ages.

Darcy went up to town early in the morning, while I went into the breakfast room to find kidneys, bacon, kedgeree and all the dishes I had been missing. It was good to have Queenie back. I went down to the kitchen to tell her that I appreciated the breakfast.

"Whatcher, missus," she greeted me, washing up the last of the breakfast pans. "I came back, just like you wanted."

"Queenie, I made it perfectly clear that we brought you back because we wanted to give you a second chance. Believe me, there are plenty of more qualified cooks, but I felt you'd been loyal and deserved to prove yourself again."

"Go on." She grinned at me. "You missed me, I know it."

"Queenie, do you know what incorrigible means?" I asked.

She shook her head. "It means . . . oh, never mind. I just came down to say that the kidneys and bacon were perfect this morning."

"So do I get my chef's jacket, then?" she asked.

"I'll discuss it with Mr. Darcy when he returns," I said. My feeling was that if she had a chef's jacket there would be no stopping her.

"Oh, and Queenie," I said, "until we find a suitable nanny for Master James, I'm afraid that Maisie is occupied with taking care of him. That means that I'm doing without my maid. Someone has to polish my shoes and make sure I have clean clothing. Maybe I can ask you to come back to your old job for a while? When you're not busy in the kitchen, of course."

"See, I knew it," she said, a big grin spreading across her face. "You did miss me. You missed having me as your maid. I knew that girl couldn't do the sort of job I did. Well, Bob's yer uncle, then. I'll be up in your room seeing what you need done as soon as I finish this lot." She paused, thinking. "Perhaps if you want me to be your maid again you can hire a scullery maid to peel the potatoes and do the washing up. If you want to give me time to look after you proper, that is."

"We'll think about it," I said.

She was still grinning. "I can't wait to tell that Maisie that she ain't your maid no more," she said. "I knew she was never as good as what I was."

"Maisie is a very satisfactory maid," I said. "But at this moment she is a full-time nursemaid. I'm sure it will all be sorted out soon enough."

"Just as long as you don't find another nanny like that last old cow," Queenie said. "She wasn't half bossy, wasn't she? And a face that could curdle milk."

"Queenie, have you forgotten you were dismissed for being rude about somebody?"

"Well, yes," she said. "But she was a duchess. I can be rude about a nanny, can't I? She's only a servant like me."

I pictured Nanny Hardbottle's face if she heard herself being compared to Queenie.

"It's not up to you to pass opinions," I said. "Your job is to cook and right now to go up to my room and see which of my shoes needs polishing."

"Bob's yer uncle," she muttered, and off she went.

I went upstairs, retrieved James and took him out for a long walk in his pram. It was good to be in the fresh air and to watch his little face showing excitement at the chickens and newborn lambs. And it stopped me from thinking too much about what Darcy had found out in London. What if he located Stanley Jones by himself and got the credit for cracking this case? Then I reminded myself that the important thing was that Stanley Jones couldn't harm anyone else. He seemed to have no feeling for how many lives he had ruined.

When we came back, I fed James his lunch. He was eating well now, opening his mouth like a little sparrow for food. Then I went down for my own luncheon, but found it hard to eat. I wished Darcy would come home, or at least telephone. I'd just finished my rice pudding and stewed plums when the phone rang.

"Mr. Darcy on the line for you, my lady," Mrs. Holbrook said.

I rushed to the phone, nearly knocking over the plinth with a potted palm on it in the hallway. "Whoops." I righted it just in time and grabbed the receiver.

"You've news?" I asked.

"We found the archives of the trial," he said. "Everything as you described it. Smithers and his friends testified that they were walking in a dark back street near the docks, having been to a pub there. There was no pavement to walk on. Suddenly the motorbike came roaring around the corner. They tried to dodge it but it struck Ben Waverly. The defendant tried to show that they were drunk and staggering and one of them fell under his wheel, but the jury gave the verdict of manslaughter. He was sentenced to twelve years in Wandsworth prison. So I wondered, since you were the one who found all the information, whether you'd like to come up to town and go to Wandsworth prison with me. It seems unfair that you should miss out now."

"Thank you," I gasped. "I'd love to."

"I'll meet you at Victoria," Darcy said. "I took the motorcar, so call for a taxi to the station."

You have never seen anyone get dressed so quickly. That was until I went to put my good shoes on. Only one shoe was on the shelf in the wardrobe. I searched around for the other one, then went down to find Queenie.

"Queenie, did you polish my shoes this morning?"

"Yeah, like you told me to," she said.

"The brown court shoes? There is only one on the shelf. What happened to the other one?"

She frowned. "I'm sure I brought them back up to your room," she said.

"Only one. I've searched and I have to go out in a hurry. Go and look where you were polishing them, quickly."

She stomped off. I waited, fuming with impatience. I could hardly go up to town in my old country brogues. At last she returned, bearing one shoe.

"It fell under the sink," she said. "It might be a bit wet."

I pressed my lips together so I didn't say what I wanted to. I put on the shoes. The right one was quite a bit wet, but I had no choice. Again I found myself questioning whether we did the right thing by rehiring Queenie. Then I went outside and paced the forecourt, waiting for the taxi to arrive. I prayed it wasn't the ancient mariner driving it again. What we needed was more than one motorcar, I thought. But on our income that was out of the question. The Bentley was Sir Hubert's to start with. We owned nothing.

After what seemed an age the taxi came. I caught an express to London and found Darcy at Victoria Station. "Sorry to keep you waiting," I said. "The taxi took a while to come."

"I shouldn't have taken the motorcar to the station this morning," he said. "I didn't think you'd need it."

We went down into the tube station and were soon on our way south to Wandsworth.

"I'm as curious as you are to find out what has happened to this person and why he was released from prison," he said. "Let's hope he has had to register some kind of forwarding address and we can nail him. He must be on parole, after all."

We came out to an afternoon that promised rain. It was a long walk from the nearest tube station, but Darcy, ever protective, held an umbrella over me. At last Wandsworth prison loomed before us, a dirty brown hulk of a building, with towers and a portcullis entrance, quite depressing. But then I suppose prisons are meant to look depressing, aren't they? As a warning against committing crimes. Darcy must have telephoned ahead to let them know we were coming because we were admitted with no fuss and shown to the warden's office.

"Stanley Jones, you say?" he asked. "I remember him well. He was a model prisoner. No trouble ever. In fact he used the time to study and better himself. Took engineering courses."

"So he was released early for good behavior?" I asked.

He looked up, surprised. "Oh no, Mrs. O'Mara. He died, three months ago. It was a bad winter and he caught pneumonia."

Chapter 33

Oh dear. It seems we've got it all wrong. Now what do we do?

Darcy and I stared at each other.

"May I ask what this is about?" The warden noticed our bewildered faces.

"We thought that Jones might have been involved in a series of crimes that happened recently, but he was already dead when they occurred," Darcy said.

"I wouldn't have said that Jones would be involved in any sort of crime," the warden answered. "He always maintained that he was falsely accused. Naturally he felt horrible about killing a man, but his version of the story was that he came around a corner on his motorbike, late at night on a dark street. These young men were strung across the road. He honked and tried to avoid them but they were drunk and staggering. As he steered to go past, one of them fell in front of his wheel. There was nothing he could have done. Then, of course, they were all from influential families. Their barrister for the prosecution made it seem that he was the drunken one, out of control on a motorbike he had just purchased. The barrister even hinted that he bore a grudge against the upper classes, but I don't think that was true. My own opinion is that he was a good bloke, in the wrong place at the wrong time. He would have been eligible for parole next year and I would have fully recommended it."

"Did he leave any family?" I asked.

"He did have children," the warden replied. "He talked about them often. His wife had died when they were very young and he had raised them alone, to the best of his ability. When he went to prison they were put into council care. One was adopted and the other went to an orphanage. He had no contact with them for years, but then the son came to visit a couple of years ago. Apparently the nuns at the orphanage would give him no details of where his father was and it was only when he was out on his own that he located Stanley."

"How old would that son be now?"

"Around twenty, I would say. His father was so pleased to see him after all these years. I gather he had found an apprenticeship working in a repair garage and was doing quite well."

"Do you remember his name?"

The warden frowned. "I believe it was Albert, but I might be wrong."

"And any idea where we might locate him?" Darcy asked.

"He would have signed the visitors' book when he came here," the warden said. "The last time would have been his father's funeral. Such a shame. I think Stanley Jones could have had a good life ahead, but he was never strong and last winter was harsh here."

We thanked the warden and went down to the front counter to check the visitors' book. "Elm Street, Tottenham," I said. "So he did at least sign the visitors' book in Wales with the right town."

"And annoyingly far away on the other side of London," Darcy said. "I suppose it's back to the tube again, unless you're too tired today and we should pursue this tomorrow."

"We have to find him as soon as possible," I said. "He's clearly avenging his father's death and wrongful imprisonment.

"Now we're so close I want to keep going. And he may be coming home after work, so a good time."

It was getting close to rush hour when we finally reached the tube station, and the underground trains were now packed. It was hard to breathe and the unwashed bodies pressed up against me were certainly not appealing. Darcy shot me a sympathetic glance. We came up at Manor House Station and then had to take a bus, equally crowded.

"I suppose we could have found a taxi," Darcy said, "but at this time of day it would have been too slow and cost a fortune."

I tried to nod agreement but at this moment a taxi felt like heaven. At last we found ourselves at White Hart Lane, a major thoroughfare through Tottenham, and set off for Elm Street. The address proved to be a butcher's shop on the corner.

"Do you think he gave a false address?" I asked Darcy.

"Only one way to find out." Darcy went toward the door of the shop. The sign already said *CLOSED*, but there was a light on, someone moving around inside. Darcy banged on the door.

"We're closed. Can't you read?" came the voice from inside.

"This is police business," Darcy yelled back.

This produced a big man in a blood-spattered apron, who opened the door a few inches and peered out.

"You don't look like police to me."

"Special Branch," Darcy said. "We're looking for Albert Jones. Do we have the right address for him?"

"Did have," the man said. "He rented the room above the shop but he moved out a couple of months ago."

"Did he say where he was going?"

"Didn't tell me a sausage," the butcher said, the colloquialism being rather apt. "One day he was there, the next he'd gone. Left a lot of stuff behind. Pots and pans, that sort of thing. The flat was furnished but he left hangers in the wardrobe. Sheets on the bed. Only took his clothes and personal items as far as I could see." He paused. "Is he in trouble?"

"He may be. We need to speak to him about several crimes."

"I thought he was a decent lad until this," the butcher said. "Always paid his rent on time, until when he left. Didn't pay the past week's rent. So if you see him tell him he owes me. Not that he'll pay up, but at least he should know."

"So he gave you no indication of where he might be headed?" Darcy asked.

"We weren't exactly on chatting terms. He paid his rent, said good evening when he saw me and went up the stairs. That's about it, really."

"Do you happen to know where he works?" I asked.

The man looked suspicious that a woman was questioning him.

"I do. He works over at Hears Motors on White Horse Lane toward Hackney. Been there a couple of years."

"And one more thing," I said. "Does he ride a motorbike?"

"He saved up and just bought one for himself. Good-looking bike too. I asked him where he planned to store it, but that was when he scarpered one night. His boss might know more. Sorry I can't help. But I tell you one thing. I never took him for a crook. He'd had a bad childhood. Raised in an orphanage by sadistic nuns, but I thought he'd turned everything around now. Liked his job, doing well. That's a pity."

"We may be wrong," Darcy said. "We won't know until we find him and have a chance to question him."

We came away.

"Probably not much point in going to the garage tonight," Darcy said. "It will be closed now. So we should just head home. Your son will be most annoyed that you've been neglecting him."

"What about you?" I asked. "He misses his father too, you know. But thank heavens that awful nanny forced me to stop nursing him. Otherwise I would still be tied to the house."

"We need to do something about finding a nanny, don't we?" he said as we stood at a bus stop. "It's too much responsibility for a young girl like Maisie to be completely in charge of him."

"I agree," I said, "although she seems very competent with him. But as soon as we've located Albert Jones and settled these crimes, I'll devote myself full-time to finding the perfect nanny . . . or at least a nanny who is perfect for me."

Darcy looked at me and grinned. Fog was creeping up from the marshes, giving the streetlights an eerie glow. Suddenly I wanted to be home, safe with my loved ones. Perhaps I wasn't made to be a sleuth. What I wanted was a safe and quiet life, but it never seemed to happen.

Chapter 34

THURSDAY, MARCH 18
LOOKING FOR MR. DEVERAUX

The next day Darcy took the motorcar and drove up to London. His plan was to join a pal at the Met to go looking for Albert. He suggested it was probably not a good idea to have a woman with him, just in case Jones turned out to be violent. I got on with life at home, pausing to listen for the telephone every ten minutes. I just wanted to hear Darcy say, "We've caught him and he confesses everything." But the day went on and I heard nothing. In the middle of the afternoon Darcy arrived home.

"What news?" I asked.

He shook his head. "We went to the garage and Jones had quit his job recently. He told his boss he wanted a bit of freedom. He'd saved up some money and was going to see the country on his new motorbike. They parted amicably but he hasn't heard from Albert since."

"So he could be anywhere," I said.

"Not quite," Darcy reminded me. "He hasn't managed to get to William Deveraux yet, and I'm absolutely sure he will try to. That's where we should be going. I've found out where Deveraux lives. Do you want to come along?"

"You bet," I said. "Let me go down to the kitchen and tell them they don't have to send up tea." I rushed down, only to be met with a scathing look from Queenie.

"And I just made the cucumber sandwiches too," she said. "Cut the crusts off and all."

"I'm sorry but I have to go with Mr. Darcy. It's important."

I didn't know why I was explaining to a servant. Nobody I knew would do such a thing. I had too much of my grandfather in my blood. Darcy had the motorcar waiting outside and we drove off as fast as the twisty lanes would allow us.

"Where are we going?" I asked. "Is it far?"

"Lucky for us he only lives across the border in Surrey," he said. "Not too far from Guildford. We should be there in half an hour."

Once we reached a major road, we surged forward as if the Bentley had sensed our impatience. William Deveraux had clearly done well for himself. He lived in an impressive pseudo-Tudor house set amid manicured grounds in the middle of Stockbroker Belt. The gates were locked and we had to press a button to be admitted. It was lucky that Darcy had telephoned to warn William that we were coming, or we probably would not have been let in. As it was, a gardener appeared to watch us driving up to the house, and the front door was opened by a footman as we pulled up.

"Mr. Deveraux will see you in his study," the footman said and accompanied us through a foyer and down a corridor into a room overlooking the back lawns and a swimming pool. There was a tennis court to one side, and an orchard beyond. The garden must have looked lovely in summer, but at this time of year it had a rather forlorn appearance. William Deveraux was sitting at an impressively large mahogany desk. He rose when we entered and he came toward us, hand outstretched.

"Lady Georgiana, Mr. O'Mara, how very nice to meet you." We shook hands.

"I believe we met years ago when we were doing the rounds of the debs' balls," Darcy said.

"Your name is certainly familiar to me," William Deveraux said, "but to tell you the truth I was more interested in the fillies at the time. I was searching for my future mate, you know, not playing the field like most of the other chaps."

"Like me," Darcy said. "It took a woman like Lady Georgie to make me settle down." He turned to me and winked.

"And did you find your future mate?" I asked as he ushered us toward two leather chairs.

"I did indeed," he said. "I must say I did rather well in all aspects. Winnie is a marvelous person, a terrific hostess and what's more she's American. Her father is in railroads so the infusion of cash has certainly come in handy." He gave an embarrassed grin. "My father has had a tough time keeping the old pile going. We've an estate in Kent, you know. Trowbridge Hall. It was pretty much falling down around us until Winnie's fortune restored it. We'll inherit one day, of course."

"Do you have children?" Darcy asked.

"Oh rather." He beamed now. "Two sons. Geoffrey and Adam. The light of my life. Such fun, inquisitive little boys."

He reached and picked up a photograph in a silver frame. Two skinny boys in bathing suits were sitting on a rock, the older with dark hair flopping over his forehead, wearing spectacles and looking serious, while the younger gave a grin showing a missing front tooth.

"Geoff is off at boarding school at Fernlea Park nearby. We see him at weekends because Winnie misses him so much. Adam will follow next year." He paused. "Look here, can I offer you something to drink? Coffee at this hour?"

"There is no need," Darcy said. "We're sorry to bother you, but something rather strange and alarming has come up and we wanted you to be forewarned and prepared."

"I say. That's a little unsettling. Do you mind elaborating?"

Darcy looked at me, giving me the go-ahead to speak. "Do you see any of your Cambridge friends these days?" I asked.

He looked surprised at this. "Not really," he said. "Once you become a family man you lose touch with the gay young bucks. I get the occasional Christmas card or bump into one of them at my club in London."

"You remember Shrimpy Smithers?" I asked.

"Shrimpy? Yes. I do remember him. He wasn't a particular friend, but we were at Trinity together. The last time I saw him was at his wedding. He got married soon after we came down from Trinity. Married a French girl who was studying there. He had a big wedding in London, at the Catholic church in Mayfair. I can't remember what the name was."

"The Church of the Immaculate Conception," Darcy said. "Otherwise known as the Farm Street Church."

"That's right." William nodded.

"We got married there ourselves."

"Oh, so you're also Roman Catholics?" There was a hint of disapproval in his voice.

"I'm a good Irish boy," Darcy said. "My father is Lord Kilhenny."

"I see." He paused. "So why this interest in my Cambridge past?"

Darcy looked to me again. "I believe you attended Shrimpy's stag party the night before the wedding?" I paused. "And after the party you were walking down a dark street with several friends when—"

"When some damned fool came at us on a motorbike," William said. "Ran straight into poor old Ben Waverley at speed, knocked him down and drove over his neck, killing him. Awful business. The brute got away with manslaughter, but they gave him twelve years, I believe. He'd still be in prison."

"He's dead," Darcy said. "He died of pneumonia three months ago."

"Good riddance," William said. "So what exactly have you come to see me about?"

"There were four other men with you, besides you and Ben, on that street that night," I said. "Sebastian Inchcliffe, Shrimpy, Rupert Warburton-Stoke and Algie Beauchamps."

Deveraux considered this for a moment, then nodded. "That's right. Pure coincidence that it was those chaps. We were all heading for the same tube station."

"They have all died very recently, in what appeared to be accidents," I said. "But we now know that they were not accidents at all. These men were cleverly and deliberately killed."

William was frowning now. "And you think I might be next?"

We nodded.

"But wait. You said this bloke on the motorbike died in prison."

"He did. But we believe his son is carrying out vengeance on his father's behalf."

"Vengeance that his dad went to prison for killing someone? The bloke had been drinking and clearly had a chip on his shoulder about upper-class boys who didn't have to work."

"That's not how he saw it," Darcy said. "The man always protested he was innocent. He said you six were blind drunk, staggering across the road. He sounded his horn at you but as he went to drive past, Ben fell right in front of his wheel. He had no time to stop."

William paused. "Well, I suppose we were all soused out of our minds," he said. "But the judge was more inclined to believe men of our sort of background. So you think the son is killing us off, one by one?"

"We believe so. Unfortunately we have no proof, only a lot of circumstantial evidence. So we came to you to warn you to be vigilant and also to see if we can set a trap for this chap."

"How do you plan to do that?"

Again Darcy turned to me. "The others were all killed doing something they were passionate about, also something that came with danger attached. Sebastian drove fast cars and went off the road into a ravine. Algie was racing speedboats. Rupert was climbing and the rope broke, and Shrimpy had just taken up open water swimming. All of their deaths were deemed to be accidents and it's impossible to prove otherwise. So you are the only one still alive."

William frowned. "Well, I certainly don't do anything risky like that. I'm a boring sort of chap. I play golf and tennis and bridge. We go on holiday to the Continent. I go to Geoffrey's school to watch him play sports. That's my life, pretty much."

"Tell me," Darcy said, "have any strange things happened to you, recently? Any near accidents?"

"I can't say. . . ." he began; then he stopped. "I did get a flat tire coming over the Hog's Back the other day. But that was just annoying. I'd stopped right before, at the bottom of the hill, to have a pint at the pub there."

Darcy looked at me and a glance passed between us. "So someone could have stuck a nail in your tire while you were inside the pub?"

"I suppose so, but flat tires happen, don't they?"

"Any other incidents?" Darcy asked.

"Not really. There was that fire in the chimney, but that was attributed to a bird's nest that had fallen down. And it was easily put out."

"What about your wife?" I asked. "Has she had any strange accidents recently?"

Again I could see the wheels turning in his head. "She did

have a near miss a few weeks ago," he said. "Remember there was a big snowstorm. She came out of the house and shut the front door rather forcefully and an icicle fell off the roof and just missed her. But that was a freak of nature. Nobody could have been hiding on the roof to make it fall." And he actually laughed.

"Shrimpy's wife was killed when she stepped off the curb," I said. "It was claimed she looked the wrong way because she was French but she had lived in this country for ten years."

"Good God." Deveraux looked startled now. "So you think it was the same person? Wanting to kill a loved one first? Wanting to make the bloke suffer?"

"It's possible," I said.

"The other accidents have all happened in the last weeks," Darcy said, "so one can assume that he'd like to get rid of you as quickly as he can. You haven't spotted a young man on a motorcycle hanging around your neighborhood, have you?"

William Deveraux frowned. "I can't say I have. This house actually has good security. When you are a banker you need to protect yourself from cranks. As you saw, you can't get in unless the gate is opened for you. And my gardeners are quite vigilant."

"Mr. Deveraux," I said, "do you have anything planned in the near future that could include an element of danger or surprise?"

Again he considered. "I've been invited to a pheasant shoot. Not something I usually do. I personally don't see any need for unnecessary killing, but this is a major client of the bank and he's invited a couple of us, so duty calls."

Darcy glanced at me. "When is that?"

"Two weekends from now," Deveraux said. "Next weekend

we'll be at Geoffrey's school as usual. There's a big cross-country meet and he'll be running. He's really good. He'll probably be leading the pack as usual." His face displayed the pride.

"I think the pheasant shoot might be just the sort of thing our man is looking for if he can't get you some other way," Darcy said.

"That's right," I agreed. "We were at Sandringham a couple of years ago when someone managed to pull off a murder and make it look as if the person was shot by accident. Everyone is so focused on the birds, you see."

"So you think I should not go?" William glanced up anxiously.

"On the contrary," Darcy said, "I think you should go. You should even let it be known that you are going, just in case this man hasn't heard about it. And we will provide backup, hoping to catch him red-handed."

"Oh, I see." He had turned a little pale. "So I will be bait."

"That's right. But don't worry. We will literally have your back."

"That's reassuring, I hope." He gave a nervous chuckle.

"Not just us," Darcy said. "I'll get Special Branch Scotland Yard involved."

"Then let's hope this chap turns up and we can nab him." Deveraux ran his hand anxiously through his hair. I could appreciate how he felt. Being offered as bait is not fun.

Chapter 35

FRIDAY, MARCH 19
EYNSLEIGH

Now we are so close I'm really hopeful that we'll catch Albert Jones. I think one gets a taste for killing. Once you have killed a person, the second and third murders are a piece of cake. You lose all feeling for humanity.

Darcy went up to London early on Friday morning to arrange everything with Scotland Yard. He also planned to talk to the owner of the estate who was hosting the shoot. I was excluded from these negotiations and was relegated to the role of wife, mother and homemaker. I put my energy into the nanny search, wondering if I should go up to London and face those agencies again. Before I could do this, Belinda telephoned.

"Georgie, I have to talk to you," she said. "I've had a bit of a shock."

"What is it?" My mind went immediately to family members being killed.

"My maid, Trudi," she said. "Georgie, I've been harboring a German spy."

"Golly," was all I could think of saying. "How did you find out?"

"I became a bit suspicious when I sensed that she had been through my drawers. Of course a personal maid goes through all her employer's clothing, but it was things like papers on my desk being moved, or the items in my jewelry box. Nothing taken, you understand. But then once when she thought I was out I heard her telephoning someone, speaking in German. My German isn't wonderful, but I heard her say, 'They have no idea.' And then apparently the other person asked her to go down to Eynsleigh again because I heard the word 'O'Mara.' They were interested in Darcy. So I sent her out shopping and searched her room. I found a gun, Georgie. A Luger. And what looked like notes on various people and places. When I looked up the words to translate one note it said 'little or no defense.'"

"Gosh, Belinda, so what did you do?"

"Well, I was rather afraid to confront her, so I thought I'd ask Darcy. He'd know the right thing."

"I'm afraid he's out today, but I can certainly tell him when he comes back. In the meantime, why don't you set a trap for her?"

"A trap? How?' Her voice sounded a bit shaky.

"Maybe write something on a piece of paper and leave it in plain sight. A letter maybe. Say something like did you know that Cousin Felix is now working at the secret weapons factory in Barking. See if she takes it or copies it."

"Crikey. That sounds very . . . spy-like."

"I thought you wanted to practice being a spy. This is your big chance. Don't do anything silly, but you want to catch her at it. Then Darcy or someone he works with can confront her and deport her."

"Oh damn," Belinda said. "Then I'll be without a maid again and have to start from square one."

"I'm still looking for my nanny," I said. "We can do the rounds of the agencies together. It's less intimidating with two of us."

"I think I've lost my faith in these agencies," Belinda said. "Sending me a German spy!"

"You can't blame the agency. She obviously made up good references."

"I suppose so. So you think I should act normally and say nothing?"

"Definitely say nothing. She might be dangerous."

"Gosh, yes. I thought she wasn't what she claimed to be. There were things any proper maid would know that she didn't."

"Absolute cheek," I said. "Those Germans. Sending maids over here to spy on people. What do they hope to gain?"

"Perhaps they are really planning for war in the future," she said.

"Golly, I hope not. My mother is still there."

"You can't persuade her to come home?" she asked.

"She adores Max and she adores being adored. Hitler is quite charmed with her, so I gather."

"Oh, Georgie. That's awful. Let's pray there will be no war. The last one was ghastly, wasn't it? And so futile. Nothing gained."

There was a pause, then Belinda said, "So what news on your end? Are you any further ahead with catching the man who killed Rupert?"

"Yes, we are, actually. We're setting a trap for him at this moment. At least, Darcy is at Scotland Yard, organizing it."

"Do we know who he is and why he's doing this?"

"Yes to both. But I'd rather not explain it over the phone. Just in case someone could be listening. Come down when the business with Trudi is finished and I'll tell you the whole story." I paused. "Oh, and tread carefully, Belinda. We don't know how dangerous she might be."

"Thanks a lot." She laughed. "Don't worry. I'll be the cool, collected spy catcher."

"And when you've caught her, come and stay."

"All right," she said. "But I don't want to be away from London for too long, because things are going rather well with Charlie. You know I mentioned him. . . . He was Rupert's climbing partner."

"Oh, so it's Charlie now, is it? Last time it was Charles and he was rather quiet and reserved."

"Well," Belinda said. "I've seen him a few times and he's quite an interesting chap. Really witty and he's traveled all over the world and done all sorts of interesting things like working on a sheep station in Australia and digging for diamonds in

South Africa. He's a younger son, you see. His brother will inherit the estate and the title."

"Title?"

"His father is an earl. Charlie is so glad he won't get stuck with the very large estate."

"So how is he supporting himself now? Does he get family money?"

"Some. Enough, I think. But he also writes books about his travels and they sell quite well."

"I'm glad for you, Belinda. But is Jago really out of the picture?"

"I think he is. I think we've both moved on," she said, and I could detect a note of sadness in her voice. "If I'd really wanted that I should have not gone off to France. So maybe in my heart I wasn't convinced that it would work for us."

"Well, don't let this one get away if you think he's right for you," I said.

"Thank you, Auntie Georgie." Belinda laughed. "Actually I've come to really envy you and Darcy and your home and family. I think that's what I want now."

"Come down and tell me all about it," I said.

We said our good-byes and I hung up the receiver. I couldn't wait to tell Darcy about Trudi. Then I realized something. Queenie had been the one who suspected her all along. "There's something about that woman that's not right." That's what she had said. Good old Queenie. Perhaps she did have her uses after all.

I went upstairs to James. He was totally absorbed, stacking blocks. I watched him with great pride. My son. I could well understand how William Deveraux had said his boys were the light of his life. James was the light of mine.

I couldn't wait for Darcy to come home. How could I not have a number where I could reach him in London? It was so frustrating. When he finally came home about eight that night I was waiting to pounce on him in the front hall.

"So you'll be pleased to know that my contacts at Scotland Yard did listen to me and are happy to supply men for the pheasant shoot next week."

"That's good news. I wouldn't feel up to tackling someone where guns were involved."

"Georgie, you wouldn't be doing the tackling!" He looked horrified.

"Maybe not, but I'd want to be there. I'm the one who did all the spadework."

"I agree," he said. "And you should be there. Just not tackling. Now, am I in time for dinner?"

"You are. The gong should go any minute. But I've something else to tell you. Something much more up your alley."

"Really?" He was looking suspicious.

Then I told him all about Belinda and her maid. "And the interesting thing," I concluded, "is that Queenie suspected her all along. She told me there was something not quite right with the maid. I thought it was just that she was foreign, but no. She saw through her, Darcy. So it's good to have her back with us."

"In case any more German spies try to infiltrate Eynsleigh?" He looked amused now.

"You never know. This woman was heard to mention 'O'Mara.' Who knows what she managed to see on your desk?"

Darcy shook his head. "It would have been at the most the number of pigs and cabbages sold. I have been in this business too long to leave anything incriminating or dangerous around. But it would be interesting to know what she had tried to look at."

At that moment a gong sounded farther down the hall.

"Dinner is served," I said. All tensions were forgotten for a moment as we walked to the dining room.

॥⁄ℇ

ALL EVENING I had been battling with an uneasy feeling. I supposed it was the thought of catching Albert Jones at a pheasant shoot, or maybe it was Belinda's maid being a German spy. Either way it still lingered as I undressed and got into bed. Darcy joined me and I snuggled up against him, waiting to feel calm and safe in his arms.

I'm so lucky, I told myself. I have such a wonderful husband and son. A picture of James swam into my head, sitting on the rug in his nursery, patiently stacking blocks, an expression of extreme concentration on his little face. So precious. So wonderful. I couldn't bear it if anything ever happened to him. I heard William Deveraux's voice in my head, talking about his sons. "The light of my life." And I sat up abruptly, pulling the covers off Darcy.

"What on earth's wrong?" he asked.

"I just realized," I said.

"What?" he repeated.

"In all the other cases, Albert Jones struck at something that meant the most to those men: Sebastian's cars, Algie's boats, Rupert when climbing. . . ." I could see Darcy staring at me as he listened. "William Deveraux is not passionate about pheasant shoots. He doesn't want to be there. He is only attending to appease a client."

"And?" Darcy asked, really focusing on me now.

"He is passionate about his sons. I realized that when I was watching James earlier today. He said they are the light of his life. And his son Geoffrey is the star of the cross-country meet. If Albert Jones is going to strike at all, it might be at William's son, not William himself. And what better time to strike than the cross-country race meeting tomorrow."

"Good God." Darcy sat up too. "You might well be right. And it's Friday night and I have no way of contacting the blokes at Scotland Yard before tomorrow morning."

"Then we have to go ourselves," I said. "As far as we can gather, Albert Jones is not dangerous himself. He's not likely to be carrying a gun. He doesn't know that we suspect him. He wants all the deaths to look like accidents."

"You're right," Darcy said. "So you think something will happen to William's son during that race?"

"Either to William or his son," I said.

"But cross-country races are five or ten miles," Darcy said. "I participated in some myself when I was at prep school. How can anyone shadow him for the entire race?"

"How are your running skills?" I asked.

He shot me a horrified look. "I haven't run since I left Downside. Not five miles anyway. You've fed me far too well and I am not in that sort of condition."

"Should we suggest that they remove Geoffrey from the race, then?" I asked.

"No. On the contrary. It's our one chance of catching this

despicable man. I'll try to alert local police in the morning, get there early enough to see a map of the route and then station ourselves at points where something could happen."

"What do you think he might do on a cross-country course?" I asked.

"I've no idea," he said. "It's not like driving a motorcar into a ravine, or blowing up a boat. Presumably it will be a route through the countryside, not too hilly for young boys."

"So nowhere really to stage an accident?"

"It may go through woods," Darcy said. "Areas where the spectators can't see what's going on. That's where he'd strike, presumably."

"Kidnap the boy, do you think? Or even stab him?"

"I don't see how. Even if he's ahead of the other boys, they'd be hot on his heels and see what was happening."

I could tell Darcy was now in full action mode. "I have to decide where to station myself and any local police I can round up."

"And me? Where should I station myself? Am I not included in this?"

He was frowning at me. "Georgie, it's not the sort of thing to involve a woman."

"You agreed he wasn't dangerous himself."

"Yes, but there is no way you could tackle him if you spotted him."

"I could sound the alarm," I said. "I could hinder him, intercept him. . . ."

"And if he was desperate enough to pull a knife on you or even knock you to the ground? I couldn't agree to that."

"But I have to come," I said. "I've been the one driving this investigation so far. I was the one who proved to you that the accidents were in fact staged. I need to be there. If necessary I'll watch the parking place to see if any motorbikes turn up."

"I suppose so," he said, reluctantly.

"Do you think we should telephone William Deveraux?" I asked.

He thought, then shook his head. "Maybe not. He and his wife might decide to pull his son out of the race and then we'd never nab this man."

"We still have to consider that Jones might be aiming at Deveraux, not his son."

Darcy frowned again. "What could he do if he wasn't going to shoot or stab him, both of which would obviously be murder?"

"He might be desperate."

"I still say we do not tell him. Let him continue to be the bait. It's our one chance to catch Albert Jones. After this his killing spree will be over. He can change his name, go to South America and effectively get away with murder."

"You're right," I said. "Maybe you can get a message to someone you know at Scotland Yard in the morning before we leave. If Jones takes off on his motorbike, it would be nice to have a police car chasing him."

"I'll do what I can," Darcy said. "Let's go to sleep. We have to be up early."

He pulled me down beside him and wrapped his arms around me.

"I don't know if I can sleep," I said. "It's horrible to think that one man can take lives so easily, can be so eaten up with revenge."

"From what we hear, he had a horrible childhood that undoubtedly scarred him," Darcy said. "Losing his father when he was ten, then being in an orphanage with nuns who wouldn't allow him any contact with his dad. Then to find out that his father was probably innocent. It's enough to make anyone angry and bitter."

"You're being very philosophical," I said.

"I'm not just a handsome devil, you know," he said. "I'm still waters that run deep."

"Irish blarney," I said, wriggling to give him a fake punch. Then he grabbed my wrist, and tensions, plans, philosophy were forgotten.

Chapter 36

SATURDAY, MARCH 20

AT FERNDALE HOUSE SCHOOL

Maybe today we'll have solved this and we can breathe easy
again. I confess to being a bit scared. What if I let this man
slip through my fingers? We don't even know what he looks
like.

Rooks were cawing madly in the big beech tree as we left the
house in the early morning. Mist clung to hedgerows and fences
as we drove through the country lanes. It was promising to be a
beautiful spring day. There were daffodils and primroses blooming and baby lambs in the fields. I'd liked to have paused to
enjoy this, but every fiber of my body was tense. Fortunately the
school was only a half hour's drive away over in Surrey. Our first
stop was at the nearest large police station, where Darcy had

some trouble convincing them to lend us plainclothes officers. He had to show them some sort of warrant card, which seemed to impress them. I've no idea what it said, but he disappeared into an inner office and came out shaking hands with the duty sergeant. From there it was a short hop to the school. We drove up an impressive driveway to what looked like a Georgian house. The words *Ferndale School* were painted discreetly to one side of the gate. At this hour there was no sign of activity, the boys presumably being at breakfast. We were taken to the headmaster in his private quarters. He too was having breakfast and none too pleased to be receiving guests. When he heard what Darcy had to say he was even less happy.

"Utter drivel," he said. "Tommyrot. Nonsense. Is this some kind of stunt?"

"Not at all, sir," Darcy replied calmly. "All we can tell you is that this man has targeted five Cambridge graduates who put his father in prison. Four of the five have died recently in what seemed to be accidents. Geoffrey Deveraux is the son of the last surviving member."

The headmaster was a nervous, twitchy sort of fellow. As he listened his eyes bulged and his mustache went up and down with his Adam's apple.

"Let me get this straight. You really believe that this maniac plans to strike during the cross-country race today?"

"Possibly," Darcy said.

"It would make sense," I added. "He has killed the other men doing something they were passionate about. William Deveraux is passionate about his sons."

The man looked at me as if I were a worm who had just dared to speak to him. "So are you trying to tell me that this man will attack Deveraux or his son?"

"We've no idea," Darcy said before I could answer. "He did kill one man's wife before killing him."

"Then for God's sake why is this not a matter for the police? Why is Scotland Yard not here? And who might you be?"

"There will be plainclothes police stationed along the route today," Darcy said, "and as for me, I usually work with the Home Office and bigger fry than this, but we have a personal connection to these men and inside knowledge that the police don't have."

The headmaster's eyes were still bulging. "If what you say is true, then we must cancel the race," he said. "I've got boys from three schools coming here, and their parents. I can't be responsible for putting them in danger."

"This is our one chance to catch this man," Darcy said. "I would ask you not to cancel. Nobody will be in danger except for William Deveraux and his son, and we're going to try our best to make sure they are watched. Ideally we'd like to catch this Albert Jones in action."

The headmaster shook his head emphatically. "I don't know. Sounds like a rum deal to me. I don't know what the world is coming to. Parents send their boys to me for a good, safe education."

"Then let's hope we catch this man today and need not worry anymore," Darcy said. "Now, do you have a plan of the course?"

"My games master has it," the headmaster said. "Down at the gymnasium. He should be there by now, making sure everything is in order."

"Then we'll go and speak to him," Darcy said.

As we turned to go I asked, "By the way, has a man on a motorbike been seen on school grounds?"

"Man with a motorbike?" He glared at me. "Outsiders are not permitted. He'd be quickly escorted off the premises. My grounds-keepers are most diligent. They walked the entire course yesterday, just to make sure there were no hazards like fallen branches."

We left him and made our way to the gymnasium.

"I don't see any reason to mention our real motive for being here," Darcy muttered to me. "We don't want to start a panic or to have him call off the event. Just follow my lead."

We spotted the games master coming out of the building with a clipboard. Darcy went up to him. "Hello," he said. "We're from the press, sent to cover this event. Do you have a minute?"

"Press, eh?" The games master looked quite pleased. "Well, yes, I suppose this is quite an important race around here."

"So we have a few questions," Darcy said. "Do you have a map of the course?"

"I do. It's going up on the easel here." He led us to a blackboard. "Quite a simple route. Starts behind the gymnasium here, past the rugby field, then through that bit of woodland, across that field, then looping back through more woodland, dropping down to cross a stream—"

"A stream?" I asked. "Isn't that dangerous?"

He laughed. "When I say stream, it's more of a trickle unless we've had a big storm. No more than ankle-deep, I assure you.

Then up the other side, more woods, and the sprint for home across the cricket pitch and finish in front of the pavilion."

"So that's the only water feature?" I asked. Darcy glanced across at me.

"Apart from one last low-lying area which is always a bit boggy and has a large puddle across the path." He grinned. "I wouldn't actually call it a water feature."

"Jolly interesting," Darcy said. "Is it an easy path through the woods? Not lots of tree roots and things?"

"Oh no. A bridle path actually. Quite easy going underfoot. Soft, sandy soil. Perfect for runners. We'll set some good times today."

"I understand that you've a boy called Deveraux from this school," I said. "Are you hoping for a good time from him?"

"Geoff Deveraux?" The man's face lit up. "Oh rather. Great little runner. If he is true to form he'll leave the others in the dust. Of course Compton School has got that big kid, but I don't think he's so good over five miles. Oh no. We're hoping for good things from Geoff Deveraux."

We left him as soon as was polite. Darcy went off to meet with the policemen, who had just arrived. We checked the car park but saw no sign of a motorcycle. Darcy had words with the groundskeepers who were putting up chairs and signs. Then we walked the last part of the course.

"No point in bothering with the first mile or so," Darcy said. "Geoffrey won't have separated himself from the pack by then. It's the last couple of miles or so that are important." We walked together, following the bunting along the route. Every now and then there were bright arrows marking the way.

"Jones could possibly turn one of those arrows to direct Geoffrey off the route," I said.

Darcy nodded. "Possibly. This will only work if he really has separated himself from the pack. If he's among other boys, then Jones can do nothing."

"And Geoff's father? What could Jones do to him?"

"One of the police is going to be standing with him. And he'll be in a crowd of spectators, so I can't see what could happen to him."

The course ended at the cricket pavilion after it emerged from the last of the woods. Where the pristine lawn met the woods there was a dip in the terrain, a drainage ditch, creating the boggy area the games master had described with the large puddle across the path. On the far side of this the path disappeared into a thick stand of birch trees and bracken. It would be possible for someone to keep hidden here, I thought, and mentioned this to Darcy.

"We'll have someone stationed at the edge of the woods," he said. "And we'll be checking everyone who comes onto school grounds."

We walked into the woods. After a few yards the path turned and we were among the trees. Our footsteps were completely muffled by the soft soil of the path, and all around was an eerie silence. I found myself looking around nervously, as if I sensed danger, but saw nothing. When a crow or rook gave a harsh call over our heads, I jumped and grabbed Darcy. When we emerged from the woodland into a plowed field, we heard the hum of traffic and realized that the field bordered a road, with the footpath going along the edge of it, beside a hedgerow and a line of old oak trees. The bank and hedge were high enough that we couldn't see the traffic on the road. All kinds of bad scenarios rushed into my head.

"Darcy, what if Albert Jones pulls up on his motorbike, grabs Geoff and kidnaps him?"

Darcy examined the hedgerow. "There's only one gap where the footpath enters into the field down there." He hurried toward it.

"Or Jones changes the arrow. Geoff runs out onto that road and is hit by a car. It seems quite busy."

Darcy frowned. "This does seem to be the one weak spot, doesn't it? The one place he can easily gain access to the boys running past. I might station myself nearby, just in case."

We had reached the gap in the hedge and Darcy peered out. "Nowhere to leave a motorbike around here," he said. "But I still think it would be wise for me to take this stretch of the race. It's close enough to the finish that Geoffrey might be ahead."

"And where should I station myself?" I asked.

"With all the other spectators," he said. "And before you complain, you can keep an eye on the car park from there."

"I should think that Albert Jones would stand out a mile among all the posh parents," I said. "Easy enough to spot if he dares to come onto school grounds. This road here seems more likely."

By the time we had returned to the school grounds, the boys were starting to come out. The runners were already in their racing singlets and shorts, their blazers or jumpers draped over their shoulders in the chilly air. I picked out Geoffrey Deveraux from his photograph—lanky, skinny, looking earnest in his round spectacles. Then he muttered something to the other boys and they all laughed. Geoff laughed too, revealing a cheeky little-boy face. My heart lurched that anything bad might happen to him. We'd do everything we could to prevent it, but would it be enough?

Other boys were emerging from the school buildings in twos and threes, and as we watched, a coach came up the drive, bearing the runners from another school. Soon they were joined by a second coach and parents started to arrive. I scanned the car park carefully, but it seemed unlikely that Albert Jones would be brazen enough to ride his motorbike onto school grounds. It seemed the most likely that the spot Darcy was guarding was where he could strike. But might he notice Darcy and thus not dare to act? I felt all my muscles tense. We were dealing with a man who had killed four other men rather cleverly. Was I wrong to suspect that he'd try to harm William Deveraux's son, and here, today? Thinking about it now, the pheasant shoot next week seemed far more likely, and men from Scotland Yard were taking care of that.

It seemed to take forever before the runners lined up for the start of the race. Darcy was nowhere to be seen. The car park only held the two coaches and posh parents' cars. I spotted William Deveraux talking to the games master. A pretty dark-haired woman stood beside him, giving a carefree laugh. William went over and ruffled Geoffrey's hair in an affectionate gesture. I moved away, around the gymnasium, so that he wouldn't see me. I didn't want to arouse any suspicion.

"On your marks!" the starter shouted. Then a pistol went off.

I jumped at this and found myself checking both Geoffrey and his father, in case the shot had been real. But the boys took off with some jostling for position and William stepped forward, clapping and cheering. I heaved a sigh of relief. First step accomplished. The boys disappeared across the school fields and I saw them enter the first stretch of woodland. Now there was nothing to do except wait. The parents were now wandering over to the finish line on the other side of the cricket pitch. I hung back and walked over to the cricket pavilion, which was at the edge of the woods, near the finish line. I decided to take up a position where I could see the runners emerging from the woods. I couldn't spot any policemen standing there, but I supposed by the time they came out of the woods, they would be observed by the parents and thus be safe.

Those of you who know me do know that I am prone to clumsiness on occasion. As I walked behind the cricket pavilion, my foot caught on something and I tripped, stumbling into the longer grass at the edge of the field. "Damn," I muttered as I stood up, embarrassed that anyone might have seen me and noticing grass stains on my skirt. But it seemed I was still out of sight of the spectators. I looked down to see what might have tripped me up. A rock, maybe. Then I saw a string or cord going through the grass. I bent down to examine it. A cable or wire of some sort. I traced it back and saw that it came from a window at the back of the cricket pavilion. Intrigued now, I started to follow it through the grass. It was black and therefore invisible against the dark soil. I followed it until it went into the puddle in the ditch, but it didn't seem to come out the other side.

What on earth?

Then suddenly I understood. I felt a great rush of fear. It was an electric cable. If Geoffrey came out of the woods first, he'd step into that water and get an electric shock that might kill him. His legs would already be wet from running through the stream. But what if Geoffrey wasn't first? Would one of the other runners be electrocuted? I didn't dare touch the cable myself, not knowing that much about electricity. I looked around to find someone to tell, but there was nobody within sight. I could stand here, of course, and warn the runners as they came out of the woods. But what if they didn't listen? What if one of them plowed ahead into the water? What if a group of boys came together—would several be killed?

I knew I had to do something, but I wasn't sure what. I hesitated, not knowing if I should stay put to warn the boys or find someone to tell about this. Then I thought, the cricket pavilion! I could find the cable and unplug it. As simple as that. I had no idea how much time I had. I hurried back, following the line of cable to that narrow window. Obviously I couldn't climb in that way. I ran around to the front of the pavilion. The crowd was all facing away from me, eyes fixed on the woods. Should I tell someone? But there might not be time to explain. Then I saw the games master. I ran over and grabbed his arm.

"Quickly. Come with me. Emergency," I gasped.

He looked at me suspiciously as I dragged him away from other spectators. "Cricket pavilion," I said, tugging at him. "Come on. Someone is trying to electrocute the runners."

"What are you talking about? Are you mad?' He attempted to shake himself free from my grasp.

"There's an electric wire coming from the pavilion into the big puddle. The first boy to step into it will be electrocuted."

"My dear woman, I really don't think . . ." he said. "You must be imagining things."

"I traced the wire myself," I said. "It came from a window in the pavilion. If you're not going to help I'll find it myself before it's too late."

I let go of him and ran up the steps into the pavilion. At the front there was a veranda where spectators could sit, then a dark, narrow hallway with doors opening from it. I stared, trying to calm my racing heart. How far along the building had that window been? Somewhere in the middle. I heard footsteps behind me and the games master appeared.

"Electric plug. Where?" I shouted.

"Equipment room?" He pushed past me to the left. Outside we could hear cheers as the first runners could be spotted emerging at the edge of the woods. He opened the door and we both surged into the dingy narrow room. Cricket bats and pads lined the walls. Someone was in there, crouched down, his hand on a switch.

"Stop him!" I yelled and threw myself at him. He flung out an arm, knocked me sideways and scrambled to stand up. "Get off me!" he shouted. The games master, a bigger chap altogether, grabbed him and held him. "What is going on here?" he asked.

"Let go of me, you bastard!" the man shrieked. "Take your hands off me."

Before he could break free I reached out and yanked a plug from the wall, giving a sigh of relief as it came out in my hand. "He was going to electrocute one of the boys," I said.

The games master was holding him around the throat. "Don't I know you? You're one of our groundskeepers, aren't you?"

I now had a moment to look at him. "His name is Albert Jones," I said. "And he is wanted on four counts of murder."

Outside there were deafening cheers as the runners raced for the finish line.

Chapter 37

I suppose one can say all's well that ends well, but it really was touch and go. Now thank heavens life can return to normal tranquility.

It was much later that I learned that Geoffrey had won. He had indeed come out of the woods first and run through that puddle. Albert Jones had been watching, his hand on the switch that would have turned on the electricity. We had only been just in time. Darcy returned to find Jones already in police custody. He looked at me, then frowned. "What happened to you?"

"Nothing. We found Jones in the cricket pavilion," I said.

"You've a big bruise on your cheek." He reached up to touch it.

"He knocked me over," I said. "I tried to tackle him."

"Georgie, what were you thinking?" He glared.

"He was about to flip the switch that would have electro-cuted Geoffrey," I said. "Don't you see how clever that was? By the time anyone reached him, Jones could have wound back the cable and nobody would ever know. They'd think it was a heart attack or something."

Darcy nodded. "And there was I, guarding the entrance to the road. You discovered it alone. I feel like a fool."

"Only by accident," I said. "I noticed the cable in the grass and followed it." I failed to mention that I had tripped over it.

We learned that Albert Jones had been hired as a grounds-keeper the month before. He certainly plotted very well. What a misuse of what was clearly a good brain.

Afterward we met Mr. Deveraux and told him exactly what had transpired. He looked shocked. "Trying to kill my boy? What kind of fiend does that?"

"Well, he's now in police custody," Darcy said. "You can breathe easy."

He took Darcy's hand. "I can't thank you enough. If you hadn't nabbed this blighter . . ." His voice cracked and he couldn't finish the sentence.

"It was really my wife who caught him in the act," Darcy said. "She was the one who figured out this whole case."

"Really?" He stared at me. "Then I am completely in your debt, young woman. Who'd have thought that a delicate aristo-cratic young thing like you could manage to track down a mur-derer?"

I was tempted to say that I'd done it before, but modesty

forbade. So I smiled sweetly and wondered how often men under-estimate women. Meetings with police followed, telephone calls to Scotland Yard, and we did not get home until late afternoon. When I entered the foyer Mrs. Holbrook appeared to tell me there had been a telephone call from Miss Belinda again. She said it was urgent. I took off my coat and asked the operator to connect me to Belinda's number. When it rang several times, I wondered if Belinda would be at home late on a Saturday afternoon. I also wondered why Trudi did not answer the phone. I began to feel anxious. What if Belinda had confronted Trudi and Trudi had shot her? On the fifth ring it was picked up.

"Hello?" Belinda's voice, slightly breathless.

I gave a small sigh of relief.

"Belinda. It's Georgie. You rang me?"

"I did. You'll never guess. . . . Trudi has done a bunk. I woke up this morning and wondered why I wasn't served my morning tea, and she had gone. Someone must have been listening in when I telephoned you and warned her. That's all I can think. Anyway, I suspect she must be on her way back to Germany by now."

"I told Darcy about it but he hasn't had time to contact anybody in the Home Office yet. We've been otherwise occupied, catching Albert Jones."

"Who?" Belinda asked.

"The man who killed your cousin Rupert and those other chaps," I said. "We caught him today as he tried to kill the son of the last remaining man who put his father in prison."

"His father in prison?" she said. "Is that what this was all about? Revenge?"

"Exactly," I said. "He believed his father to be innocent and frankly I suspect he was innocent. But he died in prison and Albert has been killing off the men whose testimony put him there."

"Blimey," she said. "And you caught him?"

"Just in time," I said. "Anyway, you'll probably have a visit from one of Darcy's lot to ask you about Trudi."

"So damned annoying," she said. "Now I'll have to press my own clothes and make my own tea."

"I'll come up to town next week and we'll go maid and nanny hunting together," I said.

"Good idea. Now I suppose I had better run my own bath and get ready. I'm going out on the town with Charlie. I have to look my best."

I put back the receiver and went to find Darcy to tell him that Belinda's maid had left. I suspected they'd want to check that she had gone back to Germany and not found a more desirable position from which to do her spying.

After all the excitement, my life went back to normal. Granddad arrived in time for Easter, which was lovely. The gardens were a mass of spring flowers. James was clearly delighted to have his mother around more of the time. He was now very close to walking, able to pull himself up and even stand for a second before plopping down again. I realized that I did not want to miss important milestones in his life, even if I did find a nanny, which was seeming increasingly impossible. Then a week later Belinda telephoned me again:

"You remember Phyllida Devlin? At school with us in Switzerland?"

I thought about this. "Irish girl? Bright red hair and green eyes. Rather stunning, wasn't she?"

"She was. Well, I met her last night at the club I was taken to," Belinda said. "She was the cocktail waitress there."

"Golly," I said. "That's rather a comedown from Les Oiseaux School."

"You're right," she said. She has come down in the world. You remember she left in the middle of a school year. And she wasn't presented at court like us."

"Oh. You're right. I remember. I thought it was because she was Irish."

Belinda shook her head. "Apparently her father lost all his money in the crash of '29."

"Just like my father," I said.

"And he killed himself," Belinda went on.

"Again just like my father."

"So the family had no money and the mother had a complete nervous breakdown. She'd always been a delicate type but she literally took to her bed and simply gave up. Well, there were four children younger than Phyllida was, including a baby of two. Then six, ten and fourteen." She gave a chuckle. "Apparently the father came home from India every four years."

"So what happened?"

"Phyllida found herself running the household, taking care of her siblings and her mother."

"Gosh, how awful."

"She did this with great devotion, apparently, for several

years. And then the oh-so-delicate mother meets a man, a fellow army officer of her late husband, and marries him. She's all set to go out to India with him, taking the younger children with her. And . . . listen to this . . . she told Phyllida it was about time she moved out and got a job. After giving up the best years of her life like that. She just tosses her daughter aside. Unbelievable."

"Poor Phyllida," I said. "So what's this got to do with my nanny?" A horrifying thought entered my head. "Oh no. I don't want a stunningly beautiful young woman as my new nanny. I know Darcy is very good these days, but there is a certain amount of temptation that no man can resist."

"Not Phyllida, silly," Belinda said. "It's their old nanny. When the family upped and went to India, the awful mother told the nanny they didn't need her anymore. They'd be using local ayahs that people have in India. The nanny who had been with them for years! Just chucked her out."

"What a horrible woman."

"She sounds it. So Phyllida felt sorry for her and took her in. They share a flat in Bayswater. Phyllida works in the club and the nanny works in a shop of some sort. Phyllida says she works as a cocktail waitress because the tips are so good, and you never know who you might meet. So she'd actually like to part ways with the nanny, as it's rather limiting to her social life to have an older woman sharing her digs. She can't exactly bring a man back for the night."

"So how old is this nanny and is she looking for a new position?"

"She can't be young because she was Phyllida's nanny and she wasn't exactly young then. But she's not decrepit."

"And does she want a new position?"

"Phyllida says she doesn't like working in a shop but she didn't want to look for a new nanny position as she didn't want to abandon Phyllida after what she'd done for her."

"Golly," I said. "Did Phyllida say what kind of person she was?"

"Very warm, apparently. Her own mother was quite remote and she remembers sitting on Nanny's knee singing 'Oh Danny Boy.'"

"Is she Irish, then?"

"She is. Got a lovely brogue, apparently."

"Darcy would like that." I smiled. "She sounds quite perfect. When can I meet her?"

"Come up to town and I'll arrange a meeting," Belinda said. "Oh, and if you're very good, I'll let you meet Charlie too. But you better make it soon, as I'm going up to Yorkshire to meet Charlie's family for Easter."

"Charlie's family? This sounds serious."

"I think it is, Georgie," Belinda said. "I really think this may be the one."

"I do hope so," I said. "It's about bloody time."

She laughed as she hung up her phone.

Epilogue

Belinda brought our old school chum Phyllida Devlin plus her old nanny to see us. Nanny Kathleen looked around with approval and settled in right away. She met Maisie and immediately expressed herself happy to have her as assistant nursemaid. More importantly, James took to her. Hearing her singing to him as I passed warmed my heart. Belinda then went up to Yorkshire and stayed for quite a while. I held my breath, hoping for an announcement. It was about time Belinda met a really decent chap who would make her happy.

I heard from Zou Zou, who was on her way to watch her horse run in the Grand National. Darcy's father was going with her, as her trainer. Was it too much to hope for a happy ending there? I had to admit that perhaps Darcy's father was too much of a stick-in-the-mud for someone who flew her little plane all over the place.

Right after Easter two letters arrived in the post. One was

from Sir Hubert, who was on his way home from Australia. The other bore a very impressive crest. Not the Rannoch crest, thank heavens. With trepidation I opened it.

Their Majesties King George VI and Queen Elizabeth request the presence of Lady Georgiana and Mr. O'Mara at their coronation on May 12th, in this year 1937.

So my tiara would be needed after all. How exciting. I just hoped that Fig had not mislaid it on purpose.

Acknowledgments

After all these books, it is still a joy to work with Michelle Vega and the team at Berkley, and with the best agents in the universe—Meg Ruley and Christina Hogrebe. Thanks also to John and Clare, who are my first readers, and to the rest of the family who put up with me.